The meow of death...

Whisker Jog, New Hampshire, is a long way from Hollywood, but it's the place legendary actress Deanna Daltry wants to call home. Taking up residence in a stone mansion off Cemetery Hill, the retired, yet still glamorous, septuagenarian has adopted two kittens from Lara Caphart's High Cliff Shelter for Cats. With help from her Aunt Fran, Lara makes sure the kitties settle in safely with their new celebrity mom.

But not everyone in town is a fan of the fading star. Deanna was in Whisker Jog when she was younger, earning a reputation for pussyfooting around, and someone is using that knowledge against her. After being frightened by some nasty pranks, Deanna finds herself the prime murder suspect when the body of a local teacher is found on her property. Now, it's up to Lara, Aunt Fran, and the blue-eyed Ragdoll mystery cat Lara recently encountered to collar a killer before another victim is pounced upon...

Also by Linda Reilly

The Cat Lady Mystery Series

Escape Claws
Claws of Death

CLAWS OF DEATH

A Cat Lady Mystery

Linda Reilly

LYRICAL PRESS
Kensington Publishing Corp.
www.kensingtonbooks.com

Lyrical Press books are published by
Kensington Publishing Corp. 119 West 40th Street New York, NY 10018

All Kensington titles, imprints, and distributed lines are available at special
quantity discounts for bulk purchases for sales promotion, premiums, fund-
raising, and educational or institutional use.

To the extent that the image or images on the cover of this book depict a
person or persons, such person or persons are merely models, and are not
intended to portray any character or characters featured in the book.

Special book excerpts or customized printings can also be created to fit
specific needs. For details, write or phone the office of the Kensington
Special Sales Manager:
Kensington Publishing Corp.
119 West 40th Street
New York, NY 10018
Attn. Special Sales Department. Phone: 1-800-221-2647.

Kensington and the K logo Reg. U.S. Pat. & TM Off.
LYRICAL PRESS Reg. U.S. Pat. & TM Off.
Lyrical Press and the L logo are trademarks of Kensington Publishing Corp.

First Electronic Edition: June 2018
eISBN-13: 978-1-5161-0417-8
eISBN-10: 1-5161-0417-X

First Print Edition: June 2018
ISBN-13: 978-1-5161-0420-8
ISBN-10: 1-5161-0420-X

Printed in the United States of America

For my aunt, Deanna White, whose love and generosity were the inspiration for Deanna Daltry.

Acknowledgments

So many folks to thank!

To my editor, Martin Biro, thank you for your encouragement and for helping to improve the story. Your inspiration and your ideas for tweaking the details made it so much better!

To my agent, Jessica Faust, who is always there when I need her. Thank you, Jessica!

To Kensington's fabulous marketing team, thank you for working so enthusiastically at getting the word out there about the Cat Lady Mysteries.

A huge thank you to Erin Alsop for naming Catalina. What a perfect name for a sweet mama kitty!

To my husband and family, thank you for your continuing love and support. I couldn't have done any of this without you. And a special thanks to my mom, Peg Gregory, for experimenting with the recipe for blueberry buckle until she got it perfect!

And hugs to all the cozy and cat lovers who have embraced the series. I couldn't have asked for more *purr*fect readers.

Claws of Death
Cast of Feline Characters

Twinkles: An orange-striped tiger cat with big gold eyes, he's fond of snoozing with his best bud Dolce

Ballou: A black, short-haired feral with an adorable white 'stache, he's gradually venturing into the orbit of the humans who love him

Munster: This orange-striped male, the sociable, unofficial greeter of all human visitors, is itching to cozy up to the chief of police

Dolce: Long-haired, solid black, and as sweet as a sugar cookie, he's usually found curled up in Aunt Fran's lap

Bootsie: Slender and gray, this lovable girl has been waiting a long time to find her forever home

Frankie: With his white chest and paws and pink nose, this gentle gray boy craves a tranquil home where he can be the only cat

Catalina: This darling white kitty with one black ear and one black forepaw is the mom to Noodle, Doodle, and Bitsy

Noodle: Mostly white, this kitten's brown, diamond-shaped mark next to her right eye pegs her as the queen of the litter

Doodle: With two black stripes encircling one foreleg like an armband, this brother to Noodle and Bitsy looks ready to patrol his territory

Bitsy: Size-wise, this tiny kitten hasn't quite caught up to her siblings, but she's frisky and curious and a definite mama's girl

Blue: A mystical Ragdoll with a creamy coat and chocolate-colored ears, paws, and tail, she materializes whenever Lara needs her to conjure up a clue

Chapter 1

"Oh God, I've got to get ready."

With the toe of her beaded blue sandal, Lara Caphart turned off the vacuum cleaner and pressed the button to retract the cord. The cord snaked into the vacuum with a loud snap. She jumped slightly at the sound.

Take a deep breath, she told herself. *She's only a movie star. She's only been nominated for three Oscars and a Tony. She's only Deanna Daltry...*

Lara was lugging the vacuum back to the supply closet when she bumped smack into her aunt, Fran Clarkson. Seven months ago, Lara had moved into her aunt's Folk Victorian home in the town of Whisker Jog, New Hampshire. Though Aunt Fran had lived in the house for well over three decades, as of the beginning of the year it officially became the High Cliff Shelter for Cats.

"Sorry, Aunt Fran. I'm rushing, and I— Oh good glory, you look gorgeous. Is that a new top?" She tucked a strand of her coppery hair behind her right ear.

Aunt Fran smiled, her green eyes beaming beneath the smidge of highlighter she'd swept along her upper lids. "Yes, it is," she said, referring to the gauzy, moss-colored top she wore over her pale gray capris. She did make for a stunning picture. "Lara, why are you so jittery? Ms. Daltry won't be here for at least another hour."

"But...but...she's Deanna Daltry! And she's going to be living in our town—in tiny Whisker Jog, New Hampshire!"

Aunt Fran chuckled. "I've never seen you so starstruck before. Remember, she's here to adopt, not to audition us for parts in her next movie."

"I know, I know. It's just—"

"And also remember, she has a reputation for being late. Notoriously late. So don't expect her to be here at the stroke of three."

Lara sighed. It was true. The famous actress, best known recently for her starring role in the Broadway hit *Take Me, I'm His*, had often been dubbed Hollywood's "late date." Never married, she was known for her string of leading-man lovers, as well as for her generous good works.

She glanced around the back porch. The official meet-and-greet room for the shelter, it boasted a sturdy square table over which a cat-themed runner had been draped. The ceiling border depicted whimsical cats—hand-painted by Lara—frolicking over a background of cerulean blue. A pine corkboard hung on one wall. Photos of cats that had been successfully adopted covered the board. Lara was pleased that four kittens and two adult cats had found good homes since the shelter opened in January.

A furry body leaped soundlessly onto one of the four padded chairs. The Ragdoll cat, blue eyes sparkling, gave Lara a curious look.

Lara grinned at Blue, the cat that had the knack of popping in and out of the scenery like a puff of smoke.

"You're always smiling at that chair," Aunt Fran said. "It must remind you of something."

If you only knew, Lara thought.

"It reminds me that I'd better get hustling and clean up. When our illustrious guest arrives, I don't want to look like something a squirrel dug out of a hole in the ground."

* * * *

It was the stroke of four thirty-five when Deanna Daltry arrived. The actress had driven herself to the shelter, her vintage cream-colored Mercedes spotless and gleaming under a mid-July sun.

Slender and silver-haired, Deanna wore her hair in a short, casual style combed away from her face. Clad in faded denim capris and a white halter top, she held out one hand.

"Forgive my bare face," she said, sounding apologetic. "I find that the less makeup I wear, the less recognizable I am."

"Ms. Daltry," Lara said, trying valiantly not to gush. "I would know you anywhere. And you look beautiful, with or without makeup." She took the woman's outstretched hand, holding it a second or two longer than she should have.

Deanna's gray eyes made a sweep of the room. "Is this room the shelter?" she asked Lara. "I'm loving the feline décor."

"The shelter is actually our home," Lara explained. "Three of the adult cats live here permanently. On adoption days, we outfit them with blue collars to indicate that they're in-house cats. This room"—she waved a hand at the table—"is where we introduce ourselves, tell you about our shelter, and enjoy tea and snacks with those who wish to partake. Is iced tea all right? With the heat, we figured…"

The actress grinned and winked at Lara. "'Those who wish to partake.' You're a dear young woman, do you know that? And yes, iced tea sounds like just the ticket on this sultry day."

Inwardly, Lara slapped herself. Why did she have to sound so goofy in front of this legend? Why couldn't she just be herself?

"Anyway," Lara went on, "my aunt, Fran Clarkson, will be here any second. She's—"

"I'm here," Aunt Fran's voice trilled from the doorway. Lara couldn't hide her smile. Her aunt's tone never warbled that way. Was she feeling a bit starstruck herself?

Aunt Fran set a pitcher of iced tea on the table, along with a small plate of cat-shaped cookies. "Ms. Daltry," she said, offering her hand to the actress, "I'm Fran, and we're honored that you've chosen our shelter. Please have a seat."

The table had already been set with tall glasses, dishes, and spoons. Lara poured each of them a glass of iced tea. "I hope you like cookies," she said. "Daisy Bowker at the local coffee shop made them especially for you. They're flavored with lavender."

Deanna's smile widened. "To match the iconic gown I wore in *Forever and a Century*? How sweet of her."

"That's amazing, Ms. Daltry," Lara said. "How did you know that?"

"First, I insist that you both call me Deanna." The actress flashed a brilliant smile, but Lara spied a touch of sadness in her expressive eyes. Ignoring Lara's question, she looked around. "Aside from these delightful cookies, I haven't seen any cats yet."

Lara laughed. "We close the door to the large parlor on adoption days, until we're ready to let visitors in." She pushed her chair back and left the room to open the door. Munster, an orange-striped darling, moved past her like a rocket. He knew that on days when that door closed and then opened again, he was about to meet new people.

Lara followed the cat to the back porch, where he promptly jumped onto their visitor's lap.

"Oh, what a darling you are," Deanna cooed, stroking his head. "But you're wearing a blue collar, so I can't adopt you, can I?" She pushed her chilled glass toward the center of the table.

"He's our official greeter," Aunt Fran said, then smiled at the slender gray cat eyeing them from the doorway. "But Bootsie here is ready for a nice quiet home, aren't you sweetie?"

Bootsie dipped her head forward and moved cautiously into the room. Aunt Fran called to her, but Bootsie made a circuitous route and wound herself around Deanna's ankle.

Deanna clucked over the cat, reaching down to run a hand along her soft body. "She's a doll, for sure," the actress said and then sighed. "I know I sound selfish saying this, but…well, I was actually hoping to adopt a pair of kittens." She held up a slender hand. "And I already know what you're thinking, that everyone prefers kittens over adult cats because they're so cute and frisky. But for me, coming back here represents a new beginning, and—" She paused and gazed up at the ceiling, the fingers of one hand lightly touching her throat.

Aunt Fran spoke first. "Ms.—I mean, Deanna, you don't need to explain. Your feelings are fully understandable. And, as it turns out, your timing is excellent."

"Three weeks ago," Lara said, "someone left a cardboard cage on our front porch. No note, no explanation—just a shy mama kitty and three very hungry kittens inside."

"The kittens are about fourteen weeks old," Aunt Fran explained, "so they're definitely ready for adoption. We've already approved an application from a woman who wants to adopt the mom and one of the kittens. As soon as the woman's recovered sufficiently from her hip surgery, she and her daughter are going to pick them up."

Deanna's gray eyes beamed. "So, the other two are still available?"

"They are," Aunt Fran confirmed. "They've both had their vaccinations, but they're due for a second round in a few weeks. We'll give you a referral to our preferred vet, who will also do the neutering and spaying when each one is ready."

Lara couldn't suppress a smile. "They're predominantly white, but the male has two black stripes above one paw that make him look like he's wearing an armband, and the female has a brown, diamond-shaped mark next to her right eye. We've been calling them Noodle and Doodle, but of course you can name them anything you'd like."

Deanna clasped her hands together. "Oh, I can't wait to see them."

Lara rose from her padded seat just as the elusive Ragdoll, Blue, slipped onto the vacant one. Blue set her chin on the table and gave a slow blink, her gaze coming to rest on Deanna. From the cat's expression, Lara saw that she approved of the woman.

"I'll get them for you," Lara said. "Last I saw, they were napping on the cat tree in the large parlor."

She scooted out of the room, returning a minute later clutching the kittens to her chest. Lara handed the male kitten to Deanna. Munster sniffed the kitten's tail but didn't vacate his comfy lap space.

"Oh, they're absolutely angelic." Deanna nuzzled the male kitten against her cheek, smiling at the female tucked under Lara's chin. "They're perfect," she declared. "I promise to give them a loving home."

"We do have an application that needs to be filled out," Lara said carefully. She didn't want to risk offending the actress, but anyone wanting to adopt had to be approved. It was part of the process designed to give their feline residents the best homes possible.

A noise from the large parlor drew Munster's attention. He leaped off Deanna's lap and went off to investigate. Lara set the female kitten in Deanna's lap.

Deanna bit down gently on her lower lip, then curled her free hand around the female kitten. Her voice grew soft. "I wasn't sure about coming back to Whisker Jog," she murmured, a pained look dimming her eyes. "But you've both made me feel so very welcome. I'm glad I'm here, and I'm grateful to both of you for giving me a private appointment. I know you're not normally open on Thursdays." She laughed. "Application process? Good! Bring it on. I assure you that once you check me out, you won't have any reservations about letting me adopt."

"Excellent," Aunt Fran said.

The kittens had gotten antsy, so Deanna set them down. Their mom appeared suddenly and sat watching them from the doorway. Her other kitten hovered behind her.

"Here's mama now," Aunt Fran said. "We've been calling her Catalina and her other kitten Bitsy, but her new owners will probably change that."

All white with one black ear and one black forepaw, Catalina looked up at Deanna. Her tail curled around her feet as she assessed the newcomer.

"So that's the mama kitty," Deanna said with a smile. "What beautiful markings."

Bitsy, slightly smaller than her sibs, padded over to Deanna and sniffed at the toes of her purple sneakers.

"I think she's checking me out." Deanna winked at Lara.

Catalina was clearly comfortable around the actress. Deanna reached down and stroked her head, eliciting a soft purr from the cat. The kittens immediately went over to their mom. Introductions over, Catalina turned and strolled from the room, Bitsy, Noodle, and Doodle following in her wake.

After that, Deanna seemed to relax. She began regaling Lara and Aunt Fran with tales from her early days in Hollywood.

"Do you ever get tired of people intruding on your privacy?" Lara asked. "I'll bet people are always trying to take selfies with you."

The warmth in Deanna's expression cooled, and her eyes narrowed. "You've hit the nail on the head, as they say, Lara. You can't imagine how many times I've wanted to hide, to disappear. How often I've wanted to seek out a place where no one can bother me or hurt me." Her thin nostrils flared slightly.

"I'm sorry," Lara said. "I shouldn't have asked. I didn't mean to pry."

The actress' smile instantly returned, as if prompted by a cue card. "Don't be silly. It was a fair question." She swallowed the last of her iced tea, then pulled her cell phone out from the tiny purse she'd brought with her. "By the way, you're both coming to the reception on Sunday, right?"

"Reception?" Lara asked.

Aunt Fran piped in. "I saw something in the paper about it. The Whisker Jog Ladies' Association is holding a welcome tea and reception for Deanna this Sunday afternoon at the historical society. I'm not a member, so no, we've not been invited."

"Bummer," Lara said.

Deanna waved a hand. "Never mind that. You *are* invited, because I'm inviting you. I'll speak to Evelyn Conley, the coordinator. Besides, I fully intend to support your shelter, and I want to make that known to everyone attending this little shindig."

"Oh, that's so kind of you. Thank you," Aunt Fran said.

Lara's mind instantly flitted to her wardrobe. As a watercolor artist, she spent most of her days working in paint-splattered T-shirts and denim. She had no idea what to wear to an event like the one to which Deanna had invited them.

But that got her thinking. Gideon, the local attorney she'd been seeing for a few months, had asked her to dinner the following Saturday at a new restaurant just outside the town limits. She'd planned to splurge on something summery to wear, but hadn't had a chance to shop. Maybe she could find something that would fit the bill for both events.

"Yes, thank you, Deanna," Lara said. "I'd love to attend."

"Fine. I'll see that invitations are hand-delivered to you by tomorrow. As for that application, is it something you can send to my private email address?"

"It sure is," Lara said. "If you give us your email address I'll get it right off to you."

Deanna's smile was genuine. "I'm so pleased that I came here today. You've both been gracious and lovely. And I promise, those kittens will have a wonderful home."

Chapter 2

The door to the white clapboard building that housed the Whisker Jog Historical Society had been propped open with a large brick. Painted barn red, the door boasted a patriotic folk art flag hanging directly below its brass knocker.

Voices drifted from inside the building. Aunt Fran went in first, Lara trailing behind her.

Lara felt good today, pleased that she'd found a flowery yellow sundress and matching espadrilles at a price she could almost afford. The dress flared at the bottom, and was adorned with two deep but discreet pockets. She'd splurged and bought the ensemble, dressing it up with the chunky gold necklace her aunt had bought at a yard sale a few months earlier. She'd tucked her cell in one of the pockets—just in case she wanted to snap a few celebrity pics.

"I've never been in here," Lara said, gazing around the large entrance that had once served as a meeting room for the townspeople. In one corner, a portable air conditioner struggled to pump out enough chilled air to cool the surrounding area.

"The reception must be in the main room," Aunt Fran said. "Since we're early, why don't you browse here for a bit. Some of the town's artifacts are quite interesting. I'll head to the back to see if anyone needs help setting things up."

"Thanks. I think I'll do that."

Lara was glad to see that her aunt was walking far better than she had been before her knee-replacement surgery. And while Aunt Fran no longer used her cane, Lara knew that her right knee still troubled her.

Lara looked forward to the day when both her aunt's knees were back to normal and pain-free.

She wandered over to a large glass case that sat in the center of the room. Beneath the glass was a yellowed map of Whisker Jog, its edges brown and wrinkled. Lara peered at the handwritten paper tacked above the map. It explained how the town got its name.

Originally called Elbern's Location, the town's boundaries had once formed a precise rectangle. Then a local farmer had claimed that a narrow slice of land at the southwest corner was actually part of his cow pasture in the adjacent county. Founder Josiah Elbern, the land surveyor who'd painstakingly laid out the boundaries, railed at the farmer, calling him a scoundrel and a heathen. But the farmer persisted, so Elbern brought the matter before a magistrate. To his dismay, the farmer had his ducks—or rather his deeds—in a row, and proved title to the sliver. The boundary line was changed, spoiling the perfectly rectangular town. Livid over the decision, Elbern changed the town's name to Whisker Jog, deeming the jog in the new boundary line a debauchery created by a sliver of land the "breadth of a cat's whisker."

Lara grinned at the story. How had she never known that?

"Lara?"

The familiar voice came from behind her. She turned to see Chris Newman, a local accountant who'd recently taken over as editor of the town's weekly paper, the *Whisker Gazette*.

"Hey, Chris, how's it going?"

Wearing a short-sleeved red shirt over a pair of khaki shorts, Chris shrugged. He held up his camera. "Not bad. I'm covering this little soiree for the paper. How are things at the shelter?"

"Great. And thanks for getting the word out. Those weekly plugs have brought in a lot of donations."

"Happy to do it," he said.

The voices in the main room rose to a swell. "I think her car just pulled in!" someone squealed.

"Deanna must have arrived," Lara said, hearing the excitement in her own voice. "Excuse me, Chris, but I need to catch up with Aunt Fran."

He nodded and waved, and Lara hurried toward the main room. Three long tables covered in lavender linen formed a horseshoe of sorts at the rear of the room. In the center table, three china teapots sat on a silver tray. Delicate and fancy, each teapot was pale pink with a golden spout, the finial at the top shaped like a butterfly.

Twenty or so eager-looking people, most of whom were women, milled about the room. According to Deanna, each of the historical society members had been permitted to bring a spouse or a guest.

The main room evidently had central air, but in Lara's opinion it could have been ten degrees cooler. She spied Aunt Fran chatting with a sixtysomething woman in a garish orange muumuu. Her aunt spotted her and motioned her over.

"Lara, this is Joy Renfield. She owns a tea shop in Moultonborough, and she also reads tealeaves."

The woman, whose graying hair stuck out from a wide purple headband, shook Lara's hand briskly. "I've been following Ms. Daltry's career for a long time, so I volunteered to supply the teas for this reception. If you enjoy them, and I'm sure you will, I hope you'll visit my shop one of these days. It's right on the main drag, in a little strip mall. I also do psychic readings, if you go for that sort of thing. May I give you a coupon for a free reading?"

Lara felt bombarded by the woman's enthusiasm. "Um, yes, sure, that would be great."

She knew that her aunt didn't put much faith in psychics, but Lara had always enjoyed having her tarot cards read. The predictions had always been somewhat generic, but it was fun believing someone might be able to see into her future.

Joy whipped out a pink card from her cross-body leather wallet and gave it to Lara. "I'll be looking for you, okay?"

"You bet. I'll try to get there soon." Lara took the card and slipped it into one of her deep pockets.

Voices around them rose. The actress was walking in their direction.

"Here's Deanna now," Aunt Fran said brightly. She tugged her niece's arm. "Nice meeting you, Joy."

Joy whirled toward the commotion as if someone had announced the arrival of the Queen of England. Her eyes glittered, and a wide smile split her somewhat plain face. "Oh my, it really *is* her. And she's on time," she added in a near whisper. "Excuse me. I have to go to the bathroom." She turned and bolted.

Lara pulled her gaze from Joy's retreating form and greeted Deanna. "Thanks again for inviting us," Lara said quietly.

"My pleasure," Deanna breathed, taking Lara's hand. Her face was made up to perfection, her silver hair framing her delicate cheekbones in stylish wisps. Wearing a teal wraparound dress that highlighted her trim figure, she leaned closer and murmured in Lara's ear. "I understand you've approved my application. Can you bring the kittens to my place tomorrow?"

"To your place? Oh, absolutely. We'd be honored."

Lara had checked out Deanna's references, one of whom was a well-known celebrity who'd nearly made her swoon. She'd stammered over her words, feeling like a silly star chaser. The man had been genial and kind, even if Lara had sounded like a giggling groupie.

Deanna nodded, and then moved on to give Aunt Fran a firm hug. "You'll come along as well, Fran, right?"

"I wouldn't miss it," Aunt Fran said.

A stout woman came up behind Deanna, almost bumping into her. Her brunette hair was worn in a style reminiscent of the 1980s, a bit too large for Lara's taste. She wore a shiny gold dress that strained slightly at the bust, divulging some serious cleavage. An engraved name tag pinned to one shoulder identified her as "Evelyn Conley, Special Member." Lara wondered what made her more special than the regular members.

"Deanna," the woman said in a slithery voice, "I think it's time I gave my announcement welcoming you to our lovely town. After that you can mingle and chat with all the Ladies' Association members."

"Nice to see you again, Evelyn," Aunt Fran said.

Evelyn's eyes popped wide open. "Oh. I— Do I know you?"

"Your granddaughter, Trista, was in my class the year before last."

"Oh, yes. I remember you now. Didn't someone say you quit teaching?"

"Only for this past year," Aunt Fran said. "I plan to return in the fall."

Evelyn flashed her a weak smile. "Well, that's...nice. Deanna, we really need to get moving. Come with me and I'll introduce you. Not that you need an introduction," she added coyly, slipping her arm through the actress's. "I still can't believe that I, your biggest fan ever, am right here with you in my own hometown!"

Deanna winked at Lara, then followed Evelyn's lead. The two stood before the center table, blocking the view of the teapots.

Joy had returned. She came up quietly to stand beside Lara. She gave Evelyn a dark look. "I didn't even get to say hello to Deanna," she grumbled. "And I'm the one who supplied the teas free of charge."

"Don't worry," Aunt Fran said kindly. "I'm sure you'll have a chance to meet Deanna in a bit."

Evelyn's booming voice made up for the lack of a microphone. Her glossy, cherry-tinted lips moved in exaggerated fashion, as if she'd rehearsed her spiel. After introducing herself, she gave a rousing welcome to Deanna.

The guests tittered and clapped, waving their smartphones in the air to capture the moment.

Deanna spoke only a few words. She thanked everyone for the warm welcome but said she would prefer to greet each guest personally. She said nothing about having lived in the area as a child. In Lara's view, Deanna was the truly gracious woman she'd always thought her to be.

"I'd like to say one last thing," Deanna said. "I recently adopted two kittens from the High Cliff Shelter here in town. The owners, Fran and Lara, are two of the most delightful women I've ever met. They're completely devoted to their feline charges. For the remainder of the month, I'm offering to pay the adoption fee for anyone wishing to adopt from their shelter—subject to their approval of your application, of course."

Murmurs filtered through the crowd, and several people clapped. A woman standing behind Lara bleated, "Application? For a cat? How silly is that?"

Aunt Fran turned and graced the woman with a radiant smile. The woman flushed and pretended to search for something in her handbag.

After Deanna concluded her speech, she began mingling with the guests. Evelyn swiveled toward a rear doorway and snapped her fingers. Two teenage boys wearing starched white jackets appeared, each holding a sizeable tray of goodies. At Evelyn's nod, they began moving through the room, offering delectable-looking delicacies to the guests.

Lara plucked a round of sliced baguette topped with smoked salmon from the tray. She sampled a bite and said, "Aunt Fran, try this one. It's to die for."

Her aunt smiled. "I don't want to go that far, but I'll take your advice." She tasted the canape and nodded. "I agree, but I'm more interested in those mini-cheesecakes that other young man is offering."

"I'm going to amble around, see if I can drum up some goodwill for the shelter," Lara said.

"Good plan."

Lara strolled among the guests, nodding and making pleasantries with anyone who offered a friendly smile. A few people asked her about the cats, and she willingly gave a plug to the shelter.

Chris Newman, camera in hand, moved around the edges of the room, snapping pictures. Lara was giving him a tiny wave when a thin, seventyish man with thick white hair and droopy-looking eyes slipped into the room. The man flicked his gaze around, as if unsure if he should join the party. He appeared to be searching for someone.

Lara stepped back slightly and watched him. Dressed in a navy jacket over beige chinos, he wore a nervous expression as he moved farther into the room. All at once, his face froze.

He was looking directly at Deanna.

Wiping his hands on his jacket, he edged through the guests toward the actress. Something about his demeanor made Lara uncomfortable. Not that he looked dangerous or anything. More like jittery or anxious.

Deanna stood in front of the middle table, her hands clasped at her waist. She chatted amiably with an elderly woman and her much younger companion, a man with a brush cut and a freakishly wide smile. Behind the table, Joy Renfield fussed with the teapots. As guests strolled up to her, she poured cups of steaming tea into china mugs.

The newcomer approached Deanna, but before he reached her Evelyn bustled over and touched the elbow of his jacket. "Sir, I'm afraid this is a private event. Are you here with one of the members?"

The man's face turned a mottled red. "Members? Uh, no—sorry, I'm not, but I was told it was okay for me to be here. I just wanted to say hi to Deen...um, Deanna."

"As does the rest of the world," Evelyn said, her smile pleasant but firm. "I'm sorry, but this event is sponsored by the Ladies' Association, and it's by invitation only. You need to—"

"It's all right, Evelyn. I know this person." Deanna's voice was silky soft. "How are you, Don? It's been a long time."

Evelyn's mouth opened. "I see. Well, then, I apologize. Please help yourself to refreshments," she told the man and then hurried off to chat up another guest.

The man's eyes filled with tears, and he shook his head. "I never thought I'd see you again."

"It's been a long time," Deanna repeated, her smile cautious.

At that point, Lara felt like an eavesdropper. Whatever was going on between the two, the man's tone made it clear that it was intensely private. She moved closer to Joy. "May I sample one of the teas?" she asked.

Joy nodded and lifted a teapot adorned with tiny yellow daisies. She poured some into a china mug and handed it to Lara. "This one's blueberry with a hint of lemon."

Lara sipped carefully from the steaming mug. The tea was the perfect temperature—not too hot, not too cold. The fruity flavor lingered on her tongue. "Wow, Joy, this is delicious. Just right for a summer day."

Joy's eyes lit up, then flickered sideways. "Thank you. In my experience, not many people appreciate specialty teas."

"There's nothing more to say, Don," Lara heard Deanna say in a rising voice. "I think it's best if you leave."

"But—"

"Please, Don. You need to go. We'll talk about this another time, okay? I promise." Deanna's voice sounded shaky, sending a wave of unease through Lara.

By then the man had attracted some attention. Evelyn, never far from the actress, had apparently heard Deanna's plea. She stormed over and hooked one pudgy hand around the interloper's elbow. "I'll see you out through the back," she said, her tone making it clear it would be pointless to argue.

The man's shoulders slumped in defeat. Red-faced, he allowed Evelyn to escort him out through a rear exit, but not before attempting to press a business card into Deanna's hand. It fluttered to the floor, landing under the center table.

Murmurs rose through the room like the buzz of a beehive. "Who was that? Is he famous?" Lara heard someone say.

Joy, teapot in hand, exchanged concerned frowns with Lara. She set down the pot, then bent and retrieved the business card. She stared at it for a moment, then came around the side of the table and gave it to Deanna. "Miss Daltry, are you all right? You look a little pale." She rubbed her beringed hand over the actress's arm in a soothing gesture. "How about some nice blueberry-lemon tea?"

Trembling, Deanna clutched the business card tightly in her fingers. "Thank you. That would be lovely...Joy, is it?"

Joy beamed. "Yes, that's right. Would you like your tea sweetened with a touch of local honey?"

"Thank you, that sounds heavenly," Deanna said. "But first you'll need to excuse me for a moment, okay?" She touched Joy's hand lightly, then turned to Lara. "Lara, may I trouble you for a favor?"

"Of course you can," Lara said.

She followed Deanna through a rear doorway. When they reached a back room that served as the historical society's small kitchen, Deanna made a beeline for one of the wooden cupboards above the chipped porcelain sink. "Evelyn said my purse would be safe here, but with all these people milling about I'd feel better if it were locked in my car. Would you mind taking it out to my car for me?" She reached up and opened the cupboard door. An elegant lavender clutch sat on a top shelf. Deanna reached for it but her fingertips couldn't quite grab onto it.

"Let me help," Lara said. "I'm a few inches taller."

She retrieved the purse and gave it to Deanna. Deanna opened the latch. She pulled out her keychain, a dainty square of burnished brass engraved with a lavender rose. In the next instant she cried out sharply. The purse flew from her hands. Two fat earthworms tumbled out and plopped, wriggling, onto the floor.

Lara grabbed a paper towel from the holder on the counter. She scooped up the squirming creatures, opened the back door, and hurried out into the parking lot. She found a grassy area adjacent to the blacktop and dumped out the worms. A mild shiver skimmed down her arms. Normally worms didn't bother Lara—she knew they were beneficial to the environment.

But someone had intended to frighten Deanna.

She went back inside, threw the paper towel in the waste can, and washed her hands in the sink. Deanna stood gawking at her, her face pale. The keychain rested on the counter next to the sink. "Did you get rid of them?"

"Yes, I found a grassy spot and dumped them."

Deanna shuddered. She was still clutching the business card she'd intended to shove inside her purse. Lara tried to read the name on the card, but all she saw was "Donald" and something that began with W-A. She thought she spied the image of a car in the lower corner.

"Deanna, are you all right?" Lara asked. "Do you want some water?"

Deanna shook her head, then forced out a laugh. "Lara, do you remember the old seventies horror movie about the giant earthworms that ravaged a seaside town?"

"Sorry, I don't," Lara admitted. It had to be *way, way* before her time.

A bit of color had returned to Deanna's face. "It was one of my first movie roles. I played the sheriff's niece. In the end, a giant worm devoured me whole." She shook her head. "I was so young when I made that silly movie. When you're a newbie in show biz, you take any parts you can get, even if they're horrible."

Lara smiled. Where was she going with this?

"All I'm saying is that whoever put those worms in my purse obviously remembered the film and thought it would be funny. It was a prank, nothing more. Believe me, it's not the first time something like this has happened."

"Yeah, but it was a mean thing to do." Lara wasn't willing to dismiss it so easily. "Do you think that man could've done it?" She slid her gaze toward the card Deanna was still holding.

Deanna flashed her trademark smile, but her eyes held a touch of worry. "You mean my uninvited guest? No, that wouldn't be his style at all."

"Is he someone local?" Lara asked.

"Let's just say he's someone I knew when I was a teen. I have no idea where he lives now."

From her odd tone, Lara suspected the man had been a boyfriend. She also figured he was the "worm man," even if Deanna didn't agree. Still, she knew it was risky to jump to conclusions.

"Deanna," Lara asked, "other than Evelyn, who else might have seen you stick your purse in that cupboard?"

The actress shrugged. "Frankly, I'm not sure I could narrow it down. I arrived here right on time, so the kitchen was busy by then. Those two waiters were scuttling in and out of the kitchen. Evelyn kept barking orders at them. Some of the Ladies' Association members came in through the kitchen door. They're apparently familiar with the layout. I saw one of them slide a covered tray into the fridge."

Lara blew out a sigh. No shortage of potential culprits.

It had been foolhardy for Deanna, with her celebrity status, to tuck her purse into a cupboard in view of other people. Evelyn Conley should have advised against it instead of urging her to do it.

Deanna looked calmer now. She touched Lara's arm. "Lara, would you mind taking my purse to my car and putting it in the trunk?" She grimaced at the keychain. "I'll probably have to throw that away, too. It was in my purse there with those…things."

"It so pretty," Lara said. "Maybe you could clean it up instead of tossing it?"

Deanna frowned. "I'll think about it. You know, I'm grateful that I didn't trade in my vintage Mercedes before I moved here. It opens with a regular key, the way a car should. Those new keyless entry systems are too high-tech for an old gal like me."

Lara scooped the keychain off the counter. "You're far from old, Deanna, but I know what you mean about those new keyless systems. I drive my aunt's old Saturn, and that's high-tech enough for me."

"Thank you, Lara," Deanna said gratefully. "I'd go out myself, but I'm afraid there might be some looky-loos hanging about. You can imagine how it is."

Lara could well imagine. Being a star came with a price, including an annoying lack of privacy.

"Happy to help," Lara said. "The trunk, right?"

"Yes, that will be fine. And can you hold onto the key for me? I noticed you have a pocket in that adorable sundress you're wearing."

"Sure thing," Lara said, warmed at the compliment. "Be right back."

* * * *

The parking lot was jammed with cars. Deanna's Mercedes was parked in the only shady spot—under the single carport at the rear of the building. According to Aunt Fran, the local Ladies' Association paid a fee to hold its monthly meetings at the historical society.

Lara shot a glance over at the Saturn she shared with her aunt. It was parked near the road, adjacent to the sidewalk. They'd left the windows tightly closed, but now she wondered if she should she crack one of them open a bit. She mulled it over only for a moment. After the car's recent servicing, the AC was in fine working order and able to cool the inside in short order.

She was heading to Deanna's car when she spied a shaggy head peering into the back seat of the Saturn. Altering her direction, she went over and found a thin, sixtyish man with a grizzled beard gawking through the window into the back seat. Lara sidled up cautiously, halting about ten feet from the car. "May I help you with something?"

The man jumped slightly. He looked at her with a bland expression, his Red Sox shirt stained with what appeared to be chocolate ice cream. "Is there a cat in there?"

"A cat?" Lara smiled. The man had obviously spotted the emergency pet carrier they kept in the back seat in the event they came upon an animal in need of rescuing. But why was he peeking inside the Saturn in the first place? Had something drawn his attention to the car?

"No, there's no cat in there," Lara said. "I'd never leave a cat or any animal in a hot car."

"Or a baby," the man said, nodding.

"Or a baby," Lara repeated. "Are you looking for someone?"

The man stared at her for a long moment. His eyes were a pale brown and somewhat opaque, like a swirl of milk chocolate. He shook his head mechanically. "No, I have to go now. I need more ice cream. I have money."

With that he turned and hustled toward the sidewalk, his long legs moving swiftly in the direction of the ice cream truck parked on the next corner. Lara watched him for another minute or so. When he didn't reappear, she shrugged and went over to Deanna's car.

Still holding Deanna's purse and car key, she was approaching the driver's side of the Mercedes when she abruptly stopped short. On the window, scrawled in what seemed to be a garish-colored lipstick, were the words TIME TO PAY THE PIPER.

Lara sucked in a breath. She moved a tiny step closer to the car. Beneath the message, in the same color lipstick, was a hastily drawn symbol. To Lara it resembled a flower of some sort, sketched within the confines of a circle.

Heart pounding, Lara stepped away from the car. She slid her cell out from the deep pocket of her dress and took a quick photo of the graffiti.

After that, she turned and hurried back inside. Deanna would need to report the vandalism. She should also report the worms.

But it wasn't the graffiti that worried Lara. It was the message itself.

Time to pay the piper.

Was it a threat? Was someone out to harm Deanna?

Chapter 3

"I can't believe we're about to enter Deanna Daltry's home," Lara said. If she'd tried, she couldn't have suppressed the excitement in her voice.

"I know," Aunt Fran said. "I feel like such a groupie, getting this giddy over it."

Today was the day—the kittens were ready for their new home. Lara had tucked their furry charges atop a thick towel inside the cat carrier, and she and Aunt Fran were delivering them to Deanna. Aunt Fran was carrying the colored-pencil sketch Lara had made of the kittens. It was the gift she presented to each person or family who adopted from the shelter.

Lara swung her aunt's Saturn onto the circular driveway and stopped in front of the old stone manse. She shut off the engine. She wasn't surprised that Deanna's Mercedes was nowhere to be seen.

The actress had been thoroughly shaken by the bizarre message someone had written on her car window. The worms had been bad enough, but those words—time to pay the piper—had raised the creep factor to a whole new level.

The police had first deemed it a prank, a cruel taunt by someone who disliked Deanna's personal style. Chief Whitley, however, had taken it more seriously and commenced an investigation. With Deanna's consent, they'd taken her vehicle into custody, but only until a forensic exam could be performed.

The discovery of the lipstick graffiti had created quite a stir at the welcome party. Much to Evelyn Conley's dismay, the gig had broken up early. While the police hadn't wanted to ruffle any local feathers, they'd nonetheless performed discreet interviews of each of the attendees. Several of the guests had voluntarily given up their lipstick tubes for analysis.

That lipstick—the color had stuck in Lara's mind. Brightly colored and glossy, it looked suspiciously like the shade of red Evelyn had been wearing. Still, she didn't want to point any fingers. There were hundreds of shades and brands of lipstick. And Evelyn clearly adored Deanna. She'd practically fallen at her feet when Deanna had first arrived.

The stone mansion sat at the top of Cemetery Hill, overlooking a family graveyard. According to Aunt Fran, the cemetery's granite markers, some worn and illegible, dated as far back as 1864. The most recent was that of Alston Blythe, who died, childless, in 1938. After his death, the property fell into disrepair, and for decades sat neglected and unoccupied. Eventually the town took it for unpaid taxes, but couldn't persuade anyone to buy it.

Until Deanna Daltry came along.

The renovations had taken nearly four years, but the results had been spectacular.

"It's strange," Aunt Fran said. "I've lived in this town all my life, but I've never seen the inside."

"Oh, but the outside is fabulous, isn't it?" Lara said. "I've already decided I'm going to paint it and give the watercolor to Deanna as a housewarming gift." Lara eyed the granite stairs that led to the open front porch, then looked over at her aunt. "Are you going to be okay walking up those steps?"

"I think so. As long as I take it slow."

Five months earlier, Aunt Fran had undergone surgery on her left knee. The procedure had gone smoothly, and after two months of physical therapy she was walking with only an occasional twinge. She still faced a replacement of her right knee, but was putting it off until the end of the month.

"We'd better get the kittens inside," Lara said. "The car's already starting to get warm."

Cat carrier in one hand, Lara looped her free arm through her aunt's and together they picked their way carefully up the granite steps. The corner column of the stone entryway was covered in ivy. A light summer breeze lifted the leaves.

A massive oak door with a rounded arch loomed before them. On the door was a grapevine wreath clustered with bright colored silk dahlias, a huge lavender bow at the top. Lara pressed a newish-looking buzzer. Within moments the door was opened by a long-faced, fortysomething woman wearing black denim capris and a crisp white blouse. "Good morning," she greeted. "Ms. Clarkson and Ms. Caphart?"

"Yes," Lara said, smiling at the woman. "We're here with Noodle and Doodle."

The woman, her thick, coal-black hair an odd contrast to her salt-and-pepper eyebrows, gave them an unsmiling nod. "Come in. I'm Nancy Sherman, Ms. Daltry's housekeeper. I'll let her know you're here." Instead of leaving, she pulled a cell phone from her pocket and tapped it twice. After a moment, she said quietly into the phone, "Your guests are here with the cats."

Without another word, she turned and went off toward a door at the rear of the foyer.

Lara gazed around in awe at the huge entryway. The floor was marble, the walls papered with scenes straight out of the French countryside. The air felt surprisingly cool. Did the mansion have central air? Or did the stone structure keep the inside from getting overly warm?

At that moment, Lara spied Deanna scurrying down a winding stone stairway into the foyer. Her pink jersey T-shirt over a pair of white shorts made her look at least ten years younger than her reputed seventy-two years. Her makeup was subtle, applied with perfection. She greeted them warmly, hugging each one in turn, but her gaze was homed in on the cat carrier.

"I have a delightful room all made up for the kittens," Deanna said, her tone rising with enthusiasm. "This place is so vast. I thought it best to restrict them to one area for a few days, and then gradually let them explore."

"That's a good plan," Aunt Fran said. "Kittens acclimate best when they start off in a small area. Even confining them to a bathroom works well for the first few days."

All true, but Lara knew that kittens' natural curiosity could get them into trouble even in a confined space.

They followed Deanna up the stairs, where a hallway covered in plush Oriental carpeting led to the rear section of the mansion. The actress opened the door to one of the rooms and ushered them inside. She closed the door behind them.

"I thought this would be the perfect starter room, so to speak," Deanna explained. "Eventually, of course, they'll have the run of the house."

"I can see why you chose this as a starter room," Aunt Fran said. "It's beautiful!"

Sunlight streamed through the rounded arches of the room's two towering windows, both of which faced east. Along the wall, below the windows, was a built-in oak seat adorned with a thick tapestry cover that stretched its entire length. A plump kitty bed sat against one wall. A fountain that dispensed fresh water rested next to a set of food bowls. One bowl contained kitten kibble. Two others were empty. A cat-shaped toy box sat nearby, stuffed with all sorts of kitty playthings.

"By the way, this is for you," Aunt Fran said, giving the pencil sketch to Deanna.

Deanna accepted it with a smile. "Oh, it's perfect," she said. "I'll ask Nancy to frame it—she's quite good at crafts. She made that wreath on the front door. Isn't it spectacular?"

"It's beautiful," Lara agreed, setting down the carrier. Doodle, the male, pressed his nose against the zippered screen door and issued a pathetic mewl. "I know," Lara said softly, "you're getting antsy in there." She laughed and unzipped the door. Doodle hopped out first. His sister peered around cautiously before following in his wake. With the two black stripes around one of his forepaws, Doodle looked like a cat assigned to patrol the room.

"Oh, look at them," Deanna said. "I desperately want to hold them, but I know I should let them explore the room for a while first."

"You can hold them in a few minutes," Lara said. "Give them a chance to look around for a bit." She looked over at the cat bed. "If you have a sweatshirt, or something you've worn and haven't washed yet, you might want to lay it over their bed for a few days. That way they'll get used to your scent."

"That's a marvelous idea," Deanna said. "And before you ask…" She went over to a side door and opened it. "When I had this place gutted and remodeled, I made sure the builders added a private bath to each of the upstairs rooms. As you can see, the kittens' litter box is all set for them. And I assure you, it will be scrupulously maintained."

Aunt Fran peeked into the bathroom and smiled approvingly. "The kittens are going to be very happy here. I can see that already."

Lara agreed. The room had been kitten-proofed for safety. Electrical cords had been wrapped and tucked out of reach. Outlets were properly covered.

Deanna couldn't resist any longer. She bent down and scooped up Noodle, hugging the kitten to the hollow of her neck. Noodle closed her eyes in sheer bliss and pressed a paw to Deanna's throat.

"She's purring. I can hear her." Deanna grinned. "Oh, I can't wait until they're curling up with me at night in my bedroom."

Lara felt a smile widening her cheeks. In spite of yesterday's drama, Deanna seemed totally at ease, elated over the arrival of her feline furbabies.

A sudden movement near the window caught Lara's eye. On the tapestry-covered bench sat Blue, her tail swishing, her eyes alight with curiosity.

Lara felt her heart thump. *How did you get here*? she asked silently.

She knew that only she could see Blue. But never before had the elusive Ragdoll ventured this far from Aunt Fran's Folk Victorian. Was she here to check out the kittens' new place? To add her seal of approval?

Blue glanced at Lara, blinked, then went back to studying Deanna. By that time, Doodle had hopped onto Deanna's right sandal and was munching happily on the strap.

Deanna reached down and picked up Doodle, holding the siblings close to her chest. "Oh, this has truly made my day, ladies. I can't wait until they're ready to have the run of the place."

Lara smiled, but something nagged at her. Nancy Sherman, the housekeeper, had yet to come in to check out the cats or to welcome them to their new digs. Had Deanna told her to stay out of sight during their visit? Or was the woman not a fan of cats? The latter thought made Lara nervous. She wondered if the housekeeper lived in the house, or if Ms. Sherman had her own home elsewhere.

"Deanna, do you think Ms. Sherman might like to see the cats?" Lara asked.

Deanna's bright smile faded. "Nancy, I'm afraid, was not altogether thrilled with my decision to adopt the kittens. She was raised to believe cats are fine as mousers, but should never be allowed inside."

Lara saw Aunt Fran's face crease with worry.

"Oh," Aunt Fran said. "That's disappointing."

"Fran, you needn't worry," Deanna assured her. "I interviewed at least eight or nine applicants for her job, and she was absolutely the most qualified. I made it clear that I intended to have cats, and she agreed that she would assist in caring for them."

Lara slid a glance over at Blue. The cream-colored feline looked relaxed and content—a sign that she was on board with the adoption.

A sigh of relief escaped Lara. Nonetheless, she wished she could get a better comfort level with the housekeeper.

"On another note," Deanna said, a frown pursing her lips. She set both kittens down gently on the floor, then faced the women. "Chief Whitley called me this morning. My car will be released to me this afternoon. Unfortunately, the police haven't made much progress identifying the graffiti artist who marked up my window."

That was no artist, Lara thought.

"Sorry to hear that," Lara said. She'd given the police a description and a pencil sketch of the man she'd caught peeking inside the Saturn the day before. No one other than the ice cream vendor had seen him or had any idea who he was. Besides, the man might've had nothing to do with the vandalism. He'd seemed like a harmless soul, interested mostly in seeking out ice cream.

Out of the corner of her eye, Lara spied a sudden movement. Blue had gone on full alert, her dark tail swishing in agitation. The cat paced back and forth on the tapestry-covered seat, her gaze fixed on the window above. In the next moment, she leaped onto the sill and peered outside.

Lara's pulse pounded. *What is she looking at?*

She forced a smile, her heart racing. "Deanna, I'd love to check out the view," she said. "This room faces the rear of the property, right?"

Deanna mumbled something, but Lara barely heard her. Lara went over to the window and looked outside. Blue had already vanished.

The yard behind the mansion was lush and green. In a landscaped pattern that looked carefully crafted, wildflowers nestled in clusters along a twisty stone walkway. Beyond that was the old family graveyard. Granite markers, worn and darkened with age, marked the burial places of Blythe family members long passed.

Lara gasped. In front of one of the grave markers, someone was slumped on the ground. Even from this distance, Lara could see that one arm was outstretched. Had someone gone on a drinking binge and collapsed in the cemetery? Or—

She swallowed, recalling the body she'd stumbled upon barely a year earlier.

"Deanna, call nine-one-one," Lara said urgently. "There's someone lying on the ground in front of one of the tombstones. I think he, or she, needs help."

Whoever it is, please let them be okay. Please don't let it be like last time...

Deanna swerved toward the window but didn't approach it. "Dear Lord," she whispered. "I left my cell phone in my bedroom!"

"I'll call," Aunt Fran said, taking her phone from the pocket of her knee-length shorts. She tapped it a few times, then calmly reported the emergency. While she continued talking to the 9-1-1 operator, Lara rushed toward the door.

"Where are you going?" Deanna cried out.

"Outside," Lara said. She tried to squelch the bile she felt rising in her throat.

The last time she'd discovered a body, there hadn't been any hope of reviving the victim. This time…she didn't know what she'd find.

But if there was the slightest chance she could save someone, she wasn't going to stand idly by and wait for the ambulance.

Chapter 4

Lara was shaking by the time the police had arrived. Even from several feet away, she'd known the man was beyond help.

The heat of the July sun did nothing to warm her icy limbs. She hugged herself tightly, as if she could ward off the horror.

She'd recognized the victim. He was the man who'd approached Deanna at the welcome event the day before. The one Deanna had had words with, and who Evelyn Conley had banished from the party. A sharp object jutted from his neck, and blood pooled around his head. White flowers had been strewn haphazardly around his body. Lara thought she'd recognized the type of flower, but couldn't think what they were called.

Chief Whitley had zoomed onto the property four minutes after Aunt Fran's call, only a few seconds behind the ambulance. After that, everything had happened in a whirlwind of activity. State and local police cars had swarmed onto the property, parking their vehicles wherever they could squeeze them among the cemetery markers.

It wasn't until four hours later that she and Aunt Fran had been permitted to leave. They'd each been interviewed separately, but had to promise to go to the police station within twenty-four hours to give a written statement.

Deanna's statement had been taken by two state police detectives in the privacy of her home. *The privilege of fame*, Lara thought. As for the housekeeper, Lara hadn't seen her since their arrival with the kittens. She assumed the police had caught up with her somewhere inside the mansion.

Lara had wanted to take the kittens back to the shelter, at least for the time being. Deanna, however, had begged her to leave them with her. "I promise, they'll receive all the love and attention they deserve. This… horrible murder won't affect their care. I give you my word."

Aunt Fran had given her consent, and Lara had reluctantly followed suit. "But please let us know if you need help in any way," Lara told Deanna. "I can be here in a flash."

"I will." Deanna hugged each of them. "Please don't worry. Everything is under control."

When they were finally allowed to leave, Lara swung the Saturn out of the driveway. They passed a sea of police cars, both marked and unmarked.

Then Lara noticed a state trooper, his hand wrapped around Nancy Sherman's arm, walking the housekeeper toward his vehicle. Lara caught a glimpse of Nancy's face as they drove past. She looked ghostly white, and a bit unsteady on her feet. From her expression, she might have been going to the gallows.

* * * *

The chief, concerned about Aunt Fran, Lara suspected, stopped at the house late that afternoon to give them a limited update. Sitting in one of the padded chairs at the Formica kitchen table, he stretched out his long legs to the side.

"His name is Donald Waitt," Chief Whitley said, consulting his notes. "Seventy-four years old, retired gym teacher. He lives—lived—in Ossipee. Also owned an auto dealership with his brother."

"Did Deanna tell you he's the same guy who crashed her party yesterday?" Lara asked him.

Whitley looked sternly at her. "You know I can't discuss that, Lara. Ms. Daltry's statement is confidential, as are yours and Fran's."

Lara sagged in frustration. How could this have happened?

"Jerry," Aunt Fran said, "did you talk to the housekeeper, Nancy Sherman? We thought it odd that she disappeared right after we brought the kittens over."

Lara gaped at her aunt. It wasn't like Aunt Fran to point fingers, if that's what she was doing. Nancy Sherman's brusque demeanor must have really gotten under her skin.

"Again, Fran," Jerry said, more gently this time. "I can't reveal any details that aren't being disclosed to the public. Unless," he added pointedly, "I feel it's something either of you can use to help us pinpoint any unknown facts."

"The fact is," Aunt Fran said, "that Ms. Sherman made herself scarce moments after we arrived. We had no idea where she disappeared to. Come to think of it, we never saw her again."

Lara shot a look at her aunt. Hadn't she noticed Nancy Sherman being led to a state police car by a trooper? Or had she been looking in a different direction?

Whitley tapped a finger against his notepad. "The medical examiner has estimated the TOD—time of death—to be around five a.m. this morning. Ms. Sherman…disappearing, as you say, would seem to have no bearing. That doesn't mean she couldn't have killed the man."

"Five a.m.," Lara repeated. "Why did Mr. Waitt go there so early? Surely he didn't have an appointment with Deanna at that hour."

Whitley took in a long breath. "As I said—"

"I know, I know. You can't reveal the details."

"I'm sorry, Lara. You know the rules."

"Can you at least tell us what the murder weapon was? It looked like a knife of some sort, but—"

"Sorry, Lara. No can do. And not to change the subject, but the media vultures have already begun to arrive. Two network trucks rolled through town early this afternoon, and I'm sure more are on their way. Ms. Daltry has assured me she'll hire private security if need be. In the meantime, I urge you both not to talk to any reporters. If they figure out who you are they'll probably hound you, so just be aware, okay?"

"I hear you, Chief." Lara slumped in her chair.

Darn! Lara wished now that she'd paid more attention at the crime scene. She'd gotten so rattled at finding the poor man's body that she hadn't taken in as much detail as she should have.

Those flowers. What were they? They'd reminded her of something used in bouquets, but she still couldn't grasp what they were called.

"Chief, I have one more question. Did anyone mention the flowers? They were scattered around the, you know, the body."

Whitley shifted his long legs, crossing one over the other. "That's one of the details, Lara, that we are not disclosing to the public. And no, I have no idea what they were. My horticultural skills are limited to deadheading the pansies in my flower boxes every summer."

Lara decided not to press it. Something told her the flowers were symbolic of whatever the reason was for Waitt's murder. If she could identify the variety, she could begin doing some research. She was sure good old Google would be glad to help.

"I understand," Lara said. "My lips are sealed."

Smiling at the chief, Aunt Fran reached over and squeezed his large hand. "Jerry, you've known me long enough to be assured that I would never reveal confidential police info."

Whitley flushed to the roots of his thick white hair. "I know you wouldn't, Fran." He snapped his notebook closed. "Remember, you both need to come down to the station in the morning to give a written statement. I won't be there. You'll be talking to one of the state police detectives."

"Understood," Aunt Fran said, lowering her head.

Lara would've sworn her aunt had winked at him. She knew the two had been having occasional dinners together, but that seemed to be the extent of it. Or was it? The chief wasn't overly enamored of cats, at least not in multiple numbers. But he cared deeply for Aunt Fran. Of that much, Lara was sure.

"Chief, I just thought of something. When we arrived this morning, I didn't see any other cars there. Where did the…you know, victim, park his?"

"Not that it's your business, but we found a vehicle parked about a half mile down the road. It's registered to Waitt. That's all I can say."

"Has his family been notified?" Aunt Fran asked him.

"They have, and they're in shock. I'm glad I didn't have to break the news to them."

A buzzer sounded at the back of the house, making Lara jump.

"Someone's at the shelter door," Lara said. "I wonder— Oh, good grief, Aunt Fran. We forgot about Kayla! We're supposed to be interviewing her today."

Kayla Ramirez was a student who'd called about a part-time job at the shelter. Lara had set up an appointment to chat with her at five that afternoon.

Aunt Fran looked suddenly flustered. "You're right. In all the confusion, it slipped my mind. You'll have to excuse us, Jerry. I'm afraid duty calls."

The chief nodded. "If it's something to do with cats, I'm outta here. I'll call you tomorrow, Fran." He rose and headed for the kitchen door, then turned and looked directly at Lara. "Not to pick on you, Lara, but remember that old saying about loose lips…" He let the thought dangle.

"I know. They sink ships." Lara squelched a smile.

They also reveal secrets about people, Lara thought.

Secrets that might lead to a killer.

Chapter 5

Kayla Ramirez turned out to be a delight. A vet tech student, she was spending the summer with her grandmother in nearby Tuftonboro. She'd spotted the ad for a part-time shelter assistant in the online version of the *Whisker Gazette*, and had immediately called for an interview.

"If I can work with cats and earn a bit of money for textbooks," she'd said in her soft voice, "my summer will be perfect."

Only Lara was aware that Blue had sat in on the interview. While Lara, Aunt Fran, and Kayla sipped pink lemonade and munched on shortbread cookies, Blue had appraised the applicant from the vacant chair. When the Ragdoll cat blinked twice and rested her chin on the table, Lara knew Kayla was a keeper.

Aunt Fran had been equally impressed. Lara knew from the twinkle in her green eyes that she was thrilled to have Kayla join the team.

"I'm ready to start tomorrow, if that's okay," Kayla said with a shy smile. She pushed her oversized eyeglasses higher on her nose.

"Perfect," Lara said. "Believe it or not, you'll be our first real employee. We have a high school student, Brooke, who volunteers when she can. But since she babysits for her little brother while her mom works, she has to work around her mom's schedule."

"I'm honored," Kayla said, flushing a bit.

"Tomorrow's an adoption day. We never know if anyone will show up, but on Tuesdays we usually have one or two visitors. Fridays and Saturdays are busier. I'll give you some employment forms. You can fill them out and return them tomorrow. Meanwhile, how about if I show you the ropes?"

Kayla's smile broadened. "Excellent."

They'd agreed that Kayla would work four days a week, on a flexible schedule, helping with litter box and cat grooming duties. She would also assist with driving felines to and from veterinary appointments. "And don't worry," she'd piped in. "I'm using my gram's car, and it has awesome AC!"

After the young woman left, Lara joined her aunt in the large parlor and dropped into a chair. "She's terrific, isn't she?"

Aunt Fran sat on the tufted sofa, the soft breeze from a table fan wafting over her face. "I agree that she seems like a dream employee, but let's not get ahead of ourselves. Let's see how it works out first."

Lara wasn't worried. Kayla was the best thing that'd happened all day.

She was more concerned about Noodle and Doodle. Lara felt in her bones that Deanna's home was the ideal environment for them. But between the awful murder and Nancy Sherman's odd behavior, how would they fare in the short term?

Her cell phone chirped. She pulled it from the pocket of her shorts and glanced at the readout. She felt her heartbeat spike. "Deanna? Is everything okay?"

"Everything's fine," the actress said. "The kittens seem to be making themselves at home in their special room. Instead of closing the door, we secured a gate across the doorway. So far they haven't tried to escape. I check on them often, and they look very content."

We secured a gate. Did that mean she and Nancy Sherman?

Deanna went on, her voice now wobbly. "Lara, I think the police are viewing me as a potential suspect, and I'm getting a bit scared. I have a lawyer in LA, of course, but I don't want to involve him unless I need to. He's mostly a contract lawyer anyway. I'm not sure how much good he could do."

"Why do you think you're a suspect? Did the police tell you that?"

"Not in so many words. But it was obvious from their line of questioning that I'm high up on their hit parade." She sighed into the phone. "One of the detectives returned here this afternoon. He'd apparently talked to Evelyn Conley. I guess she gave him an earful about my encounter yesterday with…the victim."

Lara shook her head. She hated to think what Evelyn had told the police. Lara suspected the woman had added a touch of her own drama to the story.

And what about Nancy, the housekeeper? Lara had seen her being escorted toward a state police car earlier.

"I don't know if she meant to throw me under the bus," Deanna continued. "But she gave the police the impression that I had some sort of history with Donald Waitt. The truth is, until today I hadn't spoken a word to him since before I left high school. That was nineteen sixty-four! Do you know how long ago that is?"

Way before I was born, Lara thought. *A quarter century, in fact.*

"Had he ever tried to contact you? Call you?"

"No. Never. Out of sight, out of mind. That's how I thought of Donald Waitt. He was part of my distant past. *Very* distant, I might add."

"Deanna, I wish I could help. Aunt Fran and I told the police everything we know, but, quite honestly, I'm not sure how useful it was." Lara thought about the white flowers scattered around the crime scene. Should she mention them to Deanna? Would that fall into the category of loose lips?

"I—" Deanna hesitated, then in a quiet voice, "Lara, a little bird told me you helped the police catch a killer last year. Is that true?"

Inwardly, Lara groaned. She hadn't caught a killer, not really. She'd figured out a few things, with Blue's help, that is. Then the killer had caught up with her before she could report what she'd discovered, and she'd had to defend herself.

"That's not exactly how it went," Lara said. "But I'm honored you'd think I'm that clever. Deanna, if there's anything at all I can think of that might help the police, I'll definitely follow through and push them on it. I give you my word on that."

She couldn't tell Deanna about Blue, of course. After the first murder, the spirit cat had been instrumental in pushing clues at Lara—things she'd probably never have pieced together on her own.

Deanna sounded relieved. "Thank you, Lara. I have every faith in you. You know something? You're the kind of person who gives me hope for the world. I'll always be grateful for the day our paths crossed." Her voice cracked a bit.

Lara was stunned. She hadn't known the woman all that long. The sentiment was a bit melodramatic, but at least it was heartfelt. She hoped.

"Wow. What a nice thing to say. Thank you." She phrased her next question carefully. "Deanna, do you have a favorite flower? Maybe a signature flower? I'm a watercolor artist, so I'm asking for artistic reasons."

"Oh, that sounds cryptic." Deanna's smile infiltrated her words. "Roses. Lavender roses. There's a florist in LA who used to tint them for me and deliver them to my home twice a week. I...miss that."

Lavender roses. Lara was sure the petals strewn around the crime scene had not come from roses. And they definitely hadn't been lavender. They'd been snowy white.

"Thanks. I was trying to gather some ideas for future paintings. Deanna, this is none of my business, but I saw Nancy Sherman leave earlier with a state trooper. She looked kind of scared. Is she a suspect, too?"

Deanna paused. "Nancy's had some issues in the past," she said, sounding annoyed at the question. "That alone pegs her as a suspect, I'm afraid. But

I will tell you right now that Nancy had nothing to do with what happened to Donald Waitt. I would stake everything I own on that."

"Oh, then I apologize for asking."

They chatted a while longer, then Deanna claimed she had to dash. After Lara disconnected, she gave her aunt a brief rundown of her conversation with the actress.

"I don't know what to think," Aunt Fran said. "I honestly don't see her as a killer, but then…"

Lara knew what she was thinking. The killer Lara had confronted last fall had been a shock, as well. Everyone in town had been gobsmacked.

"I hear you," Lara agreed. "And I know what the chief told us. I'm only going to keep my eyes and ears open and report anything strange or out of place. Nothing wrong with that, right?"

Her aunt gave her a quirky smile. "No. Nothing wrong with that. Just be aware of your surroundings, Lara."

"Not to worry. I learned my lesson."

Lara spent the next hour or so grooming cats. She was itching to get her fingers on her watercolor brushes, but she'd decided to set aside the evening for that.

Frankie, one of the newbies, adored the feel of the rubber brush rolling over his gray and white fur. He twisted his body every which way to allow her full access over his silky form.

Frankie's history was a mystery. A few months ago, a young couple had shown up at the shelter carrying a cardboard box with the flaps folded down. In the box was a sweet little gray cat with a white chest and paws. The couple explained that they owned a small apartment building on the opposite side of town. They'd found the cat abandoned and crying in a recently vacated unit.

Disgusted that anyone would leave a cat that way, Lara and Fran had welcomed him into the fold. They'd named him Frankie after the way he'd attached himself like static cling to Aunt Fran. And though he seemed to be thriving in the comfort of the shelter, Lara sensed he'd be happier in a quiet home where all the attention would be lavished on him.

"There you go, sweetness," Lara said, plunking him on her aunt's lap. "You can chill with your favorite gal for a while." She eyed the all-black male making a beeline for Aunt Fran. "Uh oh. Looks like you'll have to share your lap space, Frankie. Dolce is on the prowl and he's headed your way."

Her aunt smiled and patted the sofa. "You come right up here, Dolce. I can always make room."

Whiskers twitching, Dolce didn't hesitate. He hopped onto Aunt Fran's lap, then wrapped himself around Frankie like a furry protector.

"Oh, this is too adorable," Lara said. She snatched up her cell. "I'm putting this on our Facebook page."

She took the pic and showed it to Aunt Fran.

"Lara, for pity's sake. The lace trim on my camisole is showing." Aunt Fran fussed to readjust her garment. "If you're really going to put it on Facebook, you'd better take it again."

Giggling, Lara aimed her cell. Then, slowly, she lowered it. "Lace," she muttered. "Lace—that's it!"

"What?"

"Those flowers, at the crime scene. They reminded me of lace. Excuse me a minute."

Lara hopped up and returned a minute later with her tablet. She plunked down on the floor and Googled several different combinations. And there it was.

"Queen Anne's Lace. Aunt Fran, I'm almost sure these were the flowers scattered around that poor man's body today." She showed the image to her aunt.

"It's a fairly common flower," Aunt Fran said. "I've often seen them in bouquets."

"Which means they're easy to find. The question is, what does it mean? Why were they at the crime scene?"

"It might mean nothing, Lara." Aunt Fran rested a hand on Dolce. "And I think it's the job of the police to figure that out."

Picking up on her aunt's cautionary tone, Lara nodded and suppressed a smile. Because of her aunt's friendship with Chief Whitley, she just happened to have his private cell phone number.

She grabbed her phone. On the internet, she pulled up a crisp image of Queen Anne's Lace. She flicked the pic to the chief with a brief text.

Crime scene flowers Queen Anne's Lace?

There. She'd done what she promised Deanna. The police would have to take it from there.

And if any other clues happened to land in her lap?

She'd cross that bridge when she came to it.

Chapter 6

"I love adoption days, don't you?" Lara set out a covered plate of homemade sugar cookies. A tall pitcher of lemonade, wrapped in a dish towel, rested nearby.

Aunt Fran smiled, but her eyes held a touch of melancholy. "I love seeing the good we're doing for our rescue cats, yes. But as you know, my heart breaks a little each time someone adopts one of our babies."

Lara slipped an arm around her aunt's shoulder. "I know it does. I feel the same way. But remember how far we've come, and what we've already accomplished."

Nine months earlier, Lara's childhood bestie, Sherry Bowker, had asked Lara to return to her hometown to help her aunt. Locals had been calling Aunt Fran the crazy cat lady because she'd taken in more strays than she could handle. And with two bad knees, Aunt Fran had been overwhelmed trying to care for them.

At the time, Lara had been living over a bakery in Boston's North End. She hadn't seen her aunt in sixteen years—an estrangement she still didn't quite understand. A struggling watercolor artist, Lara had been making ends meet by working part-time in her friend Gabriela's bakery.

So much had happened since then. Lara had reconnected with the aunt she'd adored as a child. A murderer had been caught. And the High Cliff Shelter for Cats had gone from vision to reality.

The door buzzer to the shelter jolted Lara out of her reverie. A balding, elderly man was peering through the screen door. "Are you open yet?"

Lara glanced at the cat-shaped clock on the wall. It was only twelve-thirty; adoptions started at one. She opened the door, put on her best smile, and invited him inside. "Of course we are. I'm Lara Caphart. Welcome to the High Cliff Shelter."

"And I'm Fran Clarkson. You look familiar. Do you live in town?"

The man's filmy eyes brightened. "Sure do. Worked at the fire department, such as it is, for many years. Also did home inspections for the cooperative bank. I'm retired now. Wife died nine years ago."

"Have a seat, Mr., um…"

"Heston. Curtis Heston. Everyone calls me Hesty, so you might as well do the same." Walking at a slightly bent angle, he went over and plunked himself onto the nearest chair. "That lemonade sure looks tasty."

Aunt Fran sat, and Lara did the same. Lara poured a glass of lemonade for each of them. The man—Hesty—slurped down a mouthful and gave out a loud, "Ahhhh."

"So, um, Hesty, what brings you to our shelter today?" Lara asked.

He looked around. "Thought there'd be cats here. You run out of cats?"

Aunt Fran quirked her lips. "No," she explained. "On adoption days, we keep them in the house until we're ready to open. This porch—we call it the meet-and-greet room—is where we greet visitors and invite them to get to know the cats that are ready for good homes. Have you had cats before?"

Without warning, Blue sprang onto the vacant chair. The Ragdoll's blue eyes widened. Her chocolate-colored ears twitched in agitation.

Uh oh, Lara thought.

"Yep, I've had several of 'em," he said. "All of 'em lived to a ripe old age. Can't say I'll do the same, but I'm trying." He cackled at his own joke.

Lara fidgeted on her seat. "Did your cats live inside, Mr., um…?"

"I told you, it's Hesty." He scrunched one wrinkled eye as if it had a magic view into the past. "No, my first cat went out all the time. Back in the seventies, I think that was."

"And after that?" Aunt Fran prodded.

"After that I got married, and my wife gave me what for, if you get my drift, for letting my cat go outside."

Aunt Fran smiled. "She was a wise woman. She obviously knew that indoor cats are healthier, happier, and live much longer lives."

"You're right there, young lady. Anyway, my Tilly—that was my cat, not my wife—died seven months ago. She was seventeen. Sweetest little furry gal you ever saw." A tear crawled down one furrowed cheek. "It's time for me to have another cat."

Blue turned around in her chair and sat at attention.

Feeling unnerved at Blue's apparent distress, Lara hesitated. Then, unable to delay any longer, she rose and opened the door to the large parlor.

Almost instantly, Munster trotted over to Hesty and wrapped himself around the man's legs.

"Aw, look at this one," Hesty cooed. He scratched Munster between the ears. "Can I have him?"

At that moment, Frankie strolled in. The cat's eyes went large at the sight of Hesty. Ignoring Aunt Fran, he padded directly over to the man and leaped onto his bony lap. Frankie leaned into Hesty's chest and buried his face in his polyester shirt.

"Oh, would you look at that?" Hesty said. "This one already picked me!" He bent and rubbed his stubbled chin on Frankie's head. Frankie closed his eyes and purred, looking as if he'd found the mythical Shangri-La.

Lara bit her lip. Blue's tail was swishing back and forth. What was wrong?

"Okay, I'm picking this one," Hesty said. "How much is he?"

"Don't you want to know his name?" Lara asked. She felt her aunt's quizzical gaze on her.

"Sure," he said, "but names don't matter. I'll change it if I don't like it. Won't I, sweetie?" He kissed Frankie's pink nose.

"Hesty," Aunt Fran put in tactfully, "we're happy that you found a friend so quickly—that's Frankie, by the way. But like all shelters, we do have an application process. After it's reviewed and your references check out, we'll contact you to pick him up."

Hesty shrugged. "Oh. Well, no problem, I guess. My granddaughter can help me fill out the application. I don't see so good these days."

"There's also an adoption fee," Lara said. "All of it goes toward our shelter's expenses." She quoted the fee.

"Like I said, not a problem."

Lara nodded. Her head was beginning to throb. "Would you like us to email you the application, or—"

"Email, shmee-mail. Just give me the dang form."

A bad feeling gripped Lara. Blue had clearly given Hesty a thumbs-down. Yet Frankie had snubbed his beloved Aunt Fran and cozied right up to the man!

"Excuse me just a moment," Lara said. "I'll go print out an application."

Lara quickly left the room, puzzled by Blue's behavior. Could the Ragdoll cat be wrong about Hesty?

She returned with the application and set it down on the table in front of the man. By that time Blue had vanished—not a surprise.

As she started to reclaim her chair, she felt something push, hard, at her hand. Her lemonade glass tipped over, spilling pink liquid over the table.

"Oh my gosh, I'm so sorry," Lara said, wincing. The lemonade saturated the application and dripped onto Hesty's trouser legs.

Hesty frowned and swiveled his legs around in the chair. "Don't worry, Frankie," he said lovingly, "I won't let that sticky stuff get on you." Hugging Frankie close with one arm, he snagged his napkin and swiped at his trousers with his free hand.

Aunt Fran scooted from the room. She returned moments later with a roll of paper towels. The mess got cleaned up quickly, but Lara was in a mental tizzy.

A knock at the shelter door interrupted her thoughts. Kayla peeked her head in. "Hi," she said shyly. "May I come in?"

Lara was relieved to see her. It gave her something else to focus on. "Of course. Come right in, Kayla. Would you like some lemonade?"

Kayla nodded and stepped inside, handing Lara a sheaf of papers. Introductions were made, both human and feline. Lara poured her a glass of lemonade and invited her to sit.

"I guess I better go," Hesty said, "before something else spills on me." He kissed Frankie's furry head so sweetly that it made Lara's throat tighten.

"Let me print another application for you," Lara offered and left the room. She returned a few minutes later and gave the form to Hesty. He rolled it into a tube and rose from his chair.

"I'll be back for you, Frankie. Ladies, I'll have my granddaughter drop off the application later today." Reluctantly he handed over the cat to Kayla, who immediately took him into her arms. Frankie's gaze never left Hesty—he watched the man until he was out the door.

"He seems like a nice man," Kayla said in her soft voice. "Frankie sure liked him." The cat squirmed in her arms, and she set him gently on the floor.

"Yes, he did," Aunt Fran said, sliding a glance over at Lara.

The remainder of the afternoon went by quickly. No other visitors arrived, which didn't surprise Lara. The day had turned out to be perfect beach weather—which is probably where most people had spent the day.

Kayla worked neatly and efficiently, cleaning litter boxes and taking out the trash to the barrel behind the house. After that she spent time with the cats, getting to know each of their personalities.

"Should I come back tomorrow?" Kayla asked, pushing her glasses higher on her nose.

"Absolutely, if that works for you. I assume you read over the materials we gave you about the shelter?"

"I did. I think it's unbelievable what you're doing here."

"Thanks. Since tomorrow is not an adoption day, we'll work on some other projects. Catalina and her one remaining kitten have a vet appointment tomorrow. Do you think you can handle taking them? We have a large-sized carrier that will fit them both. I'll help you get it in and out of the car."

"I'd love to." Kayla clasped her hands under her chin. "Thank you, both of you, for having me here. This is going to be a wonderful summer—and such good experience for me."

Kayla left a little after four. Aunt Fran pounced on Lara.

"What in heaven's name was going on with you when Hesty was here, Lara?" she said, an edge to her voice. "You acted as if you didn't like the poor man."

With no way to explain about Blue, Lara hedged. "I-I can't put my finger on it, Aunt Fran. I was just getting a weird feeling about him." She held up a hand before her aunt could interject. "I know, Frankie obviously swooned over the man. The two looked like a match made in heaven."

"I called Jerry while you were working with Kayla. He's known Mr. Heston—Hesty—forever. He might not be the most polished of individuals, but he and his wife have always had cats. They gave every one of them a loving home."

"Okay, I concede," Lara said. She threw up her arms. "We'll review his application, if he ever delivers it, and check out his references. Then we'll go from there."

"Agreed," her aunt said, but she still looked a bit miffed.

Lara went over and kissed Aunt Fran's cheek. In an attempt to lighten the tension, she said, "Don't mind me. You should know by now I have paranoid tendencies."

Her aunt laughed. "I won't argue with that. But so long as it's for the good of the cats, I suppose I can overlook it."

The porch table now wiped down and the floor washed, Lara prepared an early supper for the two of them. She grilled two marinated chicken breasts while Aunt Fran whipped up a salad of romaine lettuce and fresh, local tomatoes. For dessert, they splurged on strawberry shortcake with strawberries from Daisy Bowker's garden.

After the dishes were done, they watched the news for a while. Reports of Donald Waitt's murder monopolized almost every major network. As if his death wasn't bad enough, veiled references to a prior relationship with Deanna Daltry gave the story a tawdry angle.

"I can't watch anymore," Aunt Fran eventually said.

"I'm with you," Lara said. "I'm going to work in the small parlor for a while. Catch up on some correspondence. Maybe do a little painting."

And try to figure out why Blue was so dead set against Hesty.

* * * *

Lara sat at the card table in the small parlor and pulled up Google on her tablet. The room, which had been her favorite when she was a child, served as both her office and art studio.

She started by searching Curtis Heston—a name, she was surprised to see, that popped up with some frequency. In his heyday, he'd been a captain on the Whisker Jog Fire Department. Given the town's size, it had been only a part-time job. He'd also worked as a home inspector until he retired several years earlier. Exactly as he'd told them.

A slew of commendations appeared online, including one from a grateful owner whose puppy Hesty had rescued from a drain pipe back in the late 1990s.

Lara sighed. If his application looked good and his references checked out, he'd be eligible to adopt Frankie. Maybe she could stall him while she tried to figure out Blue's objection to the man.

Or maybe she was crazy, seeing a cat no one else could see. Maybe *she* was the problem and not Hesty.

Pushing those thoughts aside, she Googled Donald Waitt. Aside from the news blasts about the murder, there was little to learn about the man. He'd been married with two grown kids. If he had any social media accounts, Lara didn't trip over them.

But that didn't mean he didn't have secrets.

Why had he been so anxious to talk to Deanna at the tea party on Sunday? Lara suspected Deanna knew more than she was saying. She also sensed that the actress had returned to her hometown to find peace and solitude. *Scratch that*, she thought. Deanna's privacy—to the extent she'd had any—had already been shattered.

Anxious about the kittens, Lara snatched up her cell. She sent off a quick text to Deanna.

Are N and D enjoying their new space?

She wanted it to sound casual, not as worried as she felt. Almost immediately, a return text came through.

Kittens loving it here. Haven't eaten much yet,
but curled up together in cat bed. Love these

*darlings! We're lying low. Media crawling
everywhere!*

Hmm. Haven't eaten much yet? Lara didn't like the sound of that. And who did she mean by "we"? She'd forgotten to ask Deanna if Nancy Sherman lived at the mansion.

As for the media and the looky-loos who'd camped out in front of Deanna's, Lara knew they weren't going away any time soon. Deanna would have to endure it for as long as it lasted. Lara felt bad for the woman, but it was, unfortunately, the price of fame.

Aunt Fran knocked lightly at the door and popped into the room. She handed a folder to Lara. "Hesty's granddaughter just dropped this off." She winked at her niece. "Oh, and I meant to give you this earlier," she said and gave her a sheet of pink paper. "I picked it up today at the library. There's a community book-slash-yard sale in their parking lot on Saturday. I knew you might want to go." She scooted right back out and closed the door.

Lara set aside her tablet and glanced at the yard sale flyer. She'd probably enjoy poking around there on Saturday, but she'd have to get back before adoption hours started. Right now, she was far more concerned with Hesty's application.

She opened the folder—a folder?—and perused the application. No red flags popped up. Hesty appeared to be a solid citizen with a penchant for helping others. Tomorrow she'd check his references and then go from there.

Her eyes burning, both from reading and from stress, Lara set up her easel with a fresh sheet of watercolor paper. From the sealed bottle she kept in the room, she poured water into two separate cups. She'd taken pics of the stone mansion earlier in the day and saved them on her cell phone. She pulled up the one she liked best, enlarged it slightly, and went to work.

An hour later, she'd managed to produce a rough watercolor of the mansion. She'd captured the sun gleaming off the stones, and the lush green of the ivy clinging to the stone columns. It needed much more detail, but she'd tackle that tomorrow.

In all the hoopla after the murder, she'd almost forgotten something else: the threatening message left on Deanna's car window. Did she dare text Chief Whitley about it? She was itching to know if they'd identified the graffiti artist. The chief would probably tell her to mind her own business. Which, of course, he had every right to do.

She texted him anyway.

Any news on Deanna's car vandal?

Wait a minute. Where was her brain? That day, when she'd first spotted the lipstick message on Deanna's car window, she'd taken a picture of it! How had she forgotten that?

Lara picked up her cell again and scrolled through the photos. Yes! There it was. TIME TO PAY THE PIPER. *The letters are printed carefully, almost childishly,* she thought. And next to that was a circle with a roughly drawn flower in the middle.

She enlarged the photo with her thumb and forefinger, shifting it to zoom in on the circle. The flower was a series of loosely connected dots—dots that formed a picture. It reminded Lara somewhat of a snowflake. Although the artwork was amateurish, Lara could see a pattern.

Unless she was imagining it, it was the same flower—Queen Anne's Lace—she'd seen scattered at the crime scene.

Chapter 7

"Where have you been?" Sherry Bowker bleated. She poured steaming coffee into a mug and pushed a bowl of half-and-half packets at Lara.

Lara shot a glance around Bowker's Coffee Stop. The pastel-painted walls graced with artifacts from the 1960s never failed to elicit a smile from her. Today she spotted several unfamiliar faces. Reporters? Media types? A few of them pounded laptops as they shoveled muffins into their mouths and guzzled the coffee shop's delicious java.

She looked back at her longtime bestie, whose raven-tinted hair sat in gelled spikes on her head. The spikes were a tad softer than usual, more curvy and feminine. "I've been lying low," Lara said quietly, using Deanna's phrase. She plopped a packet of half-and-half into her coffee. "You heard about the, um—"

"Body," Sherry announced, a bit too loudly. "Of course I did. It's all over the news. And you—you've been rubbing elbows with Hollywood royalty and haven't even called me!"

Lara gave her a penitent look. "I'm sorry. Things have been crazy. Honestly they have."

She'd driven her aunt to the police station early that morning so they could both sign written statements. The chief had been noticeably absent. She and her aunt had each spoken separately to a state police detective who'd worked quickly and efficiently. His keyboard skills had amazed Lara.

"And if my ears didn't deceive me," Sherry added, "you've gotten yourself involved in another flippin' murder."

Slowly, Lara shook her head. Is that what people were saying?

"I am not involved in another murder," Lara said. "Not even remotely." In a lowered voice, she explained how she'd happened to glance out the window of Deanna's mansion and spotted the man in the cemetery.

"Unreal," Sherry said. "You want a fresh fruit cup? Mom made them up this morning."

"Sure. Extra blueberries, okay?"

"If you insist. How's Fran doing?"

"Good. Taking things in stride." Sherry smiled. "She's a new person since she got that left knee done."

"She definitely has more energy, and less pain," Lara said. "Hey, Sher, not to change the subject, but do you know a guy named Curtis Heston?"

Her friend grinned. "Hesty? Sure I do. He and his wife lived on our street before they downsized to a smaller house. He's a super nice guy. Why?"

Omitting Blue from the story, Lara told her about his adoption application.

"Approve him," Sherry said. "You don't even need to check him out. Believe me, he'll give that kitty a great home."

"Wow. That's quite a recommendation."

"And you can take it to the bank," Sherry said. "I'll go get your fruit cup."

Lara sipped from her mug. In part, she felt relief. But another part of her couldn't discount Blue's odd behavior toward Hesty.

Sherry returned a minute later with Lara's fruit cup. In a glass dessert dish sat a mountain of blueberries nestled atop sliced peaches, pears, and strawberries. Sherry sidled away to wait on other customers.

Lara spooned fruit into her mouth, savoring the blend of flavors. Unfortunately, she didn't have time to linger. Kayla would be returning at eleven to assist with shelter duties.

"Hey, I gotta run," Lara told Sherry after swallowing the last blueberry. "We've actually hired our first official *paid* employee. So far she's terrific." She slapped her money on the counter. It was always a struggle to pay, since Sherry never wanted to accept money from her.

Sherry shot her a look, examined the money, and shoved a dollar bill back at her. "That's nice," she said distractedly. "Hey, are you ever going to introduce me to Deanna?"

"Of course I am, as soon as all this…nonsense is out of the way."

"They think she did it, you know."

Lara felt her heart lurch. "What?"

"I heard the cops talking about it this morning. As you know, I have a black belt in eavesdropping." Sherry leaned closer. "Deanna knew that guy, the one who got offed. They think it was a lovers' quarrel gone wrong."

Lovers' quarrel? Deanna hadn't seen the man in over fifty years!

Or so she'd claimed.

Had the actress lied about their relationship?

At one of the tables, a man wearing black-rimmed glasses and sporting a wicked tan cocked his ears toward Lara. A reporter, Lara suspected. No doubt he was trying to pick up on what they were talking about.

"If you hear anything else, text me, okay?" Lara begged. "Too many curious ears in here."

"Got it," Sherry said.

Lara leaned across the counter, gave her friend a quick hug, and left.

* * * *

When Lara got back to her aunt's, she noticed an older car—a Mercury, she thought—sitting in the small parking area adjacent to the shelter's entrance. The passenger-side window bore the decal of a cat curled protectively around a tiny kitten. Lara smiled when she realized their new assistant had already arrived and was waiting to be let in. Kayla sat on the porch steps, peering at her smartphone. She grinned when she saw Lara.

"Sorry if I got here too early," Kayla said. "I just couldn't wait to start!"

Wearing crisp denim shorts and a pink T-shirt patterned with tiny cats all over it, she rose and quickly pocketed her phone.

"Hey there," Lara said, smiling at their eager employee. "No problem being early. Didn't Aunt Fran answer the bell?"

Kayla shrugged. "I buzzed, but I guess she didn't hear it."

Interesting, Lara thought. The Saturn was still in the driveway, since Lara always walked the short distance to the coffee shop. She unlocked the door to the back porch and Kayla followed her inside.

"Aunt Fran," she called out.

No answer.

"Probably in the shower," Lara said. "Why don't you help yourself to some water or iced tea from the fridge, then you can get started."

"Thanks." Kayla pushed at her eyeglasses. "Should I start with scooping kitty litter?"

"That would be great. I have some references for a possible adoption I want to check out, so I'll be in my studio. Catalina and Bitsy's appointment is at two this afternoon. Since you're working till four, that should give you plenty of time to get her and her kitten to and from."

"Even if the appointment goes past four," Kayla said, "I don't mind working overtime. I don't even need to get paid."

"Thanks," Lara said. "Then…I'll leave you to it."

Kayla gave her a two-fingered salute and hurried off toward the kitchen.

She's almost too good to be true, Lara thought. Was there a catch to this wonderful new employee?

Lara heard Aunt Fran's soft footfalls coming down the stairs. She went over to let her know Kayla had arrived. When she saw her aunt, she had to stifle a gasp.

Descending the stairs, Aunt Fran was wearing a filmy, navy blue tunic top Lara had never seen before over pale blue leggings. Jeweled earrings graced her delicate ears, and her hair was fluffed in waves around her slender neck. "Aunt Fran, you look, I mean…"

"Like a woman?" Aunt Fran laughed.

"No, I mean yes, I mean…your hair. What did you do?"

"To my hair? I bought one of those curling wands. I wasn't blessed with your natural curls, you know."

Lara wished she hadn't been blessed with them, either. "Are you wearing blush? Your cheeks are rosy, and your eyes—"

"Lara, I know you're not accustomed to seeing me this way. But in spite of being your doddering old aunt, I do occasionally like to put on some decent threads."

Threads? Lara swallowed. Her fiftysomething aunt was anything but doddering. And she'd seen her aunt wearing makeup before, plenty of times. But this was different—it was far more enhanced, more elegant.

"It so happens Jerry and I are having lunch today at the new winery. We made the reservation some time ago. They're very hard to get."

Lunch? With the chief of police? With a murderer running loose?

"I can read your mind, Lara. Don't worry. We're making it a quick lunch. Jerry *is* entitled to sustenance, you know. It doesn't detract from his duties."

If there'd been any doubt about her aunt's interest in the chief, they'd been dispatched like petals in a stiff summer breeze.

"You can handle things here," Aunt Fran went on. "You always do. Was that Kayla's voice I heard?"

"It was. She got here early."

"Excellent. I'll be back by mid-afternoon. Call my cell or text me if anything comes up."

"Uh, sure thing, Aunt Fran. Have a great time. Give the chief my regards."

Less than a year ago, her aunt didn't even have a cell phone. Now she kept it with her at all times, checking the shelter's Facebook page frequently. She also seemed to text a lot. Lara could only guess who she was texting.

I've created a monster, Lara thought, then laughed out loud. It was a monster she wouldn't change for anything in the world.

Chapter 8

For the second time that morning, Lara disconnected a call with a sigh. She knew she should be grateful for Hesty's glowing references. Instead, she was at a loss.

She set down her cell on the card table and headed into the kitchen. Aunt Fran had made a pitcher of iced tea before she left, and Lara poured herself a tall glass.

For such a hot summer day, the house felt surprisingly comfortable. Lara had persuaded her aunt to install an air conditioner in the large parlor, something that had never been done before. At first Aunt Fran had resisted. The old Folk Victorian, she'd declared, had plenty of natural ventilation and didn't need artificial cooling. Then came an early heat wave that had knocked the energy out of both of them. She'd given in to Lara's prodding and had a unit installed in one window.

Lara was pleased to see that Kayla seemed to be enjoying her assigned tasks. After she'd finished with litter box duty, she'd scrubbed and replenished the cats' food and water bowls. Now she was sitting on the floor in the large parlor, a box of grooming supplies resting beside her. Bootsie lay stretched out on the Oriental carpet, reveling in the attention Kayla was giving her. Lara dropped down opposite Kayla and folded one ankle over the other.

"She's so darling." Kayla ran a soft brush along Bootsie's gray fur. "How could she still be unadopted?"

Lara smiled. "People choose different cats for different reasons. Don't worry. I feel sure she'll end up in a wonderful home. The main thing is that she's loved and cared for while she waits."

"I guess," Kayla said. "How about Frankie? Is that man from yesterday going to adopt him?"

"We're still processing his application," Lara said carefully.

"If I can help in any way let me know, okay?"

"Sure thing. Hey, listen, don't forget to take a lunch break. After you're through with the grooming, want to join me in my studio for a sandwich? I can make you a ham and cheese, or a PBJ if you'd like."

Kayla's eyes brightened behind her glasses. "I'd love that. I actually brought my own PBJ. Gram made it for me this morning."

"Great. Then it's a date."

"Um, Lara, what about the black cat with the mustache? I can tell from the tip cut off his ear that he was trapped and neutered at one time." She smiled up at the top level of the carpeted cat tree.

Lara swiveled her head around and looked up. Her heart nearly bounced out of her chest. On the top perch, Ballou, the feral cat, sat gazing intently at Kayla.

"Oh my Lord," Lara whispered. "Ballou has never ventured this far into the parlor. I swear, Kayla, I've never seen him on that tree."

"I tried to pat him," Kayla said. "He kind of shied away from me, but at least he didn't bolt. I was hoping I could brush him before I left today."

Lara shook her head. "He won't let you get that close, but I appreciate your trying."

"It's my job, right?" Kayla shrugged.

"You know," she told Kayla, "there was a time when Ballou wouldn't go near a human. Aunt Fran figured out that he'd been hiding under my bed during the day. Only after all humans were safely asleep did he venture out to eat and explore."

"He doesn't seem that scared anymore," Kayla said in her soft voice.

"He's not as frightened as he used to be, but he's wary. He definitely doesn't like to be touched."

Lara had tried numerous times to stroke the soft fur between Ballou's ears. Each time she'd been rewarded with the swipe of a black paw.

"I won't give up," Kayla said. "Somewhere behind those watchful eyes is a playful kitty waiting to come out."

Lara sat back on the heels of her hands and observed Kayla. She was impressed with the young woman. Kayla had finished grooming Bootsie and had moved on to Twinkles. Her touch was gentle, and she talked to the cats in a quiet, singsong tone.

Kayla looked up sharply. She'd caught Lara staring.

"Hey, listen, it's great having you here," Lara said. "I'm a watercolor artist, and I'm working on several commissioned projects simultaneously. With you helping out, I can devote more of my days to my artwork."

"Phew! What a relief. I was afraid you might think I didn't do enough."

"You do plenty," Lara assured her. "When you're ready for a break, pop into my studio, okay?"

"I will."

Lara rose from the floor and went into the small parlor. She'd just set her cell on the card table when it pinged with a text. Her heart raced when she saw the name. Deanna had texted.

We have a situation. Kittens not eating.

"What? Why?" Lara said aloud.

Instead of texting Deanna, she punched her telephone number.

"I had a feeling you'd call as soon as you got my text," Deanna said, a catch in her voice. "I don't know what's wrong. We bought the best quality kitten foods, the brands you recommended, in several flavors. They don't seem to like any of them. We're stymied. Completely mystified."

Lara closed her eyes and took in a calming breath. "By *we*, do you mean you and Ms. Sherman?"

"Yes, of course. Who else would I mean?"

Lara thought for a moment. "Deanna, are there a lot of cable TV trucks at your place?" She was already calculating how best to get to Deanna's without navigating a sea of reporters.

"There are," Deanna said, her quiet tone layered with bitterness. "I should be used to it, but this is really awful. The moment I try to peek outside they rush forward in a wave and shout questions at me. One of them asked me if I killed Donald Waitt." A small sob escaped her.

Oh, boy. Lara blew out a breath. "Deanna, is there another way to get to your home?" Lara thought she remembered seeing a narrow service road that snaked around from the rear of the cemetery.

"Yes, there's a windy dirt road that trickles right into the cemetery. Unfortunately, that whole area is still patrolled by police cars. They'll probably stop you before you get very far."

"Is there a way to let them know I'll be coming? I might be bringing an associate with me."

"Fran?"

"No, a new employee."

"I have a contact number for the state police investigator," Deanna said. "I'll let him know you're coming so his officers can let you through. Of course there's always the possibility he'll refuse. If he does, I'll call you right back." She gave Lara instructions for locating the access road.

Lara disconnected and went to back to Kayla. "I have a favor to ask. Are you willing to eat your PBJ in the car and go on a mission with me? We'll be back in plenty of time for Catalina and Bitsy's appointment."

Kayla's eyes widened behind her glasses. "You bet I am."

They quickly locked up the house and hopped into the Saturn. Kayla looked like an eager puppy on her way for a romp in the park. She gobbled down her sandwich in two minutes flat, wiping grape jelly from her mouth with the napkin her gram had packed for her.

Lara hadn't gotten a return call from Deanna, so she assumed the police investigator intended to let them drive onto the property. She was too anxious to eat her own sandwich. If the kittens weren't hungry, then something had to be wrong.

Following Deanna's instructions, she located the cemetery road, but not without some difficulty. It was tucked behind a stand of towering pines that only someone familiar with the property would know how to find.

Lara gripped the wheel tightly as she steered the car along the rutted access way. The Saturn rocked like a ship on a choppy sea. She had to slow her pace several times.

"I hope you don't bust an axle," Kayla said nervously. "This road is a nightmare."

They breathed a collective sigh when the rear of the cemetery came into view. "Sorry, but we'll have to hike it from here," Lara said.

Kayla grinned. "No problem. I run four miles every morning."

Lara spied a uniformed trooper motioning her into the cemetery. A shudder ripped through her. In her mind's eye, she saw Donald Waitt with that knife, or whatever it was, sticking out of his neck.

The trooper waved an arm at them, then trotted over. Lara powered down her window. A wave of July heat rolled in.

"Ms. Caphart, I presume?" He was thirtysomething, with a blond brush cut and startling blue eyes. Tiny beads of sweat dotted his forehead above his aviator sunglasses.

"Yes," she said, "we're from the High Cliff Shelter. Ms. Daltry is expecting us. She has an issue with her new kittens, and we're here to help."

The trooper stared into the back seat for what seemed at least a minute. For a few heart-stopping seconds, Lara was afraid she'd over-explained.

Then, flitting his gaze over Kayla, he directed them to the path that led to the back entrance of the mansion. "Thanks," Lara said.

They exited the car and Lara stared out past the cemetery. A row of cable TV trucks crowded the roadway in front of the stone mansion. Clusters of people milled about. Lara couldn't make out any faces, but their numbers alone felt intimidating.

"Let's hope none of the reporters spot us," Lara said. "That's all we'd need—to be chased by paparazzi!"

"I can't believe I'm about to enter Deanna Daltry's home," Kayla squealed.

"I know. That's how I felt on Monday. Remember, though, we're here to help the kittens, and figure out why they're not eating. They were scarfing food like little piglets before we brought them here."

Kayla adopted a serious tone. "I understand. I'm here to assist."

The sun baked Lara's face and arms as they made the trek along the worn path to the rear of house. Fortunately, she'd applied her daily dose of sunscreen. Her fair skin, dotted with a smattering of freckles, was a magnet for sunburn.

It was at least five minutes before they came up behind the mansion. A grasshopper leaped in front of Lara, and Kayla giggled. The young woman blinked as they reached the slate walkway to the rear entrance.

All around, wildflowers bloomed in colorful clusters. Lara didn't know most of the varieties, but she recognized the mammoth gold sunflowers, and the willowy lupine that was so prolific in New Hampshire. A pale yellow butterfly danced on the tip of a golden daisy, and a pair of gray squirrels chased each other over the granite bench adjacent to the back entryway. It was a scene so picturesque Lara knew she wanted to paint it. She was tempted to take a pic with her phone, but decided against it. She didn't know who might be watching their every move.

As if to prove her point, Nancy Sherman appeared suddenly in the doorway. Unsmiling, she stood motionless until Lara and Kayla reached the entrance. She reminded Lara of a stern overseer in a grim gothic novel.

"Good afternoon, Ms. Sherman," Lara said, and introduced Kayla. "I understand the kittens haven't been eating."

Nancy Sherman scowled. "They've barely touched their food. They sniff at it like it's poison. Follow me."

Lara felt her insides drop. She looked at Kayla, who was gawking at Nancy with an odd expression. Had she met her before?

They followed Nancy up a rear staircase, the sound of their footsteps echoing off the stone walls. When they reached the second story, Nancy opened the door and led them down the carpeted hallway to a room Lara knew was different from the kittens' original space.

"Deanna's waiting for you in here," Nancy said, her hand gripping the doorknob. "Against my advice, she's already moved the kittens." She knocked at the door and opened it without waiting for a response.

From the feminine décor and gorgeously appointed accessories, Lara knew they were seeing Deanna's bedroom.

"Lara, come in!" Deanna said, swinging her slender legs off the lavender spread that covered her king-size bed. Dressed in casual jersey shorts and a matching, sleeveless T-shirt, her silver hair was slightly disheveled and her face devoid of makeup. Atop the bed, Noodle and Doodle were tugging at opposite corners of a decorative pillow.

"Hi, Deanna. Hey, look at you guys," Lara said, grinning at the kittens. She introduced Deanna and Kayla to one another, and Deanna immediately hugged the young woman. "A vet tech student, isn't that marvelous. How lucky the shelter is to have you!"

Kayla flushed and pushed her glasses up on her nose. "Thank you, Ms. Daltry, but I'm the lucky one." She flashed a smile at Lara.

Lara couldn't stop staring around the room. The white furnishings were ornately carved, and a loveseat upholstered in pale lavender velvet rested beneath two towering windows. A delicate chandelier shimmered over the center of the room. On a throw rug near the bathroom, the door to which hung open, were two shallow ceramic dishes—one filled with water and the other with the obvious dregs of a can of wet kitten food. A huge dent had been made in the food supply—the dish was nearly empty.

"You changed their food and water bowls," Lara said. "Are they eating now?"

"They sure are," Deanna said. "For some reason, the move made all the difference. Nancy had a conniption when I brought them in here, but I told her it wasn't her decision to make." Deanna flitted a hand toward the bathroom. "Their litter box is in my bathroom now. I'm not sure if they've used it yet."

Lara sniffed the air. A sneaky suspicion was crawling up her spine.

Kayla had gone over to the bed and was totally engrossed in playing with Noodle and Doodle.

"Mind if I check out the other room?" Lara asked. "I want to try to figure out why they weren't eating in there."

"Be my guest," Deanna said.

The moment Lara entered the kittens' original room, a sharp smell assaulted her senses. She recognized it instantly—chlorine.

Frowning, she went over to the original food bowls, which still sat, untouched. She lifted the bowl of kitten kibble to her nose. "Good glory," she muttered to herself.

In the bathroom, the same powerful odor was even more persistent. It appeared that every surface had been washed down with a heavy-handed dose of bleach.

"I suppose I'll get blamed for this."

"Ach!" Lara whipped around to see Nancy Sherman standing directly behind her. "Good heavens, you scared me. I-I didn't hear you come in."

The housekeeper's thin lips curled into a snarl. Her face reddened under her dull black hair. "Those creatures were making a godawful mess in here. In my *opinion*," she went on, "which apparently counts for little, bleach is the only thing strong enough to kill the germs."

"Ms. Sherman—Nancy," Lara said. "Noodle and Doodle have been given a clean bill of health by our veterinarian. They're due for a second set of shots, and of course Doodle needs to be neutered and Noodle needs to be spayed. But we wouldn't have allowed them to be adopted if they weren't in excellent health. Did you wash their bowls with a strong solution of bleach?"

"Of course I did. They're animals; they're not humans. And now Deanna has sullied her lovely porcelain dishes with cat food and cat germs. It's a travesty!"

Nancy Sherman was clearly on a distant wavelength from Lara. And while Lara's patience was wearing thin, she knew she couldn't entirely blame Nancy. The woman had evidently been raised to believe animals were unclean and should not be allowed inside.

"Nancy," Lara said gently, "a good washing with soap and water would have accomplished the same thing, and without irritating the kittens' senses. Cats are hypersensitive to odors."

"As am I," Nancy said crisply.

Lara sighed. They were at an impasse. "If you'll excuse me, I need to talk to Deanna."

"Of course you do," she shot at Lara. "You want her to fire me, don't you?"

Lara shook her head. "Not at all. She obviously has faith in your abilities, and it's not my place to say otherwise. But I do need to go over some… procedures with her. For the sake of the kittens," she emphasized.

With that, Lara swept past her and went back to Deanna's bedroom. She couldn't help smiling when she saw Kayla sitting on the floor, Noodle and Doodle curled up together in the hollow of her crossed legs. Deanna beamed down at them from the edge of the bed, her legs tucked primly beneath her. When she spied Lara, she motioned her over. "Can we talk? Privately?" she added.

They went into an anteroom, a dressing room, apparently, and sat on a low bench. "Lara, I'm afraid things are escalating out there." Her voice shook. She tipped her head toward the window, which faced the front yard of the mansion. "Those news trucks have planted themselves there for the long haul. And they must have ordered pizza, because a delivery car pulled up a short while ago. Oh, Lara, I'm literally a prisoner here!"

Lara's heart sank. "I'm sorry, Deanna. I wish I could help, but I'm not sure what I can do. Did the police tell you not to leave?"

"No, in fact they've been very accommodating. They're going to bring my car back later."

Lara had almost forgotten about the Mercedes. The threat scrawled on Deanna's car window had taken a back seat to the murder. "Did they have any luck tracking down the vandal?" Lara asked hopefully.

"No, none at all. I'm grateful you reported the man who was hanging around that afternoon, though I suspect he was an innocent bystander."

"He probably was," Lara agreed. "But I didn't want to leave any stones unturned, just in case."

Deanna dabbed a fingertip to one eye. "You've been so wonderful, Lara. Someday I hope to repay you for all your many kindnesses."

Lara squeezed the actress's hand. "Taking good care of your furbabies is the only payback I need." She explained briefly about the problem with Nancy's heavy-handed use of a chlorine-based cleaner.

"I wondered about that," Deanna said. "Then I got consumed with this sad murder business, and I'm afraid I let Nancy take over. It won't happen again, I assure you." She set her fine-boned jaw in a resolute line. "The kittens are under my care now. Nancy will not be dealing with them."

Inwardly, Lara sighed with relief, but she knew Deanna couldn't be home 24/7. How would they fare if Deanna had to leave for any length of time? She'd have to find a tactful way to broach the subject with the actress.

"Another thing," Deanna said. "And I know this sounds silly with everything else that's going on, but when I was at the shelter on Friday, I noticed you have a board showing pictures of adopted cats and kittens with their moms and dads. I never had a chance to take one to send you, plus I'm not very good at taking selfies."

Lara grinned. "No problem. How about if I take a few pics now? Then we'll choose one for me to print out and post."

"Excellent idea!"

They returned to the main part of the bedroom, where Deanna posed with Noodle and Doodle for several cell phone photos. After several shots, they agreed on the last one—a pic of Deanna showing off her best Hollywood smile, the kittens tucked under her chin like a furry scarf.

"I'll print it out when I get home and put it up on the board," Lara promised.

Kayla joining in, they chatted a while longer about the kittens, and how to make their new environment as stress-free as possible. Lara glanced at her phone. It was after one-thirty. She made a quick call to Amy Glindell, their veterinarian, asking if they could be a tad late with Catalina and her kitten.

"No problem," the receptionist assured her. "For some reason, everyone's late today."

After exchanging goodbyes with Deanna, Lara and Kayla retraced their path to the Saturn. The trooper who'd stopped them earlier merely waved at them from a distance.

"That place was spectacular," Kayla said when they were back on the main drag, "but I don't think I'd ever want to live there." She bit her lip and frowned.

"It's not exactly my style, either," Lara agreed, something about Kayla's expression bothering her. "My aunt's Folk Victorian is so much cozier. Feels more like a real home. By the way, do you know Nancy Sherman from someplace? I thought I saw a flash of recognition on your face."

Kayla turned and stared out her window. After a few moments she said, "No. I thought she looked familiar but I was mistaken. I decided I didn't know her after all."

The remainder of the afternoon went by quickly. Kayla handled the veterinary appointment on her own, while Lara worked in her studio for a while.

The first thing Lara had done was to print out the pic she'd taken of Deanna with her kittens and tack it onto the shelter's corkboard. Once the board filled up, she'd have to figure out an alternative way to display the photos—maybe some kind of electronic viewer? For now, the corkboard did the trick.

That job done, she made some preliminary sketches of the scene behind Deanna's mansion—in particular, the wildflowers. She hadn't recognized most of the varieties, but bright purples and yellows had been prominent. She didn't recall seeing any Queen Anne's Lace. She and Kayla had been in such a hurry to help the kittens that she hadn't taken the time to look.

Shortly before three, Kayla returned with her charges. Both mom and kitten had been pronounced healthy and ready for adoption. Kayla and Lara agreed that Kayla would work on Friday that week, then they'd plan her schedule for the following week.

Aunt Fran returned from her lunch date a little after three. She tried to look subdued, but the sparkle in her eyes was unmistakable. Lara was happy for her. Chief Whitley was a good man, even if he was clueless about cats.

She was putting away her sketch pencils when her cell pinged with a text.

Feel like eating at the clam place tonight? 6:30 pick-up?

Lara's arms tingled, and she felt her mouth curve into a grin. Gideon had discovered a nameless little outdoor shack in Tamworth that served the most delectable fried clams she'd ever tasted. Open only from June through September, the place had been mobbed both times they'd eaten there. Seating was haphazard; customers either had to nab one of the picnic tables behind the shack or eat in their cars. Nobody seemed to mind—the clams were that good.

Lara texted back.

I'll be ready!

She suddenly felt like a schoolgirl again. She hadn't had a crush on someone since…well, she couldn't even think that far back. If reconnecting with her aunt and starting the shelter had felt like a wish granted, seeing Gideon again had been the frosting on the cake. He was smart, funny, kind—and yes, she had to admit, he was a bit on the gorgeous side.

After telling Aunt Fran her plans, she hurried through a shower, then put on her pink-and-white striped T-shirt and her favorite hot pink shorts. She scooped her curly hair into a twisty bun and secured it at the back of her neck with a claw clip.

Ready to roll, she thought.

She was grabbing her phone off her nightstand when she spotted Blue resting on the foot of her bed. One dark forepaw curled beneath her, the fluffy Ragdoll cat blinked twice, then closed her eyes.

"I'm happy I'm seeing him, too," Lara murmured.

Chapter 9

The broiling heat of the day had subsided to a comfy eighty degrees. Under a blue sky and a canopy of fir trees, Lara and Gideon had managed to snag the last picnic table behind the shack.

After devouring a large order of fried clams and a heaping mound of onion rings, Gideon groaned and rubbed his stomach. "Is it even possible that I ate that entire basket of whole-belly clams? Why didn't you stop me after the first two dozen?"

Lara laughed. "I don't think you ate quite two dozen, although you did snitch my last one," she pointed out.

"Snitched? Hey, I asked you, and you said you weren't going to eat it." He looked over at an imaginary judge. "What was I supposed to do, your honor, leave it for the squirrels?" He grinned, and a lock of straight black hair fell over his forehead. Lara resisted the urge to push it back into place.

"Did you ever figure out the name of this place?" she asked instead.

He shrugged, his smile like the glow of a thousand candles, his gaze like melted chocolate. It made Lara's insides go all squiggly. "Nah, but I think it's better this way. Preserves the mystique, right? Like being part of a secret club."

"Anyway, you were telling me earlier about your uncle Amico. He finally went into the assisted living place?"

Gideon wiped his lips with his napkin and crumpled it over his paper plate. "It took some cajoling, but he's in a good place now. It wasn't safe for him to stay alone anymore. I'm going to start cleaning out his place to get it ready for sale."

"I remember him from when I was a kid," Lara said. "I used to ride my bike past his house. I'd see him in the yard, tending his flowers and tomatoes. He always waved. Seemed like such a sweet man."

"You got that right. Luckily, they have a community garden at the facility. He has his own plot, and— Hey, want to stop there on the way home? It's only a few miles out of the way. My uncle would love to see you."

"He would?"

"Oh gosh, yes." Gideon bit his lip, then cautiously added, "You know, I told him about Donald Waitt, how you spotted his body in the cemetery. I think the name rang a bell with him. Uncle Amico worked at the high school back then. He was the janitor. These days they'd call him a custodial technician, but back then it was plain old janitor."

"Really?" Lara's interest was even further piqued.

They wrapped up their trash and tossed it into the oversized barrel adjacent to the shack. Fifteen minutes later, Gideon swung his sedan into the driveway of the one-story brick building where his uncle lived.

Lush shrubs along the front of the facility, along with a row of hanging petunias above the front porch, gave the place a homey look. Two senior gents sat on the porch, their chairs rocking almost in unison. They tipped their ball caps at Lara and she waved to them.

Gideon guided Lara through the front entrance. They went over to the sign-in desk. No one was around, so Gideon scribbled their names on a sheet attached to a clipboard.

"Are you sure it's okay to visit this late?" Lara asked. "It's almost eight o'clock."

"Absolutely. The receptionist leaves at seven, but they don't lock the doors until nine." He placed his hand lightly on Lara's waist, and she felt a tingle where his fingers touched her.

They strode down a central hallway. Generic prints of New Hampshire landmarks adorned the walls along the corridor. At the end of the hallway, they hung a left. Gideon pointed to his uncle's room two doors down.

The door to the elderly man's room was partway open. Gideon tapped his knuckles lightly on the door. "Hey, Uncle, you up for a couple of visitors?"

Lara peeked into the room, where a man of at least ninety sat slumped in a recliner. His head was completely bald, save for a few white wisps above his ears. His deeply lined face was dotted with age spots. At the sound of Gideon's voice, his eyes jerked wide open. "Gideon! My Lordy, it's good to see you. Well don't just stand there, boy. Come in, come in."

Gideon took Lara's hand and she followed him into the room. The tile floor was covered by a braided rug that had seen better days—or decades.

In one corner was an antique oak bureau with a badly silvered mirror. A sagging sofa covered in worn brown velvet rested against one wall. On a low table was a flat screen TV tuned to an old war movie, the sound muted. The remote was on the floor next to the man's recliner.

"I brought a friend with me this time, Uncle Amico." Gideon's smile was so genuine it made Lara's throat hurt. He released Lara's hand and took his uncle's gnarled hands in his own. "This is Lara Caphart. She grew up in Whisker Jog. She remembers you puttering in your garden when she was a kid."

Gideon's uncle dropped his jaw to his chest. Through filmy gray eyes he gawked unabashedly at Lara. "My, my, and what a darlin' friend she is. Lana, did you say?"

"Lara." She bent and squeezed the man's veiny hand. "I honestly do remember your garden, especially the tomatoes. I was always tempted to steal one and bring it home for my mom to put in a salad."

Uncle Amico laughed heartily. "Girl, I'd have loved it if you did that. So, tell me about yourself."

Lara and Gideon sat together on the sofa, and Lara regaled the man with bits of her past—which, in her view, was as scintillating as watching grass grow. But Gideon's uncle hung on her every word, his eyes brighter than when they'd first arrived. When she described the cats in the shelter, his eyes filled with tears.

"I still miss my Gracie," he said with a loud sniffle. "She passed right before I came here. I wanted another cat, but they don't allow pets here. Weird thing, though. Sometimes I'd swear she's sitting right here in my lap. I can almost hear her purr, you know?" He waved a hand. "Ah, don't mind me. I'm a crazy old man."

Lara swallowed. "That doesn't sound crazy to me. I think Gracie *is* with you."

"On another note," Uncle Amico said, after sucking in a long sniffle, "Gideon tells me it was your sharp eyes that spotted that dead man in the cemetery a coupla days ago."

Sharp eyes, prodded by a spirit cat, Lara thought. "It was really accidental. I happened to look out the window and saw his…body."

"Donald Waitt," Uncle Amico said. His face grew animated. "Name dinged a bell, so I started thinking about it. Played high school football in the sixties, right?"

Lara looked at Gideon, who shrugged. "That goes pretty far back, Uncle. Neither of us was even around back then." He winked at Lara.

"True, true." The old man rubbed his jaw. "Wish I could think…" He shook his head and frowned.

"You must have a great memory, Uncle Amico—is it okay if I call you that?" Lara asked.

"You call me anything you'd like, Lara." He tapped at his right eye with his fingers, and his frown deepened.

"He has a phenomenal memory," Gideon said, then leaned forward. "You okay, Uncle? Is your eye bothering you?"

Uncle Amico pulled his hand away from his face. "No, I'm fine. Just trying to remember something. Tough when the brain gets old. It's like oatmeal that's been sittin' in the cooker too long."

They chatted for a few minutes longer, but the old gent became too distracted to carry on a conversation. When his uncle's eyelids lowered to half-mast, Gideon rose from the sofa and went over to him. "Hey, Uncle, it was great to see you. We'll come back soon, okay?" He leaned over and kissed his uncle's cheek. Lara's heart soared at the tender gesture.

"We sure will," Lara confirmed. "Is there anything we can bring you next time?"

His eyes half-closed, Uncle Amico smiled. "Tell you what. You bring me a nice homemade blueberry buckle, and I'll give you the first tomato from my new garden."

"You got it!" Lara promised, having no idea what a buckle was or how to make one. She gave the man a hug, and he kissed her hand.

"Don't be a stranger, young lady."

"I won't."

When they were back in Gideon's car, Lara thought about everything they'd talked about. Had Uncle Amico remembered something important about Donald Waitt? He'd talked about the sixties—ancient history to Lara. But it was the 1960s when Deanna and Donald had known each other.

Lara smiled and began thinking about blueberry buckle. "I'm going to bake that buckle for your uncle," she told Gideon.

Gideon grinned. "I knew you would. Thank you, sweetie."

Sweetie. Had he ever called her that before?

Either way, she decided she liked it.

Chapter 10

Lara sighed and waved to Gideon as he pulled out of the driveway. He'd wanted to linger a bit longer, but she'd begged off, insisting she had some administrative tasks to finish up before calling it a night. The truth was that she was a coward—afraid that her feelings for Gideon, and his for her, were growing at too alarming a rate.

She didn't want to think about that now, not with everything else that was going on.

Under a sky glittering with stars, Lara turned toward the house. She climbed the porch steps slowly, breathing in the heady scent of newly mown grass. A part of her felt happy, and yet... How could she be content knowing a murderer was still out there? The killer had struck too close to home for Lara to feel safe. She also had an aunt to worry about, as well as a house full of cats.

And what about Deanna? How safe was she, alone in the mansion with Nancy Sherman? The housekeeper clearly had a disdain for cats. That didn't make her a murderer, but Lara still wondered about her. Thank heaven Deanna had known enough to move the kittens out of the first room and into her own bedroom. It was the future that worried Lara.

Aunt Fran had left the kitchen door unlocked—something Lara would have to talk to her about. Until Donald Waitt's killer was caught, neither of them could be too careful.

Munster and Frankie greeted her the moment she stepped inside, circling her ankles likes horses around a carousel. She locked the deadbolt, then lifted Frankie into her arms. "Oh, Frankie, what are we going to do about Hesty? Everyone says he's perfect for you, but I'm still not sure." She kissed him on the snout, and he squirmed to get down.

Lara freshened the cats' food and water bowls. Aunt Fran had left a small light on in the kitchen, a sign that she'd retired to bed early and was leaving things in Lara's hands. Lara suspected her aunt had made herself scarce in case Lara had wanted to invite Gideon inside.

After making quick work of litter box scooping, Lara went upstairs to her room. Frankie made a beeline for Aunt Fran's door, which hung partway open. No doubt he would spend the night on her aunt's bed, along with Dolce and Twinkles.

When Lara had first moved in that past November, two calico siblings—Pickles and Izzy—had been her nightly sleeping companions. Then a week after the shelter officially opened, a young woman who owned a lighting shop had adopted them into her life. Lara missed them terribly, especially at night, but was thrilled they'd found their forever home.

Lara glanced over at the corner cat tree she'd recently installed in her room. Now that the house was an official shelter, she thought it was high time they added more accoutrements for the cats. The kitties who used the carpeted tree still preferred the one in the large parlor. But one night several weeks ago, Lara had awakened to see Ballou staring at her from the top perch, his eyes shining in the moonlit room. It startled and delighted her, but she hadn't dared move. In the morning, he was gone, no doubt back under her bed. *Baby steps*, she told herself.

She unclipped her hair and let it fall to her shoulders. These days she was keeping it shorter, thanks to Kellie at Kurl-me-Klassy. Lara smiled when she recalled how miffed the stylist had been with her the prior October, when she'd thought Lara had accused a close friend of murder. After the real murderer had been caught, the misunderstanding between them had been quickly erased. Kellie was a friend, now, and the best hair stylist in town.

Lara undressed and threw on a sleeveless nightshirt. She turned on the window fan, then grabbed her tablet and plunked down on her bed. Munster hopped up next to her and batted a paw at the screen.

"If you want to Google something, you'll have to wait your turn," Lara told him. She kissed the top of his head. "I've got some peeps I want to check out."

She plunked Nancy Sherman's name into the search pane, groaning when she got about sixty-four thousand hits. She glanced at a few of the links, but saw right away that they weren't going to help. Next she tried narrowing the results by adding the words "New Hampshire" to the search. That didn't help either.

The expression on Kayla's face when she'd first seen the housekeeper still nagged at Lara. Though Kayla later denied it, Lara would've have sworn Kayla had recognized the woman.

She decided to go back to searching Donald Waitt's name. He was the victim, which meant he had at least one enemy. Although her earlier search of his name had yielded next to nothing, she remembered Gideon's uncle saying that Waitt had played high school football in the 1960s. This time, she Googled his name using different combinations, including the words "high school football."

Nothing significant popped up. The combinations brought up by the search engine didn't help with what she'd been hoping to find.

Lara yawned, a sudden wave of fatigue washing over her. Her eyes were burning. Maybe she should save this for morning. Her brain wasn't exactly firing on all cylinders.

She rubbed her eyes and moved on to something easy, something she hoped might yield the results she was looking for.

Blueberry buckle.

Chapter 11

On Thursday Aunt Fran rose early and whipped up Belgian waffles for breakfast.

"I don't know why I didn't think of making these before," she said, swabbing her last bite of waffle through a puddle of maple syrup. "When you were a kid, I made them for you every Sunday."

Lara licked a blob of whipped cream off her lips. "Today's Thursday, but I'll take them any time. And thanks for remembering. These were scrumptious."

Aunt Fran set down her fork and pushed aside her empty plate. "Lara, we need to call Curtis Heston today about Frankie. His granddaughter called twice last evening when you were out. She knows that his references checked out, because she followed up on them."

"I know," Lara said. "I just…" She shook her head. There was no way she could explain—not without sounding like a crackpot.

"You just what?" Aunt Fran's tone was uncharacteristically stern. "I've never seen you behave this way, Lara. You need to tell me why you object to this adoption."

"It's a feeling, Aunt Fran. I don't know how to explain it any better than that."

Her aunt looked down at the feline in question, who was meandering toward them as if he knew they were talking about him. Frankie sprang onto her lap and rubbed his head against her arm. She hugged him to her chest and sighed. "I had a feeling you'd say that, so I had another thought. Why don't you do a pop-in today? Stop over at Hesty's without letting him know you're coming. If something still doesn't sit right with you, we'll talk about it. Otherwise—"

"Otherwise Frankie is his. No further questions," Lara agreed.

Today was Kayla's off day, so Lara performed the usual feline duties. She thought about how much she'd enjoyed being with their new assistant the day before. Despite the stressful trip to Deanna's, she'd felt a kinship with the young woman.

With another stifling day predicted, Lara changed into a lightweight jersey top and a pair of flowered shorts. She twisted her hair into a ponytail to get it off her neck. After locating her sunglasses, she grabbed her tote and hopped into the Saturn. She'd added Hesty's address to the GPS feature on her cell phone. The estimated drive time was four minutes.

Hesty lived on a tree-lined street of tract homes that had been built during the 1950s. While the lots were small, nearly every home boasted a yard bursting with flowers. Many residents had tiny gardens in the back.

She turned into Hesty's driveway and parked behind an aging Buick. She let her car idle for a minute while she scoped out the house. The lawn was neatly tended, and the grass looked freshly cut. Flower boxes in both front windows overflowed with bright pink impatiens. A rolled-up newspaper sat on the bottom step of the small front porch.

With a sigh, Lara shut off the engine and swung her legs out of the car. A weird feeling clawed at her. Was Blue watching her from somewhere? Was that why she felt a chill creep up her arms?

She picked up the newspaper and climbed the three steps to the porch. A wreath of faux hydrangeas hung on the front door. Lara pressed the doorbell, and heard soft chimes drift from inside.

After another minute or so, she pushed the doorbell again. She leaned her ear close to the door. Not a single sound came from inside.

Lara turned and glanced at the house across the street. A petite woman wearing a straw sunhat and gloves and holding a garden trowel waved at her. "You looking for Hesty?" the woman shouted.

Lara nodded and set the newspaper on the top step, then trotted down the stairs and across the street to talk to her. "Yes. Is that his car? He hasn't taken his paper in yet. Maybe he sleeps late."

The woman, her long gray hair hanging loose around her shoulders, shook her head. "Hesty never sleeps late. He's up with the birds. Feeds the birds, in fact. The squirrels, too." She bit her lip and frowned. "You sure you rang the bell hard enough? That doorbell can be sticky in the humid weather."

"I did," Lara said. "And I heard the chimes."

The woman tossed her trowel on the ground and peeled off her gardening gloves. "Who'd you say you were?"

Lara smiled at her. "I didn't, but I'm Lara Caphart from the High Cliff Shelter for Cats."

"Oh, that's right! Hesty was so excited about adopting a new friend. I was wondering when he was gonna bring that cat home. He told me all about the little sweetie." She peered over Lara's shoulder at Hesty's house, her mouth curving into a frown. "You know, I don't like this. Hesty always brings the paper in early. Likes to read it while he's having breakfast. You stay right here, honey. I'm getting Hesty's key." She winked at Lara. "We keep each other's keys. You know, for emergencies. I'm Mildred, by the way."

Lara waited at the edge of the yard while Mildred hustled inside her house. A minute later, Mildred returned holding a key in the air. "Let's check it out," she said, a determined look in her eye.

"Thanks, Mildred. I really appreciate this."

Together they hurried across the street. When they reached Hesty's front steps, Mildred edged ahead of Lara and shoved the key in the door lock. She twisted it and pushed the door open, then immediately stumbled backward. "Lor-dee! It's hotter than the hinges of Hades in there!"

Lara grabbed Mildred under the arms to keep her upright as a blast of hot, fetid air slammed her nostrils. "Mildred, are you okay?"

Mildred nodded, made the sign of the cross, then shook her head. "Something's wrong. Hesty didn't turn his AC on this morning. The place is like an oven."

Lara agreed. Something about the whole scenario felt out of whack. The urge to rush inside to check on Hesty battled with her instinct to turn and flee and call 9-1-1. Her legs felt like rubber pins glued to the steps.

"Stay here, Mildred. I'm going to check to see if Hesty's in there." *And pray to God he's not.*

Mildred nodded, her face the color of bleached flour. "Bless you."

Lara moved around the woman and crossed the threshold onto a tiled entryway. Inside what looked to be a tidy home, a sour smell hung in the air. A carpeted staircase directly in front of Lara rose to an upper level. The living room was to her left. Sounds from a television game show floated into earshot. Facing the television was a reclining chair that rested next to an end table. From where she was standing, she could make out a bald head poking over the top of the chair.

Lara held her breath and swallowed. "Hesty?"

She called his name again, then forced her feet to tread farther into the room. She moved around the chair until she was facing its occupant.

Hesty sat slightly tilted in the recliner, his eyes staring dully at the floor and his jaw open. His skin had a bluish tint. "Oh, Hesty," Lara murmured. She gulped back a lump of bile, then turned and stumbled to the front door.

"M-Mildred," she stuttered. "We have to call nine-one-one."

Mildred nodded, tears forming on her pale lashes. "He's gone, isn't he?" she whispered.

"I-I think so." Lara squeezed the elderly woman's shoulder.

"I knew it. Soon as I opened that door, a bad feeling skittered straight up my arms." Mildred sucked in a shaky breath. "Let's call the police from my house. We can't go back in there."

Lara nodded, then followed the woman across the street. She felt numb. She couldn't stop thinking about Blue, how agitated the cat had been the day Hesty had announced his intention to adopt Frankie.

You knew he was going to die, didn't you? Lara asked silently.

Her face wet with tears, she trailed Mildred through a side door into a bright, cheery kitchen. Then her knees gave out and she plopped onto a chair. She dropped her head into her hands and sobbed. Mildred leaned over her and grabbed her shoulders, crying every bit as hard as Lara.

Chapter 12

"It's called an MI," Chief Whitley explained. "Myocardial infarction. A fancy name for a heart attack."

Aunt Fran set a cup of steaming tea in front of Lara, along with a wedge from an orange. "I thought you might like a squirt of citrus with it," she said kindly, resting her hand on Lara's shoulder. She looked at the chief. "So his death was from natural causes?"

"Totally," the chief said. "Evidently, Hesty had been keeping his ticker problems a secret from his kids and grandkids so they wouldn't start treating him like an invalid. His doctor was aware of his condition, of course, but he was the only one."

"The poor man," Aunt Fran murmured.

"In a way, Lara, it was a good thing you got there when you did. If he'd stayed like that much longer in the heat…" Whitley swallowed. "Well, it wouldn't have been a pretty sight."

"It *wasn't* a pretty sight," Lara snapped. She squeezed her eyes shut and sighed. "Sorry. I didn't mean to bark at you. And for the record, even if I hadn't gone over there, his neighbor Mildred would have checked on him. She knew it was strange that he hadn't brought his paper inside before breakfast."

Lara saw her aunt and the chief exchange glances. She could guess what they were thinking: *Second body this week.*

She squeezed a spurt of orange juice into her steaming mug. She tested a sip—still too hot to drink. "If his death was from natural causes, why did they detain me for so long?" Lara asked Whitley. "I was there for, like…three hours!"

"I know." Whitley spoke quietly. "It seems excessive in a case like this. But until they're fairly certain of the cause of death, they have to be sure all their Is are dotted and their Ts are crossed. Hesty's doctor helped put the pieces together."

Lara caught Aunt Fran's stare and averted her gaze. "I feel like one of those cadaver dogs," she said bleakly. "Everywhere I go, I find a...body."

Aunt Fran went over and hugged her niece. "I know it seems that way, Lara. But you've just had a string of bad luck, that's all. I'm sure it won't happen again."

Lara took a careful sip of her tea. She wished she could believe that.

She gazed down at the cat curled in her lap. Frankie had become her constant companion from the moment she'd returned from Hesty's. Lara wondered if the cat had a sixth sense that told him he'd never see Hesty again. She bent and rubbed her cheek on Frankie's soft head.

For once, she was happy that today wasn't an adoption day. She could do some vacuuming and dusting, then spend a few hours on her watercolors. Maybe she'd go back to working on the painting of Deanna's stone mansion.

"Chief, before you go...you, um, never answered my text. About the vandalism to Deanna's car?"

Whitley flushed and shot a look at Aunt Fran. "Technically, the vehicle wasn't damaged, only defaced. Unfortunately, we haven't made much progress in locating the culprit. That man you saw looking into your car? No one else reported seeing him hanging around that day."

Lara sagged. "But he bought ice cream from the truck on the corner. Doesn't the ice cream guy remember him?"

"The ice cream vendor vaguely remembers a fellow in a Red Sox tee buying chocolate cones from him. Not exactly rare in our neck of the woods. Anyway, the vendor had no clue who he was."

"What about fingerprints on the money he paid with?"

"Lara, the kid selling ice cream had been making change all afternoon. Even if he still had the money the mystery guy paid with, do you know how many other people's prints would be on it?" Whitley sounded exasperated now.

"I get you, Chief," Lara said and stroked Frankie's head.

The chief's cell phone pinged. He dug it out of his shirt pocket and glanced at the new text. Frowning, he tapped a few keys and stuck it back in his pocket. "Sorry, but duty calls. I gotta run."

Aunt Fran walked him out to his unmarked car. Lara couldn't help wondering how far their relationship would progress. They'd known each other for decades, but only recently had they started getting so cozy with each other. Plus, the chief wasn't exactly a cat lover. That had to be driving Aunt Fran crazy.

Once Lara began her cleaning routine, her spirits improved. Even in the heat, the physical labor had a positive effect on her. It helped banish the dark thoughts that refused to stop trouncing through her head.

She finished her cleaning routine by mopping the floor on the back porch—the shelter's meet-and-greet area. She'd already used a vinegar solution to wipe down the porch windows, and they gleamed squeaky clean in the afternoon sun.

Lara was squeezing excess water from the mop when a noise at the door caught her attention. She turned and saw the doorknob jiggling. Someone was trying to get into the locked shelter.

She set aside the mop and went over and peeked through the door pane. A face stared back at her—a little girl of about eight or nine. The child's dark, braided pigtails were secured with red bows, and in one hand she clutched a book. When the child realized she'd been caught trying to get in, her mouth formed a frightened O. She turned and raced across Aunt Fran's yard, her red sneakers pounding the ground.

Lara unlocked the door and whipped it open. "Wait! Come back!" she called out.

The child picked up her pace. She ran until she disappeared past the big maple at the back of the yard. She was obviously familiar with the path through the wooded copse, beyond which was a subdivision of recently built homes. The girl vanished from sight so quickly Lara could no longer see her.

"Well, that was odd," Lara muttered to herself. She closed the door but left it unlocked.

With all the stories in the news lately about missing and abducted children, she couldn't help wondering if the child had been in some kind of trouble. What if she'd been seeking refuge?

"What was odd?"

Lara jumped and whirled around. "Oh, God, Aunt Fran, I didn't realize you were right there. I guess I'm a little jittery."

"Understandable, considering everything you've been through," her aunt said. "So what was odd?"

Lara told her about the little girl who'd been trying to get in.

"And she had a book with her?"

"Yup. I couldn't make out the cover, but I'm pretty sure it was a kids' book."

"She probably lives at Lilac Heights. They have a wooded common area that backs up to my property line."

Lara recalled seeing a sign at the entrance to the subdivision when she was first reacquainting herself with the area. Lilac Heights was a neighborhood of about a dozen lookalike houses, distinguishable from one another only by their various muted colors. "Do you think she's okay? Maybe we should ask the police to check on her."

"I'll give Jerry a call, but I don't think it's anything to worry about." Aunt Fran went over and squeezed Lara's waist. "You've been on overload, Lara. Why don't you work on your watercolors this afternoon?"

"Exactly what I'd planned. But first, I have a question. Did you ever make a blueberry buckle? I want to make one for Gideon's uncle."

Aunt Fran looked surprised. "I think I made one a long time ago, but it's not one of my usual recipes. Isn't Gideon's uncle in assisted living now?"

Lara smiled. "Yeah, we visited with him last night. What a sweet guy. We made a deal—a blueberry buckle for him, and a juicy homegrown tomato for me. He told us he has a little garden plot at the facility."

"I'm sure I can dig up a recipe," Aunt Fran said. "So, did you and Gid have a good time last night? You and I never really had a chance to chat this morning." There was a lilt in her voice that made Lara squirm a little.

"Oh, sure," she said casually, feeling her face redden. "We had fried clams at that place in Tamworth, then we stopped to see his uncle. That's about it."

Lara never felt comfortable talking to her aunt about her relationship with Gideon. For starters, Gideon was the shelter's lawyer—a connection she didn't want to jeopardize. But the real reason, if Lara were truthful with herself, was that she was afraid to jinx the blossoming romance.

Aunt Fran didn't press her any further. She made a quick call to Jerry Whitley, who promised to make some quiet inquiries about the little girl without alarming anyone.

Lara worked for the next few hours on the painting of the stone mansion. Unfortunately, the more she worked on it, the less she liked the result. She couldn't stop thinking about the gorgeous profusion of wildflowers she'd seen at the rear of the mansion the day before when she and Kayla were there. The scene had reminded her of an English garden—something out of an Agatha Christie mystery. She wished, now, that she'd taken a picture when she'd had the chance.

Stretching her arms toward the ceiling, Lara glanced around at the books on the painted bookshelves. Once packed with children's books, the shelves now boasted an eclectic variety of volumes her aunt couldn't bear to part with. Among them were books about flower gardens—Aunt Fran was a lover of tulips. Maybe there was a book with photos of wildflowers?

Without warning, a fluffy cat leaped silently onto one of the upper shelves. Lara chuckled. She was accustomed, now, to the elusive Ragdoll appearing from out of nowhere.

It wasn't easy, being the only one who could see the mysterious cat. Lara knew there had to be a reason for their mystical connection. If only she had a clue what it was.

She hated to think where she'd be right now if Blue hadn't intervened last October when a murderer had confronted Lara. Only Lara knew what really happened that day; the police had been genuinely baffled.

Pushing away the memory, Lara gazed lovingly at Blue. The cat stretched out on the bookshelf, and a sheet of paper fluttered to the floor. Lara went over to retrieve it. "Oh, hey, this is that yard sale flyer," she said to the cat. "Thanks for reminding me." She wanted so badly to touch the cat, to stroke her cream-colored tummy, but she knew any attempt would be in vain. Instead, she went back to her chair in front of the easel.

When she looked up again, Blue was gone.

Lara skimmed over the pink flyer. The community yard sale, at which the library would also sell donated books, started at ten Saturday morning.

Perfect. She loved picking through other people's discarded trinkets and treasures. Much of it had little monetary value, but it was fun to poke around anyway. She placed the notice on the corner of her work table to remind her of the event.

Lara grabbed her tablet and searched the internet for images of wildflowers. A massive array of photos appeared. One image reminded her of the wildflowers she'd seen behind the mansion. The colors were similar. The lupine, in all its purple glory, stood out from among the other flowers.

On her easel, Lara set up a fresh sheet of paper, lining the edges with masking tape. If she couldn't paint from the real thing, she'd work from a facsimile. She wanted to present the watercolor as a housewarming gift to Deanna.

She hadn't talked to the actress since she and Kayla had visited the day before. She'd decided to step back for a day and give Deanna a breather. She felt sure Deanna would get in touch with her if anything was amiss with Noodle and Doodle.

Around four-thirty, Lara took a break. Her neck felt sweaty, and she needed hydration. She went into the kitchen and filled a glass with ice water. She gulped down a few swigs, set the glass on the counter, and wandered out to the front porch. Aunt Fran sat under the big maple in one of the two Adirondack chairs. A glass of lemonade rested on her chair's wide arm, her cell phone beside it.

"Reading anything good?" Lara said, trekking out to sit with her aunt. She plunked herself down and sat cross-legged on the grass.

"Oh, this book is excellent. You know how I love World War Two dramas? This one's about a brother and a sister in London who get separated during the Battle of Britain."

Aunt Fran waxed on about the book's plot, but Lara only half-listened. She couldn't stop her mind from wandering. Her thoughts bounced back and forth between Hesty's tidy little house and Deanna's stone mansion. The homes, while vastly different, had one thing in common—their owners had come into the shelter to adopt cats.

A car pulled into the driveway, a pale blue sedan with a missing hubcap that Lara didn't recognize. She exchanged looks with her aunt. "Are you expecting anyone, Aunt Fran?"

Her aunt shook her head.

The shelter had its own parking area on the other side of the house. Since it was clearly marked, Lara didn't think it was someone who'd mixed up adoption days.

The driver shut off the engine. After what seemed like an excruciatingly long time, the door opened. A woman wearing oversized sunglasses emerged from the car. Attired in dark brown capris and a coffee-colored tee, she had straggly black hair that stuck out from the edges of a green scarf. The woman glanced all around, then spotted them in the yard. Lara jumped up off the ground to greet the visitor.

"Can I help— Oh, good glory, Deanna. I didn't recognize you."

The actress, who'd removed her sunglasses, smiled wryly at her. "Good. I didn't want to be recognized. I'm driving Nancy's car and wearing one of her wigs."

Lara gave her a polite hug, then waved a hand in her aunt's direction. "Aunt Fran and I were just chatting about books. Can you join us for an iced tea or a lemonade?"

Deanna heaved a theatrical sigh. "You know what? I'd love that. I've been feeling like a hostage in that place."

That place. Her tone made Lara cringe.

"Thank heaven for whoever carved out that service road through the pines," the actress went on. She followed Lara into the backyard. "I used it to escape all the gawkers. I'm grateful for one other thing—some of the media trucks have finally left. I guess they got bored. Either that, or their bosses told them to find a real story instead of bothering an innocent person."

"I'm sure that's a relief," Lara said.

Aunt Fran smiled curiously when she saw them approach. After several seconds of staring, she recognized the actress. "Deanna, what a lovely surprise." She closed her book. "Do you have time to sit with us for a while?"

"Yes, I'd love to, and I'll take you up on that iced tea, Lara." Deanna lowered herself gracefully onto the other Adirondack chair.

Lara dashed inside the house. She returned with a glass of chilled iced tea and gave it to Deanna, then sat down again on the grass. "Is everything all right with the kittens?"

Deanna waved a hand. "Oh my, yes. They're doing wonderfully. Living large in my bedroom." She flashed a Hollywood smile. "They've been keeping me company at night," she said dreamily. "They sleep at the foot of my bed...well, you saw how large it is. When I woke up this morning, Doodle was kneading my neck. It was so adorable! After a few more days, I'm going to expand their living space to the entire top floor. The room that Nancy *over*cleaned, to put it mildly, is starting to air out."

Lara pulled up her knees and wrapped her arms around them. It was strange to see the glamorous actress hiding behind a cheap wig. Then again, that's what acting was all about, wasn't it? Playing a role. Pretending to be someone else.

"That's good to hear, Deanna," Lara said. "The thing is, and I don't mean to sound judgmental, but I'm a little worried about Nancy Sherman. It's sort of obvious she doesn't like cats. What's going to happen if you leave town? What if you have to travel, or take a vacation?"

"Or go off on a film shoot?" she said acidly. "That's what you're really thinking, isn't it?"

Feeling suddenly under attack, Lara held out her palms. "No, that's not what I—"

"I suppose you've heard rumors. I haven't made it public yet, but my acting days are over, at least for the time being. My agent and I have parted ways. We've severed our contract. I would appreciate it if you'd respect my privacy and keep that to yourselves. I'll be making an announcement over the next few weeks. This little...murder problem has set me back, I'm afraid."

Lara felt her jaw drop. Little murder problem? Is that how she thought of Waitt's horrible death?

"I didn't mean to pry," Lara said quietly, but in a firm voice. The topic of the kittens had strayed off. Lara needed to lasso it back in.

"Be assured we won't utter a word," Aunt Fran added in a kind voice. "And we're not trying to accuse anyone of anything. But, Deanna, after what we observed, we do have reason to be concerned about Ms. Sherman. Do you know very much about her?"

Deanna blanched. "Well, yes, certainly I do. I had her thoroughly checked out before I hired her. She's had some hard knocks in the past, but she's good people. Solid. I trust her without any reservation whatsoever."

Lara saw that they weren't getting anywhere. For whatever reason, Deanna had gone on the defensive about her housekeeper.

A tear slid down Deanna's pale cheek. "There was...actually a reason I came here. The police came over to question me again this morning. They'd gotten printouts of Donald's cell phone records. It seems someone pretending to be me had been sending him threatening texts before he died. The texts started around the time the announcement went in the local paper about my moving here."

Lara felt her insides churn. "What do you mean, *pretending* to be you? Can't the police track where the texts originated from?"

"That's where it gets tricky. The impostor evidently used a burner phone. I'm sure you've heard of them. You pay cash for them and buy prepaid minutes. Your identity remains totally private, which is why criminals use them." She heaved a long sigh. "Here's the worst part. A few days before the tea given by the Ladies' Association, the tone of the texts changed. They suddenly became friendly. My impersonator supposedly invited Donald to show up at the tea so we could chat"—she made air quotes with her fingers—"about the old days."

Aunt Fran looked flummoxed. "Deanna, if anyone can buy a burner phone, why are the police so sure the texts came from you? It was obviously someone pretending to be you, right?"

Or was it? Lara mused.

"That...isn't all," Deanna went on. "The last text, supposedly sent by me, asked Donald to meet me in the cemetery at five a.m. that morning—the morning of the murder. It also instructed him not to park anywhere on the property. That must be why the police found his car parked somewhere down the road."

Lara felt as if someone had struck her with a rock. For the first time, she felt a trickle of unease about the actress. From the beginning, Lara had believed in her innocence. Waitt's body had been dumped in that family cemetery to implicate Deanna in his murder; Lara had been sure of that.

The graffiti on Deanna's car—*time to pay the piper.* Clearly someone had been trying to frighten her. But the connection was flimsy. Why scare Deanna and then murder Waitt?

Another thought chilled Lara. What if all of it had been a publicity stunt? A stunt that somehow went too far and ended in Waitt's untimely demise?

Hollywood was rumored to be a tough place for aging actors. Lara had read that some of them struggled constantly to get decent parts. Was Deanna one of them? Even with her Oscar and Tony nominations, her age alone limited the available roles.

"That's what I'm trying to tell you," Deanna said in a shaky voice. "Whoever sent those texts to Donald knew my real name."

"Real name?" Lara said.

Deanna nodded. "My agent went to great lengths to keep my given name hidden as much as possible from the public. Still, it's out there if you dig deep enough. You know how it is—you search a well-known personality on the internet and their entire life story appears. True or not, people believe what they read."

"They do," Lara agreed. She realized she'd never searched Deanna's name online. Why hadn't she thought to do that?

"This has to remain among us," Deanna said, her voice fading to a murmur. "My given name is a horror, especially for someone of my celebrity. My surname was Dorkin, and my parents named me Idena after my mother's favorite aunt."

Lara stared at her. "Idena Dorkin?"

"Except that I was always known as Deeny. Deeny Dorkin. Can you imagine a more horrifying name for an actress?"

A bubble of laughter threatened to burst from Lara. She tamped it down, realizing how insensitive it would sound. "If it's any consolation, these days it would be quite a distinctive name."

"These days." Deanna barked out a harsh laugh. "These days aren't like the days of old—the glory days, as I think of them."

Aunt Fran, who'd remained quiet until now, spoke up. "Deanna, if the police seriously suspect you of Waitt's murder, then why are you here? Why haven't they taken you into custody?"

"They can't. At best, the evidence is circumstantial and they know it. They've had no luck tracing the murder weapon—a knife of some sort. And as Lara pointed out, anyone can use a burner phone and pretend to be me. The question is," she said in a choked voice, "who knew my real name?"

Someone local, Lara speculated. Someone from Deanna's past. Someone who'd read that Deanna Daltry was moving to Whisker Jog.

Lara now suspected that the threat against Deanna had been real. If Deanna hadn't killed Waitt, then someone was trying to frame her.

She got up, went over to the actress, and knelt on the grass in front of her. "Think, Deanna. Go back in time, to when you lived here. Is there anyone you might have made angry enough to hold a grudge?"

Deanna's face went slack. "I-I don't think so. How can I remember that far back?"

"Everyone remembers *some* things from their school days," Lara pointed out. "I'm not trying to bully you. I'm the last person who'd do that. I'm only begging you to think back. Was there a boy whose feelings you hurt by rejecting him? A shy girl you failed to befriend?"

"I don't know. I don't remember!"

Lara sat back on her heels. She didn't know what else to say, so she shook her head.

"Deanna," Aunt Fran put in, "I apologize for changing the subject, but if the kittens are too much for you right now, we'd be happy to take them back until things settle down."

Tears flowed down Deanna's pale cheeks. "Please don't do that to me. I adore those furry little darlings. I promise you, they'll be safe and pampered and loved. I give you my word on that."

Aunt Fran looked at Lara. Finally, she nodded. "All right, then. But in return, you have to promise that if you're taken into custody, Lara and I have your permission to pick up Noodle and Doodle and bring them back here with us."

"Absolutely," Deanna said, crossing her heart with her fingers. Her face creased with anguish. "If that happens, I will totally relinquish them."

Chapter 13

Kayla called Lara early Friday morning. Her grandmother, she told Lara, had made a last-minute doctor appointment in Concord that day, and Kayla didn't want her gram to go by herself. "If I can switch my work day to Saturday, I'll get there super early. I promise."

"No problem," Lara had told her, feeling a bit disappointed. "See you tomorrow."

With Friday being an adoption day, Lara had hoped to have Kayla get more acquainted with the process and help with prospective adoptions. So far, the young woman had been a dream-come-true employee, handling every cat with loving care.

Lara stared into her teacup and munched on a half-slice of toast.

"Everything okay?" Aunt Fran asked from across the table. Dolce, the all-black male, was curled in her lap. "You're only eating half a slice of toast."

"Yeah, I'm fine. Kayla begged off working today, but she's switching to tomorrow. Something about her grandmother having a doctor appointment in Concord."

"That should be fine," Aunt Fran said, "but I do have a suggestion. It might help if you made up her schedule a month in advance, instead of winging it week to week. That way you can plan better."

Lara smiled, then slid off her chair and kissed her aunt's cheek. "My logical, organized aunt to the rescue," she teased. "Will do. By the way, where's Frankie? Laying low today?"

Her aunt frowned. "He hasn't been his lovable self since yesterday. I know this sounds strange, but I think he senses he'll never see Hesty again. He goes off by himself and sleeps."

There are stranger things, Lara thought. "I suspect you're right. I've always thought cats had a sixth sense about stuff like that."

"You headed to the coffee shop?" Aunt Fran asked.

"Yup. I'll make it a short visit. Lots to do today." She swallowed her last bite of toast, then delivered her empty plate and mug to the sink. "I purposely ate a light breakfast. Daisy's making cinnamon-streusel muffins today. I want to scoop one before they run out."

"Grab one for me, too," her aunt said and dabbed her nose with a tissue.

"You got it. You okay?"

"Fine. Bit of a sniffle is all."

Ten minutes later, tote on her shoulder, Lara strode through the front door of Bowker's Coffee Stop. She shot a glance toward the back of the restaurant's dining area. Gideon sometimes sat there with his laptop and worked while he nibbled at a bite of breakfast.

No such luck today, but she spotted Daisy Bowker cleaning up tables from the breakfast rush. Lara waved at her and Daisy returned the gesture.

"There's my favorite cat lady," Sherry said after Lara took a seat at the counter. She poured Lara a cup of steaming coffee. Lara thought her friend's black hair looked more subdued than usual. The gelled spikes had morphed into gelled curls.

"New 'do?" Lara asked.

Sherry blushed, then shrugged. "I didn't feel like fussing with it today. I saved a muffin for you."

"I hope you saved two. Aunt Fran wants one."

"I'll talk to the lady in charge, see what I can do." She went off in the direction of the swinging door that led into the kitchen.

Lara plunked a packet of half-and-half into her mug just as the coffee shop's door opened. "Lara, oh good! I'm glad you're here."

Mary Newman, the thirtysomething owner of the downtown gift shop that opened early in May, flitted over to Lara. "I was hoping you'd be here. I have great news—I sold two of your watercolors this morning!" She slid onto a stool next to Lara.

For the last three weeks, six of Lara's watercolors had hung in the gift shop on consignment. Each one featured cats of various sorts. Lara's plan was to use any sale proceeds to fund an account for cat owners who had difficulty paying veterinary bills. For some people, it meant the difference between keeping a cat or being forced to give it up for adoption.

"Which ones?" Lara asked, her insides jumping.

"The ones titled *Calico Caravan* and *Blackjack Rummy*. The buyer—I think she was a tourist—bought both. She couldn't stop gushing over them."

"I'm so glad," Lara said. "Thanks for displaying them, Mary."

Mary pushed a strand of her dark hair behind one ear. In her sleeveless cotton blouse and blue shorts, she didn't look much older than a teenager. "Chris said he saw you at the welcome party for Deanna Daltry on Sunday."

"He did," Lara said, somewhat grimly. "The way things turned out, I'm sure he got some juicy tidbits for this week's paper." The image of the threat scrawled on Deanna's car window popped into her head. It reminded her that she needed to do more research on that flower—Queen Anne's Lace.

Sherry came over holding a steaming pot in the air. "Coffee, Mary?"

"You bet." She smiled at Sherry, who plopped a plate with a cinnamon-streusel muffin in front of Lara. "Wasn't it horrible about that teacher getting killed?" Mary went on. "And then poor Hesty!"

"Awful," Sherry said, her gaze straying to the door. "I didn't know the murdered guy, but Hesty was a sweetie."

Lara heard her stomach rumble. Her head buzzed, then she felt Mary's hand encircling her wrist.

"Oh, Lara, I'm so sorry," Mary said. "I forgot you found both—"

"It's okay," Lara said with a weak smile. "Let's talk about something else."

"Hello."

Lara jumped slightly at the voice and swiveled around on her stool. Joy Renfield—was that her name?—stood barely a foot behind her. A powerful scent clung to her. *Something with cloves,* Lara thought.

Sporting strands of neon bracelets, a tie-dyed tee, and a flowing purple skirt adorned with clusters of white flowers, she grinned from ear to ear. A massive purse made of painted burlap rested on one shoulder. "Hi, Lara. I was walking by on my way to the gift shop and saw you sitting in here."

"Oh, um, hi there. Nice to see you again, Joy."

"You remembered!"

"Sure I did." She smiled at the woman, who seemed over the moon at having spotted Lara in the coffee shop. "We met at the tea party. In fact, didn't you give me a coupon for a free tealeaf reading?"

Joy's face lit up. "I did, and I hope you'll take advantage of it soon. No time like the present, right?"

"Right," Lara said, nodding at Mary. "By the way, this is Mary Newman. She owns the gift shop."

Joy stared wide-eyed at Mary. "Well, then," she said slowly, "you're just the lady I was looking to meet. I have a side business making jewelry"—she held up her bangled wrist—"and I was hoping I could sell some at your shop. Can we chat?"

Mary looked trapped. She glanced at her watch. "I…guess I could spare a few minutes."

"Great." Joy grinned and turned back to Lara. "Lara, regarding our mutual *friend*…you know, the one we honored on Sunday?"

Lara nodded warily.

"I've been hoping, well, I mean, *wanting* to have a private tea party for her, complete with a tealeaf reading. I can also do a tarot card reading if she'd like. Lots of the stars like that sort of thing, though I believe the leaves tell it all." Joy furrowed her thick eyebrows. "Since she adopted kittens from your shelter, I thought you might be able to approach her for me. You can tell her I'd be glad to go to her home so she wouldn't have to face all the media hounds." Joy's eyes glittered.

Now Lara was the one to feel trapped. Joy was obviously a fan of the actress and was trying to get into her good graces.

"That's really thoughtful of you, Joy. I'm sure Deanna would appreciate the offer. She has a lot going on right now, but I'll mention it the next time I talk to her."

"Thank you, Lara. And don't forget—I owe you a free reading!"

Lara waved as Joy trounced off, a dazed-looking Mary shuffling in her wake.

Sherry rolled her eyes. "Poor Mary. She never even took a sip of her coffee. That woman's like a steamroller, isn't she?"

"She's energetic, that's for sure," Lara said. "I never had a chance to introduce her to you. Sorry about that."

"No prob." Sherry reached under the counter and pulled out a white bag. "Here's Fran's muffin. Mom said to let her know when you need more cookies."

"We have about two dozen in the freezer. We'll probably need more by Tuesday."

"My ears are burning," Daisy Bowker said, scooting up behind her daughter. "How's Fran today, Lara?"

"Still upright, as she likes to say. She sniffled a bit this morning. I hope she's not coming down with something."

Daisy winked at Lara. "Tell her to take Echinacea. Works for me every time. Hey, I gotta dash. My daughter's been running me ragged."

"Drama queen," Sherry shot at her mother's retreating form.

"You two," Lara said, her voice suddenly raw. A wave of emotion gripped her by the throat. "What would I ever do without you?"

Sherry looked alarmed. "What's wrong, Lara? Did something happen?"

"No." She shook her head. "Don't mind me. I'm having a weird week, that's all. First that teacher, then Hesty—"

"I know," Sherry said softly. "It's like a bad luck week for you, isn't it?" She squeezed her friend's arm. "Somehow, though, I think it's going to end on a positive note."

Lara choked out a nervous giggle. "I hope so, Sher. I sure as heck hope so."

Chapter 14

Lara began the short trek back to her aunt's, the sun baking her arms. She glanced across the street at the town library. Signs had been put up at the entrance to the parking lot, asking patrons to park on the street. Evidently, it took the better part of a day to set up for Saturday's yard sale.

Today Lara wanted to do more painting, if she could squeeze it in. She was sitting on a few commissioned projects, which, luckily, had distant deadlines. One of the projects was for Wayne Lefkovitz, a wealthy Boston art collector. The year before, he'd paid Lara a hefty sum for six watercolors of famous Boston landmarks. Each of the paintings had a unique feature—in one corner, an early colonial family gazed in awe at the sight of modern-day Boston. The money she'd earned had helped her and Aunt Fran fund startup costs for the shelter.

Her thoughts straying in a thousand directions, she'd almost reached the foot of High Cliff Road when she spied a familiar car. A big white Mercury was parked in one of the diagonal slots in front of the town's tiny park. On the granite bench at the rear of the park, a young woman sat hunched over a book, a high-tech type of stroller parked in front of her. She'd hooked one foot over the bottom of the stroller, no doubt to keep it close and her baby safe.

Memories came at Lara like a locomotive. In the fall of last year, after she'd first reconnected with her aunt, she'd been in town less than a day when she'd stumbled over a body behind that granite bench. Several days later, the killer had come after Lara. She hated to think where she'd be right now if Blue hadn't intervened.

Lara stared hard at the big Mercury. Something about it bugged her. She detoured over to it, her stomach buckling as she drew closer. On the passenger-side window was the decal of a cat curled around a kitten.

The car belonged to Kayla's grandmother.

Kayla, who'd claimed she couldn't work today because her gram had a doctor appointment in Concord. Had the appointment been canceled? Had Kayla decided to work today after all? If so, why had she parked on the street instead of in the shelter's lot?

A shard of disappointment zinged through Lara. She hoped Kayla hadn't lied to her. For now, she'd give her the benefit of the doubt. The young woman might have a perfectly good reason why her gram's car was parked there when they were supposed to be in Concord.

Lara started to walk away when something inside the car caught her attention. On the passenger seat was a pile of newspaper articles. In the top article, the headline read: MURDER IN WHISKER JOG SOLVED; DEADLY CONFRONTATION LEADS TO ARREST.

Lara's heart pounded. That article—she remembered it well. It ran in the county's largest newspaper the day after Lara had been attacked by a determined killer.

Feeling light-headed, she skimmed her gaze all around the park and the street, but saw no sign of Kayla. Lara covered her mouth with her hand. What was Kayla up to? Had she applied for the job as shelter assistant because of an obsession with the murder? Lara had read about murder groupies. Was Kayla one of them?

Lara cupped her hand around her eyes to get a better look inside the car. Several other news articles were in that pile, but she couldn't see if they were all from the same case.

She blew out a breath and rubbed her eyes, then turned and headed to her aunt's. Maybe she was making too much of it. In a way, wasn't it normal to be curious about a murder that happened so close to your employer's property?

If Kayla was at the shelter, Lara intended to question her about it.

"I'm home," she called out when she entered the house through the kitchen. She didn't see her aunt, but a bubbly face framed by fuchsia-tinted hair greeted her. Brooke Weston was sitting at the kitchen table, thumbing away at her cell phone. Munster snoozed in her lap. He yawned when he saw Lara, then went back to his nap.

"Brooke!" Lara leaned over and hugged the teenager. Brooke had been a regular visitor at Aunt Fran's from the time Lara had met her last year. Since then, the tint in her hair had gone from aqua to copper—not unlike

Lara's hair—to the current shade of pink. She'd also toned down the silver studs that had once lined her ears to few delicate faux gems per ear.

"Surprised?" Brooke said, setting aside her cell.

"Pleasantly surprised," Lara said. She dropped her tote onto a kitchen chair. "I thought you couldn't volunteer until Sunday?"

"Mom switched days with someone, so she took today off. She's taking Darryl to some dorky water park." She rolled her brown eyes at the ceiling. "Kids' stuff. Not for me. I'd rather help out here with you guys."

"Is Darryl excited about the water park?"

Darryl was Brooke's younger brother, a sweet boy who'd struggled with reading until a certain Ragdoll cat had sat beside him and read along with him. Darryl never saw Blue, but his reading skills had taken a giant leap forward. According to his mom, he was now reading at least three books a week.

"Yeah, the little nerd's all, like, dopey over it. Mom's taking him and a friend, so she'll have her hands full. Full of little monsters, that is," she added with a snort.

Lara smiled. She knew Brooke adored her younger bro, but needed to maintain the guise of the tormented big sister.

"Ms. C. said that your new assistant bailed on you today. Good thing I showed up, right?"

"I'd say your timing was excellent," Lara said.

"Oh, before we start, can I run something by you?" Brooke lifted Munster and gently set him on the floor. "I know we disbanded book club for July, but I had an idea for our next classic when we start up again in August." Brooke clasped her hands together. "Get this. What about *Old Possum's Book of Practical Cats*?"

"Brooke, that's an excellent idea!" Lara had actually read T.S. Eliot's classic book about cats, but would happily reread it. "I know Aunt Fran will love it, and I think Mary will, too."

Lara, Aunt Fran, Brooke, and Mary Newman were the members of a classics book club that met every Wednesday at the coffee shop. The original club had suffered from a shakeup of its members, so now it was only the four of them.

"Good," Brooke said. "I'll send a text to Mary. Now, where should I start today?"

"Can you wash out all the food and water bowls and replenish them?" Lara said. "I'll start scooping and cleaning around the litter boxes. Adoptions start at one, so we want the place to look—and smell—spiffy."

"Ms. C. said to remind you to take the cookies out of the freezer. She already made a pitcher of pink lemonade."

"Good idea. By the way, where *is* my aunt?" Lara went to the freezer and pulled out a sealed container of Daisy's cat-shaped sugar cookies.

"Upstairs. She said she wanted to start cleaning out her closet 'cuz it's getting too crowded. She made us some tuna salad for sandwiches."

Cleaning out her closet? Out with the old, in with the new?

"Okay, then. Let's get cracking. I'll meet you back in the kitchen at noon and we'll all have a bite of lunch."

For the next hour, they each performed cat chores. Brooke was a whirlwind of energy, washing bowls vigorously with gentle soap and refilling them with fresh water and kibble.

The litter boxes freshened and the surrounding areas scrubbed, Lara scooted upstairs to change into something presentable enough to greet prospective adopters. She was surprised to see Frankie stretched out on her bed.

"Hey, sweetheart," she said softly, sinking her fingers into his soft fur. "You look a little glum today."

Frankie's tail twitched, but he didn't purr. Lara was convinced that the cat knew Hesty was gone from his life. She bent and kissed his head. "Don't give up. You're going to find the perfect home, I promise."

She threw on a pair of sporty white capris, topping it with a loose blue tee with short, lace-trimmed sleeves. Not fancy, for sure, but perfect for adoption days. In her ears she stuck the oversized pink cat earrings she'd found on eBay. She ran a comb through her hair, shot a glance at the mirror, then lifted Frankie gently off her bed. "Come on, sweetie. You might meet your forever Mom or Dad today."

Downstairs, she set Frankie on the sofa in the large parlor. Brooke had already thrown together three tuna sandwiches. She and Aunt Fran were sitting at the kitchen table waiting for her.

"There you are," Aunt Fran said, smiling at her niece. "It seems we're like ships that pass in the night, aren't we?"

These days, yes, Lara thought.

"Lara," Aunt Fran said carefully, "would you mind if I let you and Brooke handle adoptions today? I was hoping to get a bit of shopping in before the weekend."

Shopping, Lara thought. The cupboards were stocked full, and the perishables were fresh. Even if they'd needed milk or eggs, it wouldn't take an entire afternoon.

No, Aunt Fran wanted to shop for something else.

"Of course we can," Lara said with a smile she hoped looked laid-back. "By the way, did the chief ever get back to you about the little girl I saw yesterday?"

"Not yet, but I wouldn't be too concerned. If Jerry thought it was anything to worry about, he'd be on it in a heartbeat."

"What little girl?" Brooke asked.

Lara gave her a recap of the child who'd tried to get into the locked shelter.

"It's weird that she had a book with her," Brooke said, then chomped off a huge bite of her sandwich.

They gobbled down their lunches, then Brooke and Lara went into the shelter's meet-and-greet room. Brooke had set the table with a handmade runner festooned with images of cats. The cushion covers had been freshly washed. The room smelled clean and welcoming.

It was around one-thirty when two faces peeked through the shelter's glass-paned door. Lara grinned at the blond man smiling at them, a little boy of about seven huddled next to him. The child looked excruciatingly shy, hiding his face in the man's beige polo shirt when Lara opened the door.

"Welcome to the High Cliff Shelter," Lara said, smiling at the little boy. He had short, wheat-colored hair and huge blue eyes. The sadness in his expression broke her heart.

The man gently pushed the boy into the room. "Hello, I'm Bruce Willoughby, and this is Petey." Bruce held out his hand, and Lara shook it briefly.

"Pleased to meet you. I'm Lara." She stooped down so that she was eye level with the little boy. "Hi, Petey. Thank you for coming here today. I'll bet you like cats."

The boy's eyes brightened, and he nodded.

Brooke came in just then, and Lara introduced her. Brooke winked at Petey, and he smiled for the first time since he'd entered.

"I understand this is a small shelter," Bruce said, glancing all around. "I can already see how different it is. You don't have cats in cages, do you?"

"No," Lara explained. "Our home is the shelter, and the cats pretty much have free range. All are up to date on shots and have regular veterinary care. This room"—she waved a hand around the back porch—"is where we greet people and introduce them to cats."

Bruce's face relaxed. "Wow, what a great concept. Anyway, I was hoping you might have a nice mellow cat available for adoption. A young one," he emphasized. He cupped his son's shoulders protectively and raised his eyebrows.

Lara glanced at Brooke. She had the feeling that the dad wanted to chat with her outside of his son's earshot.

"Should I get Bootsie?" Brooke piped in, as if reading Lara's thoughts.

"That would be great."

Brooke fetched the slender gray cat from the large parlor and set her down on the floor of the porch. Petey instantly dropped down next to the cat and ran his small hand over her back, his smile like a burst of sunshine. Bootsie leaned into him, then crawled up the boy's chest. Grinning, Petey pulled her close, rubbing his face against hers.

"Looks like they're already friends," Lara said quietly, signaling to Bruce to step into the next room.

They sat facing each other in the large parlor. Frankie had already disappeared.

Bruce's eyes welled with tears. "We lost Petey's mom three months ago," he said in a hoarse voice. "It's been so tough on him. On both of us."

"Oh, I'm so sorry," Lara said, feeling her throat tighten.

"Thank you. Petey's always been a shy boy, but after Beth died he became even more withdrawn," Bruce went on. "He's not a rough-and-tumble type of kid, know what I mean? He's quiet, doesn't make friends easily. But I always noticed that he seemed drawn to cats. Problem was, well…frankly, Beth was afraid of them. Because of that, we never had any."

Lara nodded. "You're thinking that a cat might comfort Petey, maybe bring him out of his shell a bit."

"Yeah, that's exactly what I was thinking." Bruce leaned forward, resting his elbows on his knees. "The thing is, I like cats, too. Always had them growing up. I never made a big deal of it, for Beth's sake. But I think it's time. Petey needs a cat, and so do I."

Lara liked this man. Her gut instinct told her Bootsie would be an ideal match for him and Petey.

She gave him a summary of the cat's history—how Bootsie and her three kittens had been rescued by a DPW worker, who'd immediately delivered them to his former teacher—Aunt Fran. Of Bootsie's three kittens, only two had survived. Both now had loving homes.

Bruce listened intently, then said he needed to go back to his son. He and Lara returned to the porch. Lara's breath caught in her throat.

Petey was lying flat out on the floor, Bootsie stretched lengthwise across his chest. Both looked as if they'd found heaven. But what struck Lara most was the sight of Blue leaning against Petey's right arm. The Ragdoll cat blinked once, then rested her chin in the crook of the child's elbow.

"Why don't you have a seat and I'll bring in some lemonade and cookies?" Lara said to Bruce. "Does Petey have any food allergies?"

"Not a one," Bruce said. "And those snacks sound awesome, right buddy?" He reached down to ruffle his son's hair.

"Yup," Petey said, his small hands resting on Bootsie.

When the treats arrived, Petey reluctantly got up from the floor and climbed onto a chair. He grinned from ear to ear when Bootsie hopped onto his lap.

The rest of the visit went smoothly. Bruce promised to fill out the application and email it to the shelter by the end of the day. He assured Lara that his references would check out. In return, she handed him a list of suggested brand names for food, toys, and kitty litter.

After they left, Brooke reappeared and began gathering up the used plates and glasses. "They loved Bootsie, didn't they?"

"They sure did. And—" Lara stopped short and stared out the window, into the backyard. "Brooke, there's that little girl again, the one who tried to get in yesterday!"

This time Lara was determined to catch up with the girl. She trotted outside, Brooke following close behind her. She waved and tried to signal the girl over, but the moment the child spotted Lara, she spun on her sneaker and fled toward the woods.

"Wait a minute," she called out. "I just want to ask—"

"Trista!" Brooke yelled. "Hey, Trista, wait up, okay?"

Abruptly, the child stopped running and swiveled around. Clutching a book to her chest, she gawked at Brooke. Recognition dawning, she smiled and walked slowly toward her.

Brooke caught up with her and slung an arm around the girl's thin shoulders. Lara saw them both laughing as they clomped toward the house.

"Lara, this is Trista," Brooke said. "She's in Darryl's class. Trista, this is Lara."

Lara smiled at the little girl. Today her braids were fastened with whimsical plastic monkeys, and her green T-shirt bore a stain of what appeared to be mustard. "I'm so glad to meet you, Trista." She pointed at the book. "What's that you're reading?"

Trista's eyes brightened. She held out her book at arm's length. "I'm reading about chimpanzees."

"Chimpanzees," Lara said in a jaunty voice. "That sounds very interesting. Trista, why did you try to get into the shelter yesterday? Were you looking for someone?"

The child hesitated, then looked at Brooke. In a tiny voice she said, "I-I wanted to read my book to a cat. Darryl told me lots of cats live here."

So that's what it was. Lara felt relieved. She smiled at the little girl. "Trista, I think that's a wonderful idea. I know some cats who would love to hear you read about chimpanzees. The thing is, you need to let one of your folks know first, okay? That way they can call us and make sure we're going to be home."

Brooke gave the girl's braid a playful tug. "Yeah, kid. You gotta check with your mom before you do stuff like that. Remember what they taught you at school about safety?"

Trista shrugged. "I guess so. Can I go now?"

Lara's heart went out to the girl. The poor kid looked worried, probably afraid she'd get in trouble. "Of course you can. Hey, listen, I have an idea. What if I call your mom later? I'll talk to her about it, and if she agrees, we'll set up a date for you to come over here and read your book to a cat."

Trista threw a hand in the air and jumped up and down. "Yay. That would be awesome!"

"Cool!" Brooke said. Laughing, she took Trista's free hand. "Come on, Trista Conley, I'll walk you home. Your mom's prob'ly wondering where you wandered off to. Can you say goodbye to Lara?"

"Bye, Lara," Trista said with a big smile. She waved, and Brooke ushered her toward the woods.

"Be right back!" Brooke called to Lara. "I'm taking the kid home."

Lara couldn't help marveling at Brooke. She was great with the cats, but impressive with kids as well. She had natural protective instincts.

Wait a minute.

Brooke called the child Trista Conley. Was she related to Evelyn Conley, the self-professed *biggest fan ever* of Deanna Daltry?

Chapter 15

Bootsie's prospective family were the shelter's only visitors that afternoon. Nonetheless, in Lara's book it was a successful adoption day. She felt sure that the sweet little female was on her way to having a forever home with people who loved her.

The shelter's residents were dwindling—both a good and a bad thing. While she and Aunt Fran were thrilled at the success they'd had so far, Lara knew there would always be strays or abandoned cats in need of rescuing.

Ballou's socialization skills were improving, but he was still wary and skittish. In Lara's view, he wasn't ready for placement, at least not yet. Having lived his early life outside, he'd been the ideal candidate for TNR—trap, neuter, release. Until the cold, rainy day he'd found his way inside Aunt Fran's and discovered he could have a comfy existence and still remain hidden from view. From her aunt's description of the day Ballou had darted into the house, Lara suspected Blue had had something to do with it.

Catalina and Bitsy were spoken for, leaving only Frankie—at least for now. The right person would come along for him, she felt certain of it. She only prayed Frankie wouldn't have to wait too long.

With so much to think about and her brain cells on overload, Lara went into the small parlor. The watercolor of the rear view of Deanna's mansion was still on her easel. She set up her painting supplies and dabbled at it for a while, but found it hard to concentrate with so many images barging into her thoughts.

Queen Anne's Lace. The sight of the wildflowers scattered at the crime scene refused to leave her head.

Lara set aside the watercolor and grabbed her tablet off the table where she'd left it. A quick search brought up scads of images and articles about the wildflower. She perused one of the more informative articles.

Queen Anne's Lace was a wildflower native to most parts of the country. Named for its lacy appearance, it was also known as wild carrot. Its tall, hairy stems bore flattened clusters of delicate white flowers, each cluster having an off-center, dark-colored floret.

The wildflower's name came from Queen Anne of England, an expert lace maker, who, according to legend, pricked her finger one day while making lace. The floret represented the single drop of her spilled blood.

The article also warned that another plant, the deadly poison hemlock, was often mistaken for Queen Anne's Lace. Similar in appearance, the hemlock's revolting scent distinguished it from Queen Anne's Lace, which was said to smell more like a carrot.

While the facts about the wildflowers were interesting, they didn't bring Lara any closer to finding the killer.

One final fact caught her eye. Queen Anne's Lace had a symbolic meaning—that of a haven, or sanctuary. It was sometimes thought of as a sign of protection.

Too distracted to work on the watercolor any longer, Lara put away her art supplies. Somehow, she had to persuade Chief Whitley to let her see one of the crime scene photos. She didn't want to see Waitt's body again—only the flowers. Either that, or ask the chief if the flowers had been identified.

Wouldn't it be helpful if someone close to Whitley could make the case for getting her that tidbit of info?

Lara smiled to herself. She knew exactly the right person for the job.

* * * *

Jerry Whitley slapped his hat on the kitchen table and graced Lara with a hard stare. "So, Lara, it seems you've already forgotten our conversation about loose lips."

Aunt Fran, suppressing a smile, said nothing. Instead she poured iced tea from a pitcher into the glass she'd set down in front of the chief.

"I don't have loose lips," Lara insisted, stroking Munster between the ears. The orange-striped cat was sitting straight up in her lap, gazing quizzically across the table at the police chief. "I have not shared anything with anyone. I only want to find out what those flowers were. Maybe I can glean something from it. Something that will help the police. Something I will share *only* with the police."

"Maybe you can glean something," Whitley repeated tightly. He shook his head, then gulped back a long swig of iced tea. "Lara, don't you think the state police homicide investigators are all over it? Don't you think— gee, here's a thought—they might have a tiny clue what they're doing?"

At that, Lara felt chastised. She hadn't meant to imply that the police weren't capable of solving the murder. Only that she might be able to offer insights that could speed up the investigation.

Choosing her words carefully, she said, "Chief, I don't think that at all. It's just that I see things from a different, well, perspective. The police are looking at everything analytically. Matching things up, figuring out what fits and what doesn't. Trying to piece it all together to come up with a logical explanation of who, and why, and how. Am I right?"

Whitley sighed with irritation. "It's far more complex than that, but what's your point?"

"I analyze things from an artist's viewpoint. For argument's sake, let's say the police know that those flowers were Queen Anne's Lace and *not* poison hemlock." Lara watched for a reaction, but he was poker-faced. She went on. "They'd probably try to determine where those flowers came from, right? Were they picked by hand, bought from a flower shop, grown at the killer's home—see what I'm saying?"

"Lara, please get to the point before I'm tempted to seek out poison myself."

"Okay. If those flowers were Queen Anne's Lace, I'm going to ask myself why. Why that particular flower? What does it represent to the killer?"

The chief shot a look at Munster, who was getting antsy. Lara suspected the cat wanted to climb across the table and plop into the chief's lap.

"Lara, do you take us for a collection of dunces? Don't you think we're doing that, too?"

She felt herself flushing. Maybe she'd pushed it too far. "I'm sorry. No offense intended. I know the police are working twenty-four/seven on the case."

"You have to leave it alone, Lara. You know what happened last time."

Lara shuddered. How could she forget?

"What happened last time had nothing to do with my investigating the murder. It was a fluke, remember?"

Whitley's expression softened, and he rubbed his eyes with the fingers of one large hand. "All right, I concede that point, but only that point." He chugged down the remainder of his iced tea. "Thanks, Fran. That hit the spot."

"Any time, Jerry." Aunt Fran reached over and gave his wrist an affectionate squeeze. For some reason the gesture irritated Lara.

"I'm going to leave now before that orange one"—he narrowed his gaze at Munster—"decides to do a lap dance on my thighs." He snagged his hat off the table and rose.

Lara had hoped to question him further about Deanna. Was she still under suspicion? Were the police close to making an arrest?

The problem was, she'd already pressed her luck with the chief to the edge of the cliff—one tiny push and it would plunge into the abyss.

"Thanks, anyway, for listening to me," she said coolly.

Hat in hand, Whitley paused for a moment. "Lara, look at me."

Annoyed at the command, Lara waited a moment before meeting his gaze.

"Ask me again if those flowers were Queen Anne's Lace," he said.

Lara's felt her heart race. "Were those flowers Queen Anne's Lace?"

Whitley gave her a quick nod and slapped his hat on his head. "Now, if you'll excuse me, ladies, duty calls. Pick you up at six, Fran?"

Aunt Fran smiled. "I'll be waiting."

"Another date with the chief?" Lara asked, after Whitley had left.

Aunt Fran scooped the empty glass off the table and went over to rinse it in the sink. "Just dinner and a movie. Nothing earthshattering."

Dinner and a movie is a date, Lara felt like pointing out. She realized she was being childish. Why shouldn't her aunt date the chief? They were two consenting adults, weren't they? Even if one-half of the equation did have an aversion to cats.

"You seem surprised," Aunt Fran said quietly. "Is something troubling you, Lara?"

"No, nothing," she said. *Except everything*, she was tempted to add.

She wondered if she should tell her aunt about seeing Kayla's grandmother's car earlier in the day. Their new assistant hadn't shown up or called, so Lara assumed she planned to work on Saturday, as scheduled. No, she'd wait until tomorrow, after she'd had a chance to question Kayla privately.

"Sorry, don't mind me," Lara said. "I think I'll check to see if Bruce Willoughby emailed his application yet. The sooner we approve them, the sooner Bootsie can move in with her forever family."

"I'm sorry I didn't get to meet them." Aunt Fran looked wistful. "They sound like lovely people."

"They're going to be great for Bootsie. I feel it in my bones."

Her aunt laughed. "And your bones are usually right. Lara, why don't you go to bed early tonight? You've had a grueling week."

"That sounds like a plan. I'll finish up a few things, then jump into bed by ten." She also wanted to feel bright-eyed and bushy-tailed, as her dad would have said, for her date with Gideon on Saturday. While she might want to carry a stylish handbag, she did not care to sport bags under her eyes.

"And don't forget the community yard sale at the library tomorrow," Aunt Fran reminded her.

Lara blew out a sigh. "I'm thinking of skipping it. Kayla will be here by eleven, and I want to have a chat with her before she starts."

"Oh," Aunt Fran said. She sounded concerned. "Everything okay with her?"

"Yeah, fine. I think. I just want to ask her something. What about you? Are you going?"

"No, I think I'll pass on this one. I'm stocked up on books for a while, and I don't need any more gently used tchotchkes."

Lara headed into her studio. She was too distracted to work on the watercolor of Deanna's mansion. It would probably look as if a five-year-old painted it. Instead she checked the shelter's email inbox to see if Bruce Willoughby had sent in his application.

She was pleased to find it there, attached to a brief email. She reviewed it carefully, as she did all applications. Everything looked good—no red flags. The references he supplied were both local. If they checked out, as Lara suspected they would, Bootsie's adoption could be put on a fast track.

Lara picked up her cell phone. She started to call one of the reference numbers when a sheet of pink paper fluttered to the floor, landing next to her chair. She bent to retrieve it.

Huh.

It was the community yard sale notice she'd set on her work table. How the heck had it floated this far over? There wasn't so much as a breeze in the room that could have sent it sailing through the air.

A pair of blue eyes regarded her from the edge of the bookshelf. Blue blinked once, and in the next instant she was gone.

"Why am I not surprised?" Lara whispered.

Chapter 16

On Saturday morning, the parking lot of the Whisker Jog Public Library was jam-packed with vendors. A section of the lot near the library's rear entrance had been reserved for used books. Volumes no longer wanted by the library, along with full bags donated by patrons, had been set up in neat rows along portable tables. The greater portion of the lot was crammed with homemade crafts and yard sale treasures. At a kiosk in one corner, browsers could buy coffee and doughnuts. Lara was tempted to snag a glazed doughnut, but then decided not to stuff herself too early in the day. Gideon was treating her to dinner this evening, and she wanted to be hungry enough to enjoy it.

A plump woman with bright blue eyes greeted Lara from across a table covered with knitted baby accessories. "Great turnout," the woman said, skimming the crowd. "Got any little ones to buy for?"

Lara smiled at her display of hand-knitted dresses and tiny blankets made from all shades of colored yarn. "These are wonderful," she complimented the woman. "Right now, I don't know anyone with an infant or a toddler, but I wish you luck with the sale."

The woman nodded and began rearranging her wares. Lara moved along, strolling among the other tables at a leisurely pace. At one table, a man with a beard and a long ponytail sold soy candles and bags of fragrant potpourri. With so many cats in the house, she and her aunt never burned candles. As for potpourri, she could already picture tiny shredded bits scattered all over the house by curious paws. She passed on to the next table, where trays of chunky-style costume jewelry had already snagged her attention.

"Hi!" said the cheery young vendor, who in Lara's mind looked about twelve. "Most of this stuff came from my grandma's estate, but some of it I bought at an antique shop that was going out of business."

"You have some interesting pieces," Lara noted. A jewel-encrusted elephant brooch caught her eye. She picked it up and examined it, then noticed that the clasp in the back was broken. She set it back down. Another tray held colorful plastic brooches shaped like various flowers.

"Those were popular in the seventies," the young vendor said. "Kind of like the circle pins were in the sixties?" She flashed a smile displaying a row of nearly invisible braces.

Not familiar with either of those early fashion trends, Lara chose a pink tulip from the bunch. The clasp was intact, and the brooch in perfect condition. "My aunt would love this," she said. "How much is it?"

"Those are all four dollars. If you buy three, I can do ten bucks total."

None of the others appealed to Lara. "Thanks, but the tulip alone will be fine." She dug four dollars out of her tote and gave it to the girl, who wrapped it in a tiny square of tissue. "Hope your aunt likes it," she said, sounding a bit disappointed.

Lara thanked her again and moved on. She shot a look at her watch. It was nearly eleven. She wanted to get back before Kayla arrived.

She was heading toward the sidewalk to walk back to her aunt's when she passed by a table lined with neatly arranged cardboard boxes. The boxes contained leaflets, postcards, and wall calendars, all from earlier eras. At the end of the table, another box held the largest collection of men's tie tacks Lara had ever seen.

Tempted to browse, Lara gave the table a quick once-over. Then Kayla popped into her mind, and Lara remembered that she wanted to be home when the shelter assistant arrived.

All at once, something furry brushed her ankle and she jumped a little. She looked down and caught of glimpse of cream-colored fur that vanished as quickly as it came.

"You okay?" From behind the table, a thin woman with deeply wrinkled skin and piercing brown eyes gawked at Lara. "You looked like something scared you."

Lara swiped at her ankle and smiled at the woman. "No, it was nothing. Probably one of those giant ants."

Or Blue, trying to stall her.

Was her Ragdoll guardian urging her to stop at this table?

She backtracked a few steps and glanced over the woman's offerings. One thing instantly got her attention. It was a cat calendar from 1974, with adorable photos of kittens depicted on each of the twelve months. A sticky-note on which someone had scribbled 2019 was attached to the top.

"Two thousand nineteen?" Lara asked. "What does that mean?"

"Oh, my sister stuck that on there. The days of the week in nineteen seventy-four are the same as they're going to be in two thousand nineteen." She shrugged. "In case anyone cares."

Lara cared. What a cool vintage calendar! "What's the price?" she asked.

"Will eight be okay? It's in great condition."

Lara thought about it. "How about seven?"

"You got it."

Lara paid the woman, then carefully slid the calendar inside her tote. "Thanks, and have a great day," she said. She started to walk away when her tote caught the edge of the tie tacks box and sent it plunging to the pavement. "Oh no, I'm so sorry. I don't even know how that happened. I guess I bumped the box with my bag."

"Not a problem." The woman scrambled over to retrieve the dozen or so tie tacks that had fallen from the box. "Most of them stayed right in the box. No harm done."

Lara examined her tote, baffled as to how it could have knocked over the weighty box. "Again, I'm really sorry. I hope none of them broke."

The vendor set the box back on the table. "They're fine. You can't hurt these old things. My grandfather collected them." She smiled, and her gaze grew watery. "In his day, he considered himself quite the dapper gentleman. Loved his tie tacks."

Feeling guilty for having tipped over the box, Lara smiled and began fishing through them. "Oh look, this one's a sword." She held it up.

"Check this one out," the vendor said, holding up an enameled pheasant.

"Cute." Lara's heart did a sudden pole vault over her ribs. A white, flower-shaped tie tack about the size of a quarter made her breath catch in her throat. She lifted it from the box and placed it in her palm.

"Isn't it funny that you picked out that one," the woman said, growing animated now. "I have a booklet about that. Let me see…" She began to riffle, one by one, through a box of old leaflets, but Lara couldn't stop staring at the tie tack.

"Is it…do you think it's Queen Anne's Lace?" Lara asked her.

"I know it is. Oh, here's what I was looking for." She slid a yellowed booklet out from the box and handed it to Lara. "Be careful handling it. The paper's quite thin."

Still holding the tie tack, Lara took the booklet from the woman. "The Wild Carrot Society," she read from the cover. "A society for the protection of women."

Lara's pulse pounded in her veins. She felt dots of perspiration populate her upper lip. Wild carrot was another name by which Queen Anne's Lace was known. What were the odds of her stumbling onto this booklet?

Zero, unless you counted the nudge from a certain Ragdoll cat.

"I should have remembered," the vendor scolded herself. "That booklet and the tie tack go together. My head isn't where it should be anymore."

"This society," Lara quietly asked her. "Do you know anything about it?"

"Not much. My grandfather's been gone for a long time, but I recall my grandmother telling me he joined it back in the sixties. It was some sort of secretive group, I guess, but it disbanded before it ever got off the ground."

Lara needed to leave, but she couldn't let these items go. "Are you selling both?"

For the first time, the woman's face creased with sorrow. "Everything has to go, I'm afraid. My husband died a year ago, and I'm moving to a small apartment. I can't take this stuff with me. Plus, I need the money..."

"I hear you," Lara said, feeling terrible for the woman. "What do you want for them?"

"I guess I can take fifteen for both," she said with a sigh.

Lara reached into her tote and pulled out a twenty. "Take this. I don't want any change."

The woman looked immensely grateful. "Thank you. What a kind gesture."

After waving a quick goodbye, Lara hurried off.

She couldn't wait to get back home and examine her findings.

Chapter 17

When Lara got back to the house, Kayla was already there. The big Mercury was parked in the shelter's lot, in the space farthest from the entrance. Lara silently commended their new assistant. Since today was an adoption day, Lara knew Kayla was making room for any visitors who might come by hoping to adopt.

Right now, assuming Bootsie's placement with the Willoughbys went through, Frankie was the only cat available for adoption. It made Lara wonder if they should be reaching out to other shelters, especially since most were overcrowded.

Although Frankie was in good health for his six or seven years, Lara thought of him as having special needs. She knew he would thrive only in a quiet home, preferably without other cats. A family with kids and dogs wouldn't suit him at all.

Kayla was sitting at the kitchen table enjoying a glass of iced tea with Aunt Fran.

"There you are," her aunt said at the exact moment Kayla said, "Hi, Lara."

Aunt Fran laughed. "Did you pick up anything interesting at the yard sale?"

"Actually, I did. In fact, I have a present for you." She dug the tulip brooch out of her tote bag and handed it to her aunt.

Aunt Fran unwrapped the square of tissue. "Oh, my favorite flower. Thank you, Lara." She held the pink tulip up to her left shoulder. "How does it look?"

Kayla grinned and pushed her glasses farther up her nose. "Gorgeous. Didn't I see you in a navy top the other day? That pin would give it a burst of color!"

"You're right," Aunt Fran said.

Kayla drank the last of her iced tea. "I guess I should get to work."

Lara slung her tote over one of the kitchen chairs. "Can we chat first, Kayla? Out in the shelter room?"

Something in Lara's tone must have alarmed Kayla. The young woman's smile faded from cheery to confused. "Um, sure. No problem."

Kayla followed Lara out to the back porch. After Lara closed the door, they sat facing each other at the meet-and-greet table. "First, I wanted to ask how your grandmother did yesterday," Lara asked. "Is she okay?"

Kayla straightened in her chair. "Oh. Well, she did fine, thanks for asking. Her regular eye doctor wanted her to see a specialist in Concord. Her optic nerve had gone fuzzy. Turned out she'd had some sort of mini-stroke in her eye."

"I'm sorry to hear that," Lara said, feeling her heart twist. "Can it be treated?"

"Luckily, yes. Her primary care doctor is putting her on stronger blood pressure medication. She'll have to keep going to Concord for tests—for a while, anyway. Kind of a pain, but at least she has me to drive her."

Lara nodded. Now she felt terrible for interrogating the young woman. Nonetheless, she felt she should question her about seeing her car in Whisker Jog late Friday morning. And those articles about the murder on the front seat.

"That's a relief, I'm sure," Lara said. "To both of you."

Kayla's eyes welled up. "Lara, is something wrong? You're acting like you're mad at me."

"No, I'm not mad at you," Lara said, feeling like a monster now. "The thing is—Kayla, I saw your grandmother's car yesterday. It was in front of the park here in town, not far from my aunt's vacant lot."

Kayla flushed. She twisted her hands on the table. "I was parked there, yes," she admitted. "I had research I wanted to do at the library. Since my gram's appointment wasn't until three, I figured I'd have time to do what I needed to do, get back to Tuftonboro, and drive her to Concord."

Lara was silent for a few moments. "Why didn't you park at the library?"

"I couldn't. They had the parking lot blocked off so they could set up for today's book sale."

Lara felt like slapping herself. Kayla was right. Lara had seen the signs herself, asking patrons to park on the street.

"I'm sorry. I saw those signs. I should have remembered that."

"That's okay," Kayla said in a near whisper.

Lara decided to plunge ahead. "Kayla, when I passed by your gram's car, I saw some stuff on the front seat. There was an article about the murder in Whisker Jog last year—the one I ended up being involved in."

Kayla looked down at her hands and shook her head. "I'm so sorry. I didn't intend for anyone to see that. You're probably thinking I— Oh, God, I can't even imagine what you're thinking."

"It's all right. I told you, I'm not mad. The thing is, I can't help wondering if that murder case had anything to do with why you applied for the assistant's job here."

"No!" Kayla said. "Absolutely not. I wanted to be here because I love working with animals, especially cats." She pulled off her glasses and swiped at her eyes with the heel of one hand. "If I can ever afford to get my veterinary degree, I'm going to specialize in cats."

"Kayla, I'm sorry I even brought it up," Lara apologized. "You've already proven yourself to us. We're lucky to have you here." She smiled. "And so are the cats."

Kayla stuck her glasses back on her face and sniffled. "Thanks. Listen, I can explain about that article. Since I was a kid, I've always been a true crime aficionado. I don't know why. Stuff like that has always just fascinated me. Anyway, I collect articles from bizarre cases and save them. The ones you saw in my front seat? I was taking them to a copy place. I always copy the newspaper articles and then scan the copies into my computer."

"That makes sense," Lara said. "Newspaper articles get all yellowed and flimsy if you keep them for too long."

"Exactly." Kayla looked more relaxed now, but then her brow creased. "Here's the thing," she added softly. "You were right when you thought I recognized Nancy Sherman. Her face was so familiar to me. But for the life of me, I couldn't think why."

That got Lara's attention. "Is that why you went to the library?"

"Yeah, I wanted to look at some old news articles from fifteen years ago. I found out the Whisker Jog library has copies of newspapers from all over the state on microfiche. I'd already tried finding them on the Web, but I wasn't landing on the right links."

"Fifteen years ago," Lara said, grinning. "Weren't you in grade school then?"

"Yeah, I was a bratty first-grader." She bit down on her lip. "But about six months ago, there was a program on TV that stuck in my mind. It was about an old case, but it wasn't a murder. It was about this guy who'd been robbing banks all over New Hampshire. Turned out he'd been forcing his wife to commit the robberies with him. She'd distract one teller while he robbed another. They got away with it for several months before they slipped up and got caught."

"No one ever got hurt?"

"No," Kayla said slowly. "But I'll never forget the look on the wife's face when they were shoving her into the police car. She looked, I don't know, relieved and terrified at the same time? Her attorney worked out a deal, so she only had to serve a year for testifying against her husband. The coercion was a big factor in her getting a light sentence."

"The wife—do you think it was Nancy Sherman?"

"Yeah, I do. Only she had a different name then, so I'm not totally sure it was her. That's why I wanted to get to the library. A picture's worth a thousand words, right?"

Lara smiled. "I guess so. Did you find what you were looking for?"

"No, I ended up not having enough time. I didn't want my gram to be late for her eye appointment, so I headed back."

Lara mulled over everything Kayla had told her. If Kayla's suspicions were correct, it might explain why Lara had seen a state trooper escort Nancy off the property on the day of the murder. Nancy's unfortunate criminal past probably pegged her as an automatic suspect, even if she didn't have anything to do with Waitt's death.

Lara thanked Kayla for confiding in her, then they both went to work. Adoptions officially started at one, so they had to be ready.

With Frankie the only cat now available for adoption, Lara once more thought about contacting another shelter. Summers always brought an increase in kitten populations. Right now, the High Cliff Shelter could accommodate more cats. If they offered help to one of the area shelters, it would be a win-win for all.

With Kayla there to assist with feline duties, Lara took the opportunity to duck into her studio. She closed the door, itching to peruse the tie tack and leaflet she'd bought at the yard sale.

She started by setting the tie tack on her work table. Up close, it was clear that it was designed to look like Queen Anne's Lace. Made from what appeared to be painted enamel, it had a tiny crimson floret in the center. She set it aside and picked up the leaflet. The printing date inscribed on the back was August 1962.

"The Wild Carrot Society," she read, flipping open to the second page. After that, she read silently.

A woman you know is in fear of her husband, the opening paragraph began. It went on to describe the abuse many women endured at the hands of a spouse. Most had no place to turn to, and were forced to suffer every day in silence.

The society was named after Queen Anne's Lace, or wild carrot, because of its symbolic meaning—that of a haven or sanctuary. It meant protection.

Lara read on. The society's founder, a man named Wilbur Tardiff, was passionate about the topic. He pointed out that the police didn't treat spousal abuse, or "husband and wife dust-ups" as they dismissively called them, seriously. Tardiff urged good men to join the group, and to wear the tie tack that signified a safe haven. Their own wives were expected to play a key role—that of recognizing signs of abuse in their female friends and acquaintances.

After reading a bit more, Lara felt herself getting depressed. No person or animal should have to live in fear. The Wild Carrot Society had the right idea—offering a safe refuge to women who had no place else to turn. Had the group ever gained momentum? How many men had actually joined? The woman who'd sold her the items claimed that the society had disbanded before it ever got off the ground.

The room was getting warm. Lara pressed one hand to the back of her neck, which felt slightly damp. She'd stuck her hair into a twisty knot that morning and secured it with a comb at the back. Now she felt tendrils sneaking out, curling around her face.

A knock at her door made Lara jump. She'd been so engrossed in reading the leaflet she'd lost track of time.

"You busy in here?" Aunt Fran popped into the room, clutching Frankie to her chest, his head resting on her shoulder. "Kayla and I are setting up the back porch. I'm hoping this little guy might find a mom or dad today." She kissed the cat's head.

Lara quickly got up and shoved the leaflet under her watercolor supplies. "Sorry, I had some things I needed to work on."

Aunt Fran studied her curiously. "Anything I can do to help?"

"No, I'm all set. But what do you think about this idea?" Lara explained her thoughts about contacting other shelters and possibly taking in other cats.

"It's strange that you said that. I've been thinking the same thing. We're not a traditional shelter, but we could definitely accommodate more cats without comprising the care we give."

"Then let's talk about it later, okay?" Lara suggested. "And by later, I mean tomorrow. Tonight, I'm dining with Gideon at a fancy new restaurant in Moultonborough."

Aunt Fran winked at her, something she rarely did. "Ah, that's right. You mentioned that earlier. Tomorrow you'll have to tell me all about how your date went. Well, maybe not *all* about it…"

Lara felt herself blushing to the roots of her hair.

Chapter 18

Two different families visited the shelter that afternoon. Both had kids of varying ages. Both had been hoping to adopt a kitten.

"Sorry, Frankie," Kayla said after the last group had left. "None of those people were right for you, anyway. Your special day is coming, so don't you worry." She bent and lifted the kitty into her arms.

Lara realized once again how lucky they were to have found Kayla. Crime aficionado or not, she was a true animal lover. She had a way with cats that was a joy to observe.

"Hey, have you gotten any updates about Noodle and Doodle?" Kayla asked.

"No, and I should call Deanna," Lara said. "I'm assuming no news is good news, but maybe I shouldn't assume."

Especially after Kayla's revelations about Nancy Sherman. If the housekeeper was the same woman as the one who'd helped her husband rob banks, what did that say about her character?

Two days earlier, Deanna had lamented that she was being targeted by the police. Did they still believe she'd made threatening calls and texts to Donald Waitt from a burner phone? Had there been any updates since then? Lara didn't dare ask Chief Whitley, not without risking a repeat of the "loose lips" lecture. She wondered if any of the news vans were still hunkered in front of Deanna's mansion.

Kayla left a little after four-thirty, having insisted on staying late to clear the table and wipe down the floor in the meet-and-greet room. They'd agreed she would take Sunday off—she'd already made plans to attend a family barbecue with her grandmother and some cousins. Lara thanked her once more, then scurried upstairs to get ready for her date. Gideon had promised to pick her up at six, and he was always punctual. It was one of the many things she admired about him. Gid was never late.

Her cell pinged with a text. Expecting that it might be Gideon, she snatched her phone off the table. The text was from Deanna, and she'd attached three snapshots of Noodle and Doodle frolicking in her bedroom. Lara breathed a sigh of relief; the kittens looked happy. Deanna's message read:

> *Loving my furbabies.*

Lara sent off a quick text thanking her and promised to call her on Sunday.

Lara took a shower and washed her hair, then pulled her new sundress out of her closet. At the welcome tea for Deanna, she'd worn the same dress with her aunt's chunky gold necklace. This evening, however, she wanted to wear something more delicate around her neck.

Lara fished through her jewelry box, the same one she'd had since she was a girl. Made of white padded plastic, it had a ballerina that danced to a tune when the cover was opened. It made her think of her mom, who she hadn't seen in well over a year.

This past winter, Brenda "Breezy" Caphart—now Brenda Caphart-Rice—had taken a trip to Vegas with a gal pal and met a slick-looking, self-professed country music virtuoso. Three weeks later, the two had gotten married. They'd been promising to visit Lara and Fran, but so far hadn't made an appearance. Lara hated to be a pessimist, but she wondered if her mom's quickie marriage would even make it to the one-year mark.

Her gaze landed on the slender gold necklace with a blue topaz pendant she'd had since high school. Her dad, now deceased, had chosen it for her when she'd turned sixteen. She lifted it from the box and secured it around her neck. Tears came to her eyes. *I miss you, Dad.*

At precisely five fifty-eight, Gideon appeared on the front porch. He peeked through the screen, knocked lightly, then stepped inside. His brown eyes glittered when he saw Lara. "You look amazing," he said, kissing her lightly on the cheek.

"As do you," she said, her insides warming at the sight him. He wore a light gray blazer with dark trousers, his ever-present Superman watch on his wrist.

"Our res is at six-thirty. I hope that's not too early."

"Are you kidding?" Lara teased. "I'll be half-starved by then."

After bidding a quick goodbye to Aunt Fran, they headed toward Moultonborough.

The restaurant, named Mélange, was as colorless a place as Lara had ever seen. The all-white décor was blinding. Even the roses placed precisely in the center of every table were a crisp, snowy white.

Their server, dressed completely in black, was a thin, middle-aged man with a slight French accent and an efficient manner. He suggested the chef's special—grilled filet of bass with champagne sauce. Lara and Gideon both chose it.

Over glasses of chardonnay, they sampled an assortment of local cheeses and warm, buttery rolls. Preceded by an endive salad, the bass turned out to be heavenly—perfectly seasoned, the champagne sauce as light as air.

During dinner, Lara gave Gideon an overview of the events of her week. Although she and Gideon had shared fried clams a few days earlier, they hadn't had a chance to really sit down and chat in a leisurely fashion. She told him everything, beginning with the worms in Deanna's purse to Kayla's disclosures about Nancy Sherman.

"You really *have* had quite the week," Gideon said with concern.

Lara took a sip from her water glass. "I just thought of something else. It's funny how things keep popping up in my head. When Deanna came over yesterday in that crazy getup, she was wearing a horrible-looking wig."

"Not surprising," Gideon said, forking up his last bite of bass. "It's probably one of the disguises she uses to avoid the public. I bet a lot of celebrities do that."

"Yeah, but I just remembered something else. She said she borrowed one of Nancy's wigs. It wasn't even her own. Why would Nancy have wigs?"

"I wouldn't read too much into that," Gideon said. "People wear wigs for all sorts of reasons. If she did help her husband rob banks, she might have used them to disguise her appearance."

"You're right. I didn't think of that." Lara made a face. "I'm sorry. I guess I can't stop stressing about all of this. I'm starting to get a little paranoid. I see murderers around every corner." She grinned at Gideon across the table. Against the glaring whiteness of the room, he looked even more handsome than ever.

"You're far from paranoid." Gideon's brown eyes gleamed at her. "Lara, I'm so glad you moved back home," he said in a husky voice. "I…can't imagine my world without you anymore."

Lara swallowed. She felt tongue-tied. "Thank you," she managed to choke out.

For so many years, Boston had been Lara's home. She'd loved her tiny studio apartment above a North End bakery. But she had to confess, reuniting with Aunt Fran and returning to Whisker Jog was the best thing she'd ever done. Growing closer to Gideon over the past several months felt so natural, so right. Right now, she couldn't imagine her world without him, either.

Lara swallowed the last bite of her bass. "That was unbelievable. My compliments to the chef, as they say."

Gideon smiled at her. "I hope you left room for that chocolate soufflé."

The soufflé had to be requested at the beginning of the meal, as the dessert chef required forty minutes to prepare it.

"Oh no, I didn't really order that, did I?" she groaned.

"You did, but never fear. I'll share it with you."

A tingly feeling came over Lara. The wine? The meal? Or was it the company that had her feeling suddenly giddy?

Their server delivered the soufflé in a white, straight-sided dish edged in gold. He supplied them each with a spoon, and before long Lara was scraping the bottom.

After Gideon paid the server they strolled out to his car, his arm wrapped loosely around her. The night air had cooled, but her skin felt warm. She felt as if she were glowing from the inside out. "Gorgeous evening," she said. "Thank you for such a wonderful time."

Gideon squeezed her waist. "It was great, but it was you who made it special, Lara." He said it seriously, not in his usual joking way.

He'd started to open the car door for her when she spotted something. Adjacent to Mélange's parking lot was a small strip mall of only three shops. One appeared to be a florist, another a dry cleaner. The third one had a sign overhead that read Joy's Tea Room. A neon sign in the window proclaimed the shop open.

That had to be Joy Renfield—the woman who'd supplied the teas for Deanna Daltry's welcome event! The same person who'd begged Lara to stop by for a tealeaf reading. She told Gideon about her invitation from Joy.

Gideon shook his head and laughed. "This will be a first for me—a tealeaf reading."

"Yeah, for me too," she said. "Come on, it'll be fun." She playfully looped her arm through his.

They hopped into Gideon's car, and he drove into the adjacent parking lot over the access drive shared by the restaurant and the strip mall. Only two cars were in the lot, a black sedan with a dent in its driver's side door, and an aging, pale green VW beetle.

Both the florist and dry cleaner were dark inside, but lights shined through the glass door of Joy's Tea Room. The door opened with a cacophonous jangle of bells. The scent of cloves and myriad other spices overpowered

Lara's senses. If the restaurant had been the absence of all color, Joy's Tea Room was the presence of every hue in the spectrum.

Hanging from the ceiling was an array of paper lanterns in all shapes and colors. The back wall was lined with shelves on which a jumble of metal tea tins rested, each having a unique color scheme and design. Near the far end, to their right, were two round tables covered with bright red tablecloths. Atop each table, two teacups rested upside-down on corresponding saucers.

"Be right with you," a female voice trilled from somewhere in the back of the shop.

Gideon looked at Lara and shrugged, then closed the door as gently as he could. They glanced around. Two teenaged girls browsed in front of a glass case that held an assortment of bangle bracelets and oversized earrings.

From behind the tables, a beaded curtain abruptly whooshed aside. Joy Renfield emerged into the shop, wearing a full-length, flowing pink dress. A matching headband imprisoned her flyaway hair, keeping it away from her face. Her fingernails were painted cerulean blue, and she wore a heavier than usual layer of makeup. "Hello, I'm Joy. May I— Oh my, it's you, Lara. I'm so happy to see you!" In flowered flip-flops that slapped the tile floor, she strode over and gave Lara a brisk hug.

"Great to see you too, Joy." Lara said, a bit unnerved by the intensity of the hug. She smiled and made the appropriate introductions. Gideon, ever the gentleman, politely shook her hand.

"Are you here for your free tealeaf reading?" Joy clasped her hands under her chin.

"I am, but there's a problem. I forgot to bring the coupon you gave me."

"Don't be a ninny," Joy chided. She held up a finger, tipped her head to the side, and addressed the teenaged girls. "Find anything you like, girls?"

The teens looked up sharply and shook their heads. In the next instant, they opened the door and hurried outside.

Joy rolled her blue-lined eyes. "Those two—always browsing, never buying," she said with a twinge of irritation. "But you're both here, so I'm tickled to death." She ushered them over to one of the tables, and pulled a third chair from the adjacent table. "Sit," she said in a chirpy voice. "Are you both having your leaves read?"

Gideon held out Lara's chair for her, then sat down. "Sure, why not. I could use a glimpse into my future." He grinned at Lara.

Lara stifled a giggle. Gid was such a good sport. He probably thought it was pure silliness, but was going along with it for her sake.

"Fabulous!" Joy batted her mascara-coated eyelashes at him, then turned over both teacups so that they were face up. The teacups were white and nearly translucent, with a row of tiny violets encircling the edges of both cup and saucer. Joy reached behind her, and from a low shelf brought out a moss green tea tin shaped like a Chinese pagoda.

"That's a lovely tin," Lara commented.

Joy nodded but said nothing. She opened the tin, and into each cup she shook out about a tablespoon of fragrant tealeaves. "Oolong," she said, by way of explanation. "I use a bit more than some tealeaf readers. That way I get a better reading. Do either of you take sugar or lemon?"

"Sugar for me," Gideon said.

Lara smiled. "I'll take lemon."

Joy excused herself. She returned a few minutes later with a tray that held a steaming white teapot and a double-sided ceramic dish containing both sugar packets and lemon wedges. Holding the lid on the teapot, she poured boiling water into each of their cups. "You can prepare your tea now. Don't worry about disturbing the tealeaves. It's all part of the process. The powers that be are present to guide you from a higher plane."

Lara and Gideon glanced at each other, then followed Joy's instructions.

"I'm going to leave you for a few minutes while you enjoy your tea. Let the leaves settle a bit first. As you sip, try to clear your minds of all negative thoughts. Drink as much of the tea as you can but leave a bit of liquid at the bottom." Without another word, she rose and slipped back behind the beaded curtain.

Lara felt a chuckle trying to escape her lips, but clamped it off. She didn't want to be disrespectful to this eccentric but kindly woman. She noticed that Gideon's expression had turned serious. Lara wondered if he'd bought into Joy's mystical spiel.

They finished their tea quickly. Lara found the flavor to be citrusy and quite appealing. She almost wished for a second cup.

Joy returned and sat before them. "I'll start with you, Lara. I'd like you to begin by swirling your cup three times clockwise—because time moves forward, not backward. Then carefully invert the cup and set it down on the saucer."

"Three times clockwise," Lara repeated. She did as Joy directed, then watched the liquid drain from the cup into the saucer.

"Now, tap the center of the cup three times with your right knuckle."

Lara tapped. Joy reached over and pulled both cup and saucer toward her. With great care, she lifted the teacup and set it right-side up next to the saucer.

Lara suddenly felt her nerves tighten. What if Joy saw something bad in her tealeaves? Would she be able to dismiss it as a lot of nonsense?

Joy gazed into the teacup, studying the patterns made by Lara's tealeaves. Her eyes took on an odd gleam. She turned the cup around several times. After what seemed an eternity to Lara, Joy's lips flattened into a straight line.

"Nothing too horrible, I hope," Lara said, unable to bear the suspense any longer. She felt Gideon go still beside her.

"So much to do," Joy said quietly. "Others need you, both animal and human. I see a hand with cupped fingers. That means you're juggling multiple tasks."

You got that right.

Joy pointed to a cluster of leaves close to the cup's handle. "The symbols closest to the handle represent events happening now. I clearly see the letter C."

A no-brainer, Lara thought. Cats.

"The shape is more curved at one end. It might also be a tail."

A cat's tail.

"Or a G," Joy added.

Without touching the cup, Joy's finger moved slowly around the rim. "I see a cross," she said. "Usually that means a recent loss, or a loss you fear in the near future."

Hesty, Lara thought. Though she hadn't really known the man, his death had been a blow both to her and to Frankie.

Joy's finger moved to the point on the cup that was opposite the handle. Her plain face widened into a smile. "Here I see a circle—a ring. It's thick and solid, which signifies something unbreakable in the future. Because of its distance from the handle, however, time and many challenges will first intervene."

She's quite glib, Lara thought. Accustomed to telling people what they hoped to hear.

Joy went on to relate future successes and happy times. While Lara didn't want to put much stock in the reading, she found herself breathing a sigh of relief.

"You're easy to read," Joy said, setting the cup aside. "You don't hide your feelings. You wear them like a badge."

Lara laughed. "That's sort of true, I guess."

"But you have a secret, don't you, Lara?"

She felt her body jerk slightly. "Um, a secret?"

"Not a bad secret," Joy clarified, "but it's something you feel unable to share."

Lara felt a blush creeping up her neck. Joy couldn't possibly know about her spirit cat by looking at a bunch of random tealeaves. She started to deny it when Joy added, "Unburden yourself, Lara. You'll find others more receptive than you think."

Gideon grinned and elbowed her playfully. "Okay, Lara, spill it. What's your secret?"

With a wave of her hand, she heaved a theatrical sigh. "Okay, you've caught me—it's true, all true. I'm actually a spy for the country of... Catatania. Where felines rule, and humans are subject to their every whim."

Gideon belted out a laugh. "You know, I half believe you."

Lara smiled to defuse the tension she felt building in her head. Joy's revelation had unnerved her more than she wanted to admit. "Don't laugh, because you're next," she warned Gideon.

Joy repeated the same ritual with Gideon. "Aren't you a curious one," she said, staring into the dregs of his teacup. "You don't have only one secret—you have many. Secrets you'll never share with anyone."

"I concede that. My job requires me to keep confidences." Gideon shot a look at Lara. "Do you see a ring in my future, too?"

Joy's brow furrowed, aging her ten years. "I see two rings. One is broken—"

"Uh oh."

"And one is complete. The question you need to ask yourself is, which will come first?"

The mood instantly dampened. Joy sensed it, and wrapped up Gideon's reading quickly.

Anxious to be out of there, Lara thanked Joy for her free reading. Gideon insisted on paying for his. He followed Lara to the checkout counter at the front of the shop.

"You were both fun to read," Joy said, accepting a twenty from Gideon.

"Well, I enjoyed it," Lara said. She didn't want Joy to think she'd taken the reading too seriously, either hers or Gideon's. "Maybe I'll try it again sometime."

"By the way, Lara, your friend Mary Newman was very receptive to me. She's going to let me put a display of some of my handmade jewelry in her shop."

"Joy, that's great. Mary is a terrific person. I'm sure you'll enjoy working with her."

Lara turned to leave when she noticed a good-sized framed photo, about eleven by fourteen, hanging on the back wall behind the counter. The pic was black-and-white, a medium she favored. In the photo, a family of three adults—a man and two women—and four kids posed before a fireplace on which a row of stockings had been hung. Except for their expressions, the women could've been twins. One woman glowed with happiness, while the other looked off to the side with a cheerless, vacant stare. From the fashions and hairstyles, Lara guessed that the picture dated back to the late 1950s or early sixties.

"Is that your family?" Lara asked. "It's a great photo."

Joy's face softened. "Yes, isn't it? I never married, so they're the only family I've ever had." She reached up and touched the face of the smallest child in the photo—a boy of about four or five. "A neighbor took the picture for us. It's my mom, dad, my aunt Agnes, me and my sisters, and my little brother. My last sister died a few years ago. It was almost a blessing. She didn't have a very good life."

A look of intense sadness came over Joy, so stark that it made Lara's heart catch. Lara suspected that the rest of Joy's family had also passed, so she decided not to question her any further.

Then something in the photo caught Lara's eye. The father, dressed formally in the picture, had a white flower plunked in the center of his tie. It looked exactly like the one Lara had bought at the library sale!

"Is that your dad?" Lara asked, her pulse racing.

Joy smiled, and her eyes grew watery. "Yes," she said. "The kindest, most caring man you could ever know. We...lost him far too soon."

"I'm sorry," Lara said. "It's so weird, though. I saw a tie tack just like that at the library's yard sale today." She omitted the fact that she'd bought said tie tack.

"That was one of Dad's favorites," Joy said. "He wore it all the time. I don't know where it ended up. I left home right after high school, so I don't have any family heirlooms."

Joy had no doubt been too young to remember, but Lara pressed her anyway. "Did he ever say why he liked it so much?"

"Not that I recall, but hey, I was only a kid at the time." She pointed to the photo again, this time at a little girl with unruly curls that jutted at all angles from her head. "This is me. Don't you recognize the hair?"

"Ah, yes," Lara said. "Which one is your mom?"

Joy pointed to the woman with the huge smile. "Right here. Wasn't she pretty?"

Not pretty in the traditional sense, Lara thought, but contentment radiated from the woman's wide-set eyes. "Very attractive," Lara agreed, still focused on the tie tack.

Joy glanced at the teapot-shaped wall clock. "Well, guess it's time to close up." She bit down on one lip, then, "Lara, did you ever have a chance to ask Deanna if she'd like me to do a special tealeaf reading for her? I can bring everything I need, even the teapot and cups."

"Sorry, but I haven't," Lara said. "In fact, I haven't seen her or spoken to her for a few days."

"Oh." Joy sounded disappointed.

Lara's heart went out to the woman. Joy struck her as being a gentle but lonely soul. A bit of attention from a celebrity of Deanna's caliber would no doubt make her day, if not her entire year.

"I told Deanna I'd call her tomorrow," Lara said, "so I'll be sure to mention it to her."

"Thanks." Joy's face brightened. "I'd be honored if she'd allow me to do that for her. It wouldn't hurt my business any, either, if you know what I mean." She winked at Lara. "Thanks again for coming here, both of you."

Lara and Gideon murmured their goodbyes, then headed outside toward Gideon's car. It was still light outside, but a faint glimmer of the moon was visible in the eastern sky.

"What was that all about?" Gideon asked, opening the passenger-side door for Lara.

She slipped inside the car and snapped her seat belt into place. A moment later, Gideon did the same.

"Are you talking about the photo?" Lara asked.

"Of course I'm talking about the photo. I certainly didn't buy into that spiel about you having a secret."

"Really?" Lara joked, deflecting the question. "So, you don't find me mysterious enough to be harboring a deep, dark secret?"

Gideon leaned over as far as his seat belt would allow, then turned her face toward his and kissed her lightly on the lips. "I suspect you have many deep, dark secrets. But I was talking about the photo. What was it that was so intriguing?"

Loose lips, Lara reminded herself.

She was so tempted to share with Gideon what she'd seen the day she found Donald Waitt's body. She knew she could trust him to keep it confidential. On the other hand, if he thought she was asking too many questions, he'd only worry needlessly.

"It was just...weird. I saw a tie tack like that one at the library's yard sale today. I mean, what are the odds, right?"

Gideon sat up straight and started his engine. "I didn't want to bring this up at dinner, Lara, but I'm worried."

"Why?" she asked, already knowing the answer.

"You had a bad experience last year, and now another man's been murdered. I'm worried that you're getting pulled in because you want to help Deanna."

Lara felt all of her emotions flood her face. Joy was right; she wore her feelings like a badge.

"I do want to help Deanna," she admitted. "You're right about that part. But remember, Gid, two of our kittens are in that mansion."

He shook his head, his forehead creased. "It's more than that, Lara. You have this way of wanting to set the world straight, of needing to rescue everything and everyone you come in contact with. It's one of the things I lo…I mean, that I admire so much about you." His face reddened and he slid the gearshift into Drive.

He was about to say love before he caught himself.

"Gid, I promise, I'm not doing anything that would put me in danger. What happened last year was something no one could've predicted. And I just remembered—I haven't even told you about our new assistant, Kayla."

"Uh, yes you did. She's the one who thought she recognized Nancy Sherman."

"Oh, right. Well, I told you about her, but I didn't really go into detail. Gid, she's an absolute treasure. We are so lucky to have her."

If her sudden change of topic bothered Gideon, he didn't protest. He listened patiently as she described Kayla's attributes, commenting at all the appropriate places. But Lara knew he wouldn't stop worrying.

Tomorrow would be the perfect day to bake a blueberry buckle and deliver it to Gideon's uncle Amico. The sweet old guy remembered things from the past. Maybe not clearly, but he'd definitely recalled something about Donald Waitt's high school football days.

"Are you going to visit your uncle tomorrow?" Lara asked.

"Wish I could, but I promised myself I'd devote tomorrow to my backlog. If I don't, I'll be starting off the week at a distinct disadvantage."

"I should do the same," Lara said, a vision of her unfinished art projects spinning on a mental wheel through her head. "Gid, would you mind if I visited your uncle myself? I promised him a blueberry buckle. I don't want him to think I'm breaking that promise."

Gideon smiled, his eyes remaining fixed on the curve in the road. "Lara, that's a great idea. He'd love that. You sure you have time?"

"I'll make time," she said. "We don't do adoptions on Sunday. I'll Google a recipe, unless Aunt Fran can dig one up."

"She's pretty cozy with the chief these days, isn't she?" Gideon commented.

Lara turned sharply toward him. "What do you mean? Where did you hear that?"

Gideon shrugged. "Oh, you know...around." He looked at her. "I didn't mean to imply anything. I think it's nice that they're such good friends."

"I do, too," Lara said. "It just...seems awfully fast."

"They've known each other for a long time, though, Lara. Sort of like...us."

Like us.

Lara swallowed.

"In fact"—Gideon cleared his throat—"and at the risk of sounding cliché, would you care to come up to my apartment for the proverbial nightcap?"

Gideon lived in the apartment directly above his office. She'd been there only a few times, but had never lingered.

Take a risk, she told herself.

"A proverbial nightcap sounds delightful," she said.

Chapter 19

Lara got up earlier than usual on Sunday to perform all the usual feline duties. With the cats fed and the litter boxes scooped, she hopped into the Saturn and drove directly to the Shop-Along.

The market opened early. Lately they'd been carrying produce from local farms. The blueberries were a tad pricey, but worth every cent. For Gideon's uncle, she wanted the freshest ingredients, not the watery, frozen stuff. The recipe called for two cups of the berries, but she bought an extra pint. They were delicious to eat alone, in cereal, or even in salads.

Her date with Gideon had left her on an emotional high, and she found herself humming an old Beatles ballad, one that her dad had always liked. Munster danced around her ankles, no doubt hoping to catch of drop of spilled batter. She'd already given him a blueberry, which he'd sniffed for a solid minute before finally chewing and swallowing. Lara had read that an occasional blueberry was healthy for cats, so long as they didn't overindulge.

Instead of asking her aunt to dig up a recipe for the buckle, Lara had found one on the internet. She propped her tablet against a canister so she could read it while she worked. Aunt Fran came into the kitchen just as Lara was popping the batter-filled pan into the oven.

"You're an ambitious one today," her aunt said in a voice that sounded clogged. Clad in a pair of white cotton slacks topped by a light blue jersey tunic, she clutched a crumpled tissue in one hand. Dolce trailed behind her.

"You don't sound so good," Lara said.

"I've picked up a summer cold. Don't get too close to me. What are you baking?"

Lara smiled. "I decided to make Gid's uncle Amico that blueberry buckle I promised him. I figured I'd drive over to the facility later and bring it to him." She set the timer on the stove for twenty-five minutes.

"Isn't Gideon going with you?"

"Nope. He's playing catch-up today with his workload. We might take a late afternoon bike ride if he gets enough work done. We're playing it by ear."

Aunt Fran ran some water and put the teakettle on the burner. "So, how was last night? Did you and Gideon like that new restaurant?"

"The food was great," Lara said, avoiding her aunt's gaze. "We both had the grilled bass, and we shared a chocolate soufflé—it was all yummy. The décor was a bit underdone for me. I think they're aiming for the minimalist look—but it certainly didn't detract from the meal."

"I'll have to try it sometime." Her aunt snagged a tissue from the cardboard box on the counter. "Lara, I think I'll skip church today. I'm sure Pastor Folger wouldn't appreciate me contaminating his entire congregation."

"I agree. Stay home and rest. Dolce and Frankie will keep you company." She sensed that her aunt wanted to question her more about her evening, so she quickly switched topics. "I think I'll call Deanna while this buckle is in the oven. She texted me yesterday and said the kittens are fine, but I'd feel better hearing it from her directly."

Aunt Fran dropped into a chair. Dolce leaped onto her lap and curled into a circle, his chin resting on his tail. "You're still worried about the housekeeper, aren't you?"

"Now that you mention it…" Lara told her the story Kayla had related about Nancy Sherman.

"Interesting," Aunt Fran said. "If that's true, then I honestly feel bad for the woman. If she was coerced by her husband into robbing banks, she probably feels terrible guilt over it. It might account for her unfriendly manner."

The kettle whistled. Lara prepared her aunt's tea and one for herself, then delivered both mugs to the table.

"I know what you mean, Aunt Fran. And maybe she does feel guilty. But I'd be more empathetic if the woman liked cats. It bothers me that she thinks they all belong outside."

"A lot of people still think that way," her aunt said, shaking her head. She sneezed into her tissue. "Lara, I think I'll take my tea upstairs. You don't need my germs flying all over you."

"Want me to bring it up for you?"

"No, I'll be fine." She gently dislodged Dolce, rose from her chair, and picked up her cup.

"What about medicine? Anything I can pick up at the drug store for you?"

"Not a thing. I have a medicine cabinet full of stuff for colds and flu. You do your own thing today and I'll rest."

"Okay, but text or call me if you think of anything you need. Should I postpone my visit to Uncle Amico?" After the evening she'd spent with Gideon, she felt as if he were her uncle, too.

"Absolutely not," Aunt Fran said, pushing her chair closer to the table. "I'm fine. It's only a cold, and a mild one, at that." She waved and shuffled off, Lara staring after her. Lara picked up her cell phone and tapped Deanna's saved number.

"Yes, Lara?" came a cheery voice.

"Good morning, Deanna. You're sounding chipper today."

The actress sighed. "Well, I'm trying to keep my spirits up. Quite frankly, I'm bored. I hate going out because I'm afraid people will recognize me. Nancy's very efficient, but, well, sometimes she goes into a quiet mode. Not always the best company."

Lara could well imagine. She wondered if Nancy ever took any days off. It sounded as if she was there all the time. "Are any of the cable news vans still there?"

"No! Thank goodness, they've finally all left. Fools. What did they think they were going to gain by hanging around here?"

"A story, I guess," was all Lara could think of to say. "The kittens looked adorable in those pics you sent. How are they doing?"

"They're doing really well." Lara heard the smile in Deanna's voice. "I'm so glad I adopted them. And I swear, they've grown at least an inch since last week. You should see them. I'm still keeping them upstairs, but this coming week I'm going to bring them downstairs for a few hours a day. It'll give them a chance to explore a bit. Soon they'll be able to eat in the kitchen, and we can move their litter box to a more convenient spot."

We? Lara wanted to ask. Did that mean Deanna and Nancy?

"Kittens sure do grow fast," Lara said. "I can't wait to see them again. Have you heard anything new from the police?"

"Not a thing," Deanna said acidly. "I told you, their so-called evidence turned out to be a dead end. They don't even know who vandalized my car, let alone who killed poor Donald."

"That's so frustrating," Lara said.

"I don't suppose *you've* learned anything useful," Deanna prodded.

"I'm afraid I haven't," Lara said, "but I'm keeping my eyes and ears open."

Lara desperately wanted to ask her about the Queen Anne's Lace, but she knew that fell into the forbidden category. Still, it would help if she knew whether or not the police had revealed the tidbit about the flowers scattered at the crime scene.

Maybe she should attack it from a different angle.

"Deanna, when Kayla and I were there several days ago, we couldn't help admiring the wildflowers in the yard behind the mansion."

"They do make for a pretty scene, don't they?" Once again, Lara knew the actress was smiling.

"They sure do, but it made me start thinking about plants, and how some are poisonous to cats."

"Yes, I've read that," Deanna said. "We haven't ordered any plants for the house yet, but maybe you could give me a list of what to avoid?"

"I'll do that," Lara promised, mentally adding it to her "to do" list. It was probably something she should have done sooner, for all of the new cat moms and dads. "I noticed in the yard you had some lily of the valley, and something that reminded me of poison hemlock." That part was a fib, but a necessary one in Lara's mind. "Queen Anne's Lace, maybe? I'm not sure. I'm not really a plant expert. Anyway, both lily of the valley and poison hemlock are deadly to cats. If you're thinking of cutting any of the wildflowers and bringing them inside, be sure to check first to see if they're poisonous. Feel free to call on me if you need help."

"Will do, Lara, though I certainly hope there's no poison hemlock out there." She laughed nervously. Then, in a ragged voice she said, "It's the little things, isn't it? The things you don't give any thought to that can trip you up."

Something in Deanna's tone told Lara she'd hit a nerve, although Lara's mention of Queen Anne's Lace hadn't seemed to jog her at all.

"Yes, that's all I'm trying to say. Have you thought any more about what we talked about? Did you think of any kids from your school days who might be holding a grudge?"

After a long silence Deanna said, "I did, but nothing rang a bell. To be honest, Lara, I don't think turning the clock that far back is going to be of any help."

Lara decided to back off. She'd planted the seed. For now, that was all she could do.

"Deanna, there's another reason I called. Do you remember the nice woman who supplied the specialty teas at the welcome event?"

"Yes, I think I do. Joy or Joyce something."

"Joy Renfield," Lara said. "A friend and I were having dinner out last night when we spotted her tea room in the adjoining strip mall. The shop was still open so we popped in, and she read our tea leaves."

"Oh, that sounds like a hoot. All nonsense, of course, but I can see the appeal. Did she tell you anything you didn't already know?"

"Not really." Lara had already known she carried a huge secret—no surprise there. "But Joy is a big follower of yours, and she offered to come to your home and do a special reading for you. She'll bring all the teas, the pot, the cups—the whole shebang. I told her I'd float the idea to you, but couldn't promise anything."

"You know," Deanna said in a weary voice. "I could probably use the distraction. Besides, who knows—maybe she'll be able to tell me who killed Donald Waitt."

Lara wasn't amused by the actress's flippant remark. Nothing about murder was funny.

"Probably not," Lara said flatly, "but I wanted to let you know about her offer."

After a moment Deanna said, "I didn't mean to sound callous, Lara. I'm just so mentally drained from all this. Would you give me that woman's number?"

"Sure." Lara supplied Deanna with Joy's contact info.

"Lara," Deanna said in a much softer tone, "would you and Fran like to come for lunch today? Nancy's going to make a quiche. I can ask her to whip up a fresh spinach salad. And you can both play with Noodle and Doodle to your heart's content. You'll be able to see for yourself what a wonderful home they're living in."

That made Lara smile. "Thanks, Deanna, but I've made plans to visit someone today. He recently moved into assisted living and could use some company. Aunt Fran has a summer cold, so she's taking it easy."

"Oh, that's too bad."

"Some other time, maybe?" Lara said, feeling bad now. She really did want to visit the kittens, and lunch at the mansion sounded like fun. Plus, it would give her a chance to chat a bit with Nancy Sherman.

"Certainly. Let's aim for one day this week. Please give your aunt my regards. I hope she feels better soon."

They disconnected, and in the next moment the buzzer went off on the stove.

The buckle smelled heavenly—warm blueberries, butter, and cinnamon all blended into the same whiff. Lara grabbed a pair of potholders and pulled the pan out of the oven, then set it on a rack to cool. She was sticking the potholders back on their hook on the fridge when Aunt Fran's landline rang. Lara grabbed the receiver.

"Hello," a woman's soft voice filtered over the line. "I hope it's okay that I called this number. I know your shelter is closed on Sunday."

"It's fine," Lara said. "I'm Lara Caphart. Can I help you with something?"

"Oh, then you're probably the gal I'm looking for. We've never met, but I'm Jennifer Conley. Trista's mom?"

Trista. The little girl who loved chimpanzees and wanted to read to cats.

"Of course. Trista paid us a visit a few days ago. She'd heard we had cats and wanted to read her chimpanzee book to them."

"I'm awfully sorry she tried to barge in like that," Jennifer apologized. "She knows better. My husband and I raised her better than that."

"No need to apologize. Trista was very sweet, and polite. I explained to her that she needed to have you call us first to be sure we're going to be home."

Jennifer laughed softly. "That was a tactful way to put it. Actually," she said, after a slight hesitation, "that's kind of why I'm calling. I was wondering—and this is awfully pushy of me—but if you're going to be home today, could Trista maybe read to one of your cats? Only for about fifteen minutes. I think that would satisfy her. She has a cousin who visited a shelter in another town, and they have a program where kids read to cats. Now Trista has it stuck in her head that she has to do the same thing."

Kids reading to cats. Lara loved the concept. She'd heard of at least one shelter in New Hampshire that was doing the same sort of thing. She didn't know exactly how it worked, but after today she planned to find out.

To make it work at High Cliff, they'd have to set parameters and decide how to match up each kid with a cat. Some parental supervision would be required, but that shouldn't be difficult. Maybe with Kayla's help, they could get a program started before the end of the summer.

Right now, a little girl she knew wanted to read to a cat.

"I have plans for the afternoon," Lara told her, "and I was hoping to make the noon service at Saint Lucy's. It's quarter to ten now. Do you have time to bring Trista over this morning, say around ten-thirty?"

"Oh, that would be perfect," Jennifer said. "My, you people really are nice. I didn't think it would be this easy."

"It's only because we're such a small shelter," Lara explained, "that we can be this flexible. We don't have as many cats as a traditional shelter, but I think I have the perfect cat for Trista to read to. I would ask that you stay in the room with them, though."

"Well, actually, Lara, I was hoping it would be okay if my mother-in-law brought her over. Trista usually spends Sundays with her anyway, and I've got about a million ongoing projects at my house I'm trying to tackle."

"That's fine. As long as she's accompanied by an adult, we're good."

"Oh, excellent. You're a life saver." Jennifer thanked her again and hung up. Lara felt encouraged by the call. It gave her all kinds of new ideas for the shelter.

* * * *

Lara's suspicion had been correct. Evelyn Conley was Trista's grandmother. The two arrived right on time, Trista flashing a big smile and Evelyn a cautious one.

"We meet again," Evelyn said. Clad in long pants and a short-sleeved flowered blouse, she stepped into the meet-and-greet room clutching her granddaughter's hand. "And I understand you already met Trista."

"I sure did." Lara smiled at the child. "How are you today, Trista?"

Instead of pigtails, today the girl sported a thick ponytail. Wearing a mint-green jersey over matching leggings, she held up the same chimpanzee book she'd had with her on Friday. "I'm good," she said. "Mom and Grandma said I can read this to a cat."

"You may, and I have the perfect cat for you."

She'd already chosen Munster, their official greeter, to sit with Trista while she read. Gentle and loving, Munster rarely extended a claw. He was more likely to crawl into Trista's lap and purr while she read.

Evelyn dropped onto a chair and rested her arm on the table. "That walk through the woods nearly did me in," she said with a slight grunt. "I knew I should've taken the car." She looked all around. "It's quite pretty in here, isn't it? Very welcoming."

"We try," Lara said. "Can I get either of you something to drink?"

"No, we're fine," Evelyn said firmly. "I suspect we're bothering you enough just by coming here."

"Honestly, it's really not a bother. I'll go get Munster."

Trista giggled at the name.

"Do you mind if Trista sits on the floor?" Evelyn asked. "It's her favorite way to read."

After assuring Evelyn that Trista could sit anywhere she liked, Lara went into the large parlor and retrieved a sleepy Munster.

Trista's eyes widened with delight when she saw the orange-striped cat. "Oh, Grandma, look at him!"

Evelyn glanced at the cat and nodded. "Very cute," she said.

The child had already settled on the floor, her back propped against the wall under one of the windows and her legs stretched out in front of her. Munster instantly strolled over and rubbed his head against the girl's arm. After that, he plunked himself onto her lap, and Trista began to read.

"Trista's read that book a hundred times," Evelyn quietly explained. "It's about a twelve-minute read, if that's okay." She pulled a paperback book from her purse and set it on her lap. "While I wait, I might as well get a bit of reading in myself."

"Perfect." Lara smiled. "I'll leave you guys alone. Be back in fifteen."

It was close to eleven when Lara stepped back into the meet-and-greet room. The chimpanzee book was on the table. Trista was stretched out on the floor with Munster tucked against her chest. The child wore a blissful expression as she gently stroked the cat's neck.

Evelyn instantly rose and shoved her paperback into her purse. "Lara, we can't thank you enough. I think Trista had more fun today than she's had in a long time." She held out her hand to the child to signal it was time to leave. "What do you say to Lara?"

Trista made a face, then got up off the floor. Lara suspected the girl would opt to stay for several more hours if she could.

"Thank you," Trista said politely, then her gaze wandered to the corkboard hanging on the wall. "Grandma, can I look at that?"

"Only for a minute," Evelyn said. "We don't want to wear out our welcome."

"Those are pictures of our successful adoptions," Lara proudly explained. She thought about asking Evelyn if Trista's family was looking to adopt, but then decided to wait. With all cats except Frankie currently spoken for, the timing wasn't ideal.

Trista came over and tugged on her grandmother's wrist. "Grandma, see this lady over here?"

Looking bored now, Evelyn followed her granddaughter over to the corkboard.

Trista plunked a finger over the picture of a smiling Deanna holding her two kittens. It was the pic Lara had taken at the actress's home and tacked up on the board herself.

"She used to have long hair," Trista declared. "I saw her in that book you have in your attic."

Evelyn narrowed her eyes at the photo, then sucked in a breath. A flush crept into her cheeks. "I don't know what book you're talking about, Trista, but we really need to get going."

Looking frustrated, Trista pulled at her grandmother's sleeve. "The *book*, Grandma. You know, the big book with all the pictures and stuff pasted in it. I found it in your attic. It has a million pictures of this lady. Some looked really old."

A scrapbook, Lara thought.

Evelyn shot Lara an odd look. "Well, enough of that. We've wasted Lara's time for far too long already. Let's get going."

Lara assured them once again that it had been no trouble. And once again Evelyn thanked her, then hustled her granddaughter out the door. Lara watched through the porch window as they trekked across the yard toward the path through the wooded buffer. Evelyn's feet were moving so fast that Lara wondered if she'd picked up a tailwind.

It begged the question: Why did a woman who was at least in her sixties have a scrapbook filled with photos of Deanna Daltry?

Chapter 20

Lara slipped out of her pew after the service at Saint Lucy's and made a beeline for the Saturn. Normally, she and her aunt would hang around and chat with friends after church. Today she wanted to make a fast exit. She was anxious to see the look on Uncle Amico's face when she showed up with his freshly baked blueberry buckle.

The facility looked busier today than it had been when she and Gideon had stopped there during the week. The parking lot was packed with cars. Lara assumed Sundays were probably big visiting days. She wondered if the facility held any special activities for the residents on weekends.

She stepped inside the lobby. A girl who looked barely out of high school greeted her at the reception counter. On the desk in front of the girl was a textbook—math, Lara noticed with horror. When Lara was in school she'd dreaded the subject, favoring the arts and literature end of the learning spectrum.

Lara explained why she was there.

"Just sign the clipboard," the girl said. "Do you know which room he's in?"

"Yes, thanks. I was here a few days ago."

"Okey dokey." The receptionist went back to her textbook.

Lara wrote her name on the clipboard sheet, along with the time she arrived. She went directly to Uncle Amico's room. His door was wide open. He sat in his recliner, looking perky in a red bow tie and plaid shirt. His television was tuned to a black-and-white movie on one of the classic film networks.

"Well, if it isn't Lara," he said, beaming at her. "What a wonderful surprise. Is my nephew with you?"

"No, it's just me today, Uncle. Gideon's tackling his backlog today, but I wanted to bring you a surprise." She set her tote on the floor and kissed him lightly on the cheek.

He handed her the remote. "Would you mute that for me?" he asked. "I can never find the right button."

Lara muted the TV and set the remote on his side table. She pulled the foil-covered blueberry buckle out of her tote and set it down beside the remote.

"Oh, don't tell me you made me that buckle," he said. He reached for her hand and squeezed it with his own gnarled one.

Lara laughed. "I did, but it's my first one so I have no idea what it tastes like."

"Oh, I already know." His faded gray eyes brightened as he watched her peel back the foil. "I can tell just by lookin'. Can we sample it now?"

Lara was glad she'd thought to bring a short stack of paper plates, napkins, and some plastic utensils. She cut a large square and set it on a plate for Uncle Amico. The blueberries looked gooey and luscious.

Uncle Amico took his plastic fork and dug right in, his smile growing wider with every mouthful. "Delicious," he kept repeating. "Marvelous," he added.

Lara sat on the sagging sofa and sampled hers. She was thrilled with the way the buckle had turned out. Although she'd worked in a Boston bakery for a few years, she'd never done any real baking. But this dessert had been a breeze to prepare. She'd definitely have to make more buckles in the future.

After he finished a second helping, Uncle Amico said, "Lara, remember when you and my nephew were here a few days ago, and we talked about that Waitt fella?" He wiped his mouth with the napkin Lara had supplied.

Lara nodded, her mouth stuffed full of cake and blueberries.

"Well, I guess I couldn't get it out of my head, 'cause I kept thinkin' about him. Sometimes things get all jumbled up here"—he tapped his temple—"and I can't make sense of 'em. But that night, after we'd talked, something hatched out of my brain like a baby chick from an egg."

Lara sat up straighter. She dabbed her lips with her napkin. "It did?"

Uncle Amico nodded. "You recall me saying that the Waitt boy played high school football?"

"I do," Lara said.

"Well, I started mullin' it over, and it finally triggered a memory. There was this other boy, a classmate of his, name of Jimmy Rousseau. Jimmy played football, too, but he wasn't nearly as good. Kid's dad pushed him into sports, I think, but the poor boy would've rather tinkered with a hammer and nails. He loved buildin' things."

Jimmy Rousseau. Lara made a mental note of the name, though she wasn't sure of the spelling.

"Did something happen to Jimmy?" Lara prompted.

Uncle Amico let out a long sigh. "Yeah, it did. I was working at the school in those days. Gid probably told you I was the janitor. Anyways, the coach had the team practicin' after school one day. Poor Jimmy. They say he dropped nine out of every ten passes Waitt threw to him. Waitt finally got mad and stormed right up to the kid. He tossed the ball at his face, hard, from about six feet away. Jimmy was a slender kid, light-boned. He came away with a damaged eye socket."

Lara felt her stomach sway. "That's...awful. Was the damage permanent?"

"I never really found out, but Jimmy graduated and went on to start his own carpentry business. Did real well, I guess. Everyone loved his work. Died a few years back. Lung cancer, I heard."

"Does Jimmy still have family in the area?"

"Hmm, let me think on that one." He put his head back and closed his eyes. "I know he had a boy who moved to Arizona. Not sure about the girl..."

"That's okay, I was just wondering."

Lara mulled it all over in her head. Uncle Amico was a wellspring of information.

A sudden wave of guilt swept over her. She hadn't come here to extract information from the man. Her motive had been a genuine one. She really had wanted to bake him that buckle. But then he'd started remembering, and she couldn't stop asking questions. How could she pass up the opportunity to learn more about Waitt's early years?

Gideon would say she was getting too involved. Okay, maybe she was being a tad nosy. But nothing she'd done so far had put her in any danger. She felt sure about that. Besides, she reasoned, anything that helped Deanna also helped her kittens.

"Uncle Amico," Lara said, "did Waitt ever get punished for what he did to that boy?"

"Not so far as I recall. There was talk of suspension, but nothin' ever came of it. Back then kids got away with stuff like that—not like it is now. Anyways, about a week after it happened, Jimmy's father was toolin' around in a brand new Chevy Corvair. Not surprisin' as Waitt's dad owned a Chevy dealership." He grinned. "Everyone figured old man Rousseau got himself one heckuva deal on that car."

Bribery, Lara thought. She realized now why Uncle Amico had tapped his eye that day. The story about Rousseau had been stuck in his subconscious. Her mention of Waitt had jiggled it free. What other memories might be buried in there, waiting to bob to the surface?

But there was one hitch, in Lara's mind. Even if one of Rousseau's family members had nursed a grudge against Waitt, why wait so long to kill him? That's the part that didn't make sense.

A perky teen in a pink uniform and wheeling a food cart in front of her stopped short in the doorway. She peeked into the room. "Juice, anyone? I have cranberry, grape, pineapple"—she peered into a pitcher—"and about enough orange left for one more glass."

Gideon's uncle opted for the cranberry, and Lara chose the grape juice. The teen gave them their drinks in small paper cups. "Have a great day!" she chirped, then wheeled her cart down the hallway.

Lara gulped down a mouthful of juice. She was thirstier than she'd realized. "Uncle Amico," she said, "I know I'm testing your memory, but do you remember Donald Waitt having a girlfriend in high school?"

He rocked back in his recliner, his eyes creased in thought. "He had different girls, as I recall. One of 'em stood out though. Pretty as could be, she's that gal who became an actress."

"Deanna Daltry?"

"I guess that's her name now. Used to be something else. Durkin, Dorkin...something like that. Isn't she the one who bought the old stone mansion? Gid told me something about it."

"Yes, that's her. Her name was Idena Dorkin when she lived here."

"Yup. Sounds right." He shook his head, and his eyes misted. "I'm embarrassed to admit this, Lara, but I don't read the paper anymore. Even the obits don't interest me the way they used to, so long as my name's not in there." He gurgled out a laugh. "The news is always so bad, it makes my heart hurt. I only knew about Waitt because Gid told me. These days, I only watch the entertainin' shows. Old movies, comedy reruns, stuff like that. Can't stand to watch the real world anymore. I'm too old for it, Lara. Too darned old and weary."

Lara felt her own heart hurt for him.

He reached out with a gnarled hand and touched hers. "But you, you've added a beam of light to my world. Don't know if you and Gideon are serious about each other, but I sure hope you are. That way you'll stay in my life, too—for as long as I got left, anyways."

Lara touched a finger to her eye. "That's one of the nicest things anyone's ever said to me, Uncle. And no matter what happens, you'll always be in my life. You're my friend."

"Good! And now I'll have another slab of that buckle, if you're inclined to cut one for me."

Lara grinned, set down her paper cup, and gave him another huge helping. While he ate, she tucked the foil over the rest of the buckle and then slid the pan into his mini-fridge. He could enjoy what was left at his leisure.

"Uncle, I hope I'm not bothering you," Lara said, "but I have one more question."

"Fire away," he said, wiping crumbs off his fingers.

"Did you ever hear of the Wild Carrot Society?"

His eyes popped wide open. "Wild Carrot Society. My God, I haven't heard anyone mention that in an elephant's age."

"You *have* heard of it?" Lara wanted to pump her fist.

He nodded slowly. "Well, yeah, but there's not really much to know. There was this fella—Will something-or-other—got it started back in the sixties. Problem was, he didn't have a good way to reach enough people to get 'em signed up. It was all word of mouth, and kind of secretive at that. It wasn't like today, what with the Web, and all that online social malarkey you kids go for."

Lara smiled to herself. As sweet as Uncle Amico was, in some ways he was a relic.

"Do you know why the group broke up?" she asked.

"Sure I do. In fact, I was about to join those fellas myself when the guy who started the whole thing died. After that, no one wanted to pick up the ball where he'd dropped it. His death seemed like a bad omen, if you get my drift." He snapped two knobby fingers together. "Tardiff, that was the name. That's the fella who started it."

Wilbur Tardiff. The man who'd penned the leaflet.

It had to be him.

Uncle Amico leaned his head back and nodded, his eyes beginning to close.

Lara desperately wanted to learn more, but she couldn't press the man any further. He was getting tired. She vowed to make him more blueberry buckles, as well as other baked goodies.

Last evening with Gideon—which had stretched into the wee hours—had been, well, magical. The memory made her blush and smile at the same time. If things progressed further with Gid, and she hoped they would, she'd be seeing a lot more of this gentle old man.

"Jimmy Rousseau!" Uncle Amico's eyes bolted open. "I just remembered where I saw his daughter. She works at that big nursery in Tamworth."

Lara's heartbeat sped up. "A nursery for kids?"

"No, not kids—flowers." Uncle Amico dipped his chin toward Lara's cell phone, which she'd left resting beside her on the sofa. "I bet if you Google it on that phone of yours, it'll give you directions right to the place." He winked at her.

Lara chuckled. He wasn't as technologically challenged as he pretended. She left him with a kiss on the cheek and a promise to return soon.

"Next time you visit I'll have that tomato for you," Uncle Amico promised. "Gotta give it time to ripen first."

"I'll hold you to that."

The moment Lara climbed into the Saturn, she turned on the engine and cranked the AC. She Googled the nursery, and found the link within seconds. She wouldn't even need GPS to find it, for it was on one of the main routes in Tamworth.

* * * *

The entrance to Blossoms was a rocky driveway that led to a wide patch of dirt set aside for parking. At least a dozen cars were parked in front of the main building—a red, barnlike structure that seemed to stretch the length of a ball field.

Lara got out of the Saturn and slammed the door shut. Everywhere she looked she saw bursts of pink, yellow, and purple. Seasonal flowers—pansies, geraniums, impatiens, and some early chrysanthemums—rested in plastic pots atop a sea of wooden pallets.

A twentyish man sporting multiple earrings and wearing a canvas apron lugged a hose between two rows of pallets. One by one he watered each plant, his head bobbing to a tune only he could hear. He didn't appear to notice Lara, so she cleared her throat and loudly said, "Excuse me."

He turned and looked at her. "What can I help you with?" he said in a lackluster tone.

She hadn't really thought about what she was going to say, so she plunged ahead. "I'm trying to find Jimmy Rousseau's daughter. Someone told me she works here."

The boy looked at her as if she'd suddenly sprouted warts. "You happen to know her name?"

"I'm sorry, I don't." Lara felt like a dolt. She should have asked Uncle Amico if he remembered it. Or at least gotten her surname.

The young man aimed a thumb at the building. "Go talk to Ant'ney. He should be inside." Without another word, he went back to his watering.

"Thank you," Lara said.

She headed inside the building, which housed even more plants. Along the entire back wall were refrigerated cases that held cut flowers in tall glass vases. Lara felt her pulse spike. Was there any Queen Anne's Lace here? She gave the cases a quick scan, but didn't see any.

Lara then spied a man with curly gray hair and a doughy face arguing with a customer over the price of a geranium plant. The man wore the same style canvas apron the boy outside had worn. She moved closer and peered at his name tag. "Anthony," it read.

She waited.

The customer finally persuaded Anthony to give him a discount over a broken stem, then stalked off toward the checkout counter. Lara moved in quickly before Anthony could get away. "Excuse me"—she stepped in front of him—"but someone told me Jimmy Rousseau's daughter works here."

Anthony's jaw dropped, and he gawked at her. "Who wants to know?"

"Well, actually, I do," she said. She held out her hand. "I'm Lara Caphart from the High Cliff Shelter for Cats in—"

"She don't want a cat, I can tell you that much." Ignoring her outstretched hand, Anthony sidled around her and went over to a row of impatiens. He fiddled with the plants, deadheading a few and collecting the shriveled flowers in his hands.

"That's not why I'm here," Lara said. She summoned every ounce of patience she could muster. "I just want to ask her if she remembers something about her dad. Something from the past. I'm…doing research for an article I'm writing." She cringed inwardly at the lie. *Desperate times*, she told herself.

Anthony narrowed his eyes at her, suspicion tightening his jaw. "What is it you want to know?"

Should she tell this ogre what she was looking for?

"Nothing you'd be familiar with," she said, then instantly realized her mistake. Now he really wouldn't help her.

"Write your name on a piece of paper," Anthony grunted. "If she wants to call you she will. If she don't…" He shrugged and went back to his deadheading.

Lara was glad she'd made up business cards for the shelter on her aunt's printer. She started to whip one out of her tote when she caught herself. The cards had their address on them—exactly what she didn't want Rousseau's daughter, or anyone in this nursery, to know. She regretted, now, that she'd mentioned the shelter. She hoped Anthony wouldn't remember it.

Digging deep, she found a small pad in her tote and tore off a page. She wrote her cell number on it, along with her name. "Here's my cell number," she said, giving him the slip of paper. "I'd be grateful if she'd give me a call."

Anthony looked at the paper, then shoved it into his shirt pocket.

"Thank you, Anthony. Can you tell me her name?"

The way he glowered at Lara, someone would have thought she'd asked for the woman's social security number and weight. "Claudia," he finally replied. Then he turned his back on Lara and strode away into a rear storage room.

Pleasant fellow, Lara thought to herself.

Lara decided it was a perfect time to peruse the refrigerated flowers. She started at one end, her gaze traveling over all the vases until she reached the wall at the other end.

No Queen Anne's Lace.

Disappointed, she hustled out to the car and back to her aunt's.

She hadn't been in the house for one minute when her cell phone pinged.

Chapter 21

Lara's insides dropped. The text was from Gideon.

Can't do bike ride today. Buried in work.

That was it. No niceties, no smiley face. No promise to call later.

Lara choked back tears. They'd talked about so many wonderful things last night. By the time he'd driven her home, it was well after two. She'd been certain Gideon's feelings for her were both deep and heartfelt. Had she read him completely wrong?

She shoved the phone into the pocket of her capris and went upstairs. Her aunt's door was partway open. Aunt Fran was propped up in bed by two fluffy pillows, with two even fluffier felines tucked on either side of her. Dolce and Frankie looked so adorable that Lara had to smile. "You two monkeys," she said. "Are you taking good care of Aunt Fran?"

"They've been sticking to me like glue," her aunt said with a chuckle. "Cats always know when their humans are sick, don't they?"

What if their human is heartsick? Lara wondered. "Are you feeling any better?" she asked her aunt.

"A little bit. I've been trying to read, but I keep dozing off."

"Want some juice? Tea?"

"No, I'm fine. I went downstairs a little while ago and made myself another cup of tea. I'm ready for a nap."

Lara left her aunt resting and went back downstairs. Her tablet was in her studio. She retrieved it and carried it into the kitchen. Images of a boy with a damaged eye slithered through her mind.

Jimmy Rousseau. She plunked his name into Google's search pane, using the French spelling of the surname. She knew it could also be spelled R-U-

S-S-O, but with a huge portion of New Hampshire's population being of French Canadian heritage, she took a shot at the first spelling. She added the words "Whisker Jog" to narrow the results.

He hadn't been hard to find. A master carpenter, Rousseau had apparently worked until his death a few years earlier. Lara studied his image. Sandy hair, sharp cheekbones, one eye dipping slightly lower than the other. The result of aging, or something else?

From the accolades people had left in the comments section of his obituary, his carpentry business had thrived.

There was no mention of children, although Uncle Amico had mentioned a son who'd moved to Arizona. As for Claudia—whatever her surname was—Lara didn't hold out any high hopes of hearing from her.

Her cell phone rang. It was Sherry. Her bestie usually texted before she called. Something must be up.

"You didn't stop in today," Sherry said, sounding a bit annoyed.

"Sher, I'm sorry," Lara said. "Aunt Fran's got a cold, and things kind of spiraled out of control this morning." She told her about Trista coming over to read to Munster, and also about the buckle she'd baked for Gideon's uncle.

"Okay, I'll let it go this time. Sooo...how was last night?"

Lara eyed the orange-striped cat strolling in her direction. She patted her lap and Munster hopped aboard. "It was fun," she said evenly. "We had a great meal."

"Nothing else to report?"

"I'm afraid not," Lara said. She nuzzled Munster's nose, and he revved up his purr.

"I wish I could see your face right now," Sherry said. "That would tell me everything."

You don't hide your feelings. You wear them like a badge.

"I know a certain tea lady who would agree with you," Lara said.

"Tea lady? What the heck are you talking about?" Sherry said, a sudden hitch in her voice.

Lara's mental antennae went straight up. "Sherry, is something wrong?"

"No," her friend said quickly. "It's just—look, I didn't want to tell you this before, but...well, I kinda met someone."

"What? When?"

"He came in to the coffee shop a few weeks ago." She spoke quietly. "He...kind of travels on business."

Light dawned. Lara now knew why Sherry's normally spiky coiffure had grown softer over the past week.

"I can't talk now. Mom's close by." She groaned into the phone. "It's really hard, Lara. I had to tell him I still live with my mother. It was so mortifying."

"There's nothing wrong with sharing living space with your mom, Sherry. I live with Aunt Fran."

"I know, but that's different. You guys run a shelter."

"Sherry," Lara said. "It sounds like we both need to talk. Today's been really weird for me."

"Yeah, tell me about it. Tonight's out, though. Mom invited that old battleax aunt of hers—Aunt Phyllis—to eat wings with us and then play cards. Aunt Phyl's bringing her famous pineapple upside-down cake. It's famous for how awful it is. She's the most horrid woman. Her critique of me will start the second she walks in and continue until she's out the door."

"Bummer," Lara said. She remembered Sherry's past descriptions of her super critical great aunt. "But don't let her get to you. Tomorrow for sure, then, we'll find a way to get some private time to chat."

"Sounds like a plan." Sherry sighed.

On that agreement, they disconnected. Lara set Munster on the floor, then went over to the fridge. The kitchen had gotten warm. She pulled a pink plastic ice tray from the freezer, popped out a cube, and set the cube on one of the cat dishes. She'd made the cubes a few days earlier, adding juice from a tuna can to the water. In this kind of weather, the cats loved the frozen treat, especially when the ice melted enough to expose the chunk of tuna hidden in the center.

As Munster licked the cube, Lara poured herself a glass of lemonade. She was carrying it over to the kitchen table when a familiar face peeked through the storm door.

Evelyn Conley.

Lara's glass jerked in her hand. What the flipping heck was she doing back here? Heart thumping, she set her glass on the table and opened the door. Evelyn held up a hand in a tiny wave.

"Hi, Evelyn. Nice to see you again." Her fib quotient for the day was rising.

Evelyn smiled, but Lara saw pain in her eyes. "I'm sorry to come by without calling," she said through the screen, "but I need to speak to you. May I come in for a moment?"

A creepy feeling of déjà vu all over again skidded down Lara's back.

"Uh…sure you can. Would you like something to drink?" Lara opened the screen door and waved her inside.

"No, nothing, thank you." She glanced around the kitchen. "It was so generous of you to let Trista read to that cat this morning. You really made her day. She can't stop talking about it."

"I enjoyed it as much as she did," Lara said. She smiled over at Munster, who was licking the fishy ice cube with an expression of sheer delight. "And Munster was in his glory."

At the sound of his name, Munster looked up and shot a glance at Evelyn. Lara knew he was trying to decide between greeting the unexpected visitor or sticking with his delectable ice cube. When he went back to licking the cube, Lara pointed at one of the kitchen chairs. "Evelyn, please sit. You don't have to stand there."

"Trista's always loved animals," Evelyn said, lowering herself onto the nearest chair. Her eyes welled. "Lara, I'm sure it didn't escape you this morning that my granddaughter was referring to a scrapbook when she talked about my having a book of pictures of Deanna Daltry." She sucked in a jerky breath. "From the mouths of babes, right?"

"Evelyn, don't worry about it," Lara soothed, sitting down opposite the woman. "You should see the crap I collected when I was in high school. Only I didn't put them in a scrapbook, I—"

"Lara," Evelyn interrupted. "I wasn't in high school. I was far beyond that. And, well, what with this murder hanging over all our heads, I really feel I need to explain."

Then explain to the police! Lara wanted to beg.

"Go ahead, Evelyn."

Evelyn folded her hands on the table. "I've never told many people, but, back in the day, I wanted to be an actress. Starring in all those school plays got in my blood, I guess." She blushed a hearty pink. "Deanna Daltry was starting to get known right about then. I felt a kinship with her. I knew she'd grown up around here, which made her even more special."

Lara wondered if Evelyn knew Deanna's real name.

"I used to imagine we were close friends," Evelyn went on, "living on opposite sides of the country. I-I got a little obsessed. Even after I got married, I still had one of those fangirl crushes on her. That's why I filled a scrapbook with her pictures. Oh, and she was so striking back then!"

"She's a beautiful woman," Lara agreed. "Full of grace and charm."

Evelyn squashed a tear from her cheek. "I loved that she never married. Oh sure, everyone knew she had plenty of boy toys. But it was Hollywood. That sort of thing was to be expected."

Lara had to smile at that.

"I'll get to the point," Evelyn said, looking more nervous now. "We—my husband and I—had saved enough money for a vacation for our first anniversary. It was nineteen seventy-nine. I nearly fainted when he said he'd take me to Hollywood! He encouraged me to write to Deanna and ask if I could meet her. He even suggested—bless his heart—that I should ask for a walk-on part in her next movie."

Evelyn's husband sounded like a caring man. Clueless, but caring.

"I wrote her the most wonderful letter. It took me days to get it perfect. I even bought special stationery, lavender to match what all the magazines said was her favorite color."

Lara felt for the woman, but she was also a bit unnerved. Evelyn's obsession seemed over the top.

"I explained that I was from Whisker Jog and would be honored if we could meet, even briefly, when my hubby and I visited Hollywood." Evelyn leaned to one side. She pulled a tissue out of her pants pocket and blotted her eyes.

"Are you sure you don't want some water?" Lara asked.

"No, I'm fine." She sniffled. "Well, I waited and waited. And while I waited, I worked on a special gift for Deanna. I bought some lavender-blue hydrangea flowers and glued the petals onto a sheet of ivory linen. It was painstaking, but it came out so gorgeous. I framed it and wrote on the back 'to my friend, Deanna.'"

"Sounds beautiful," Lara said. The woman's fangirl confessions were making her more uncomfortable by the second.

"Then one day, almost two months later, I received a letter in the mail from Deanna's personal assistant. My heart just about burst. In the envelope, she'd tucked an autographed photo of Deanna. 'With love to Evelyn' it read in the corner."

"That sounds nice," Lara said, wondering if the actress herself had signed it. She suspected the photos had been mass-produced for Deanna's thousands of fans.

"The personal assistant invited me to meet Deanna at the studio. She listed the days when Deanna expected to be there. She even enclosed a tiny photocopied map of the studio lot." Evelyn gave a nervous laugh.

"So, you went to Hollywood," Lara prompted.

Evelyn nodded. "We went to where the assistant had told us to go. It took us a while to navigate all the check points. Finally, we got to the right building. Some young twit of a boy directed us to a waiting room. We sat for the longest time with some extremely odd-looking people. The AC wasn't even working, for God's sake, and it was June. I was ready to pass out when a woman finally came out. She was the width of a carrot stick, and had matching hair." Evelyn glanced at Lara's hair and flushed. "She brought us into a room totally devoid of décor—an outer office, I guess. It had three folding chairs, a metal desk, and a wastebasket. She sat us down and apologized profusely, but said Deanna was shooting a movie in Nevada and wouldn't be back until the following week."

"Oh, Evelyn, I'm so sorry."

"She s-said if I left my name and address, she'd see that I got an autographed photo of Deanna. I told her I already *had* an autographed photo—she'd sent it to me herself!"

Whoa. Obsession might be too mild a word for the way Evelyn had felt toward the actress.

Evelyn barreled on. "And then I couldn't help myself—I burst into tears. It was so humiliating. The assistant gave me this weird look, and I could see the pity on her face, pity mixed with revulsion. I swear, Lara, it was the worst day of my life."

Lara squirmed on her chair. What did all this have to do with the scrapbook?

Evelyn pressed her crumpled tissue to her eyes. "My husband kept giving me signals with his eyes. I realized he was reminding me to give her the gift I'd made for Deanna. I pulled it out of my shopping bag and gave it to the assistant. She promised to give it to Deanna, thanked us for coming, and hustled us out the door."

"Well, at least you accomplished that much," Lara said, grasping for anything that might comfort the woman.

A tear flowed down Evelyn's cheek. She shook her head. "Turned out I'd left my purse on the floor next to the folding chair I'd been sitting on. I went back in for it. The beautiful framed flower I'd made for Deanna w-was in the wastebasket!"

Oh, Lord. Poor Evelyn. Hollywood had not been kind to her.

"There are all kinds of people, Evelyn," Lara said softly. "That woman sounds like one of those mean girls. I'm sure Deanna would have loved your gift. She'd probably have been horrified to know what that woman did with it."

"I-I suppose you're right," Evelyn said. "After I got back home, I tucked my Deanna scrapbook away in the attic. It's been languishing in a file cabinet for decades. Who knew my curious little granddaughter would go digging for treasures up there?" She smiled and hiccoughed at the same time.

Lara didn't know how to respond. She barely knew Evelyn.

"I'm sorry I bothered you, Lara, but I just felt I needed to explain. I felt like such a fool when Trista brought up my scrapbook this morning. You must've thought I was some kind of nut." She dabbed at another tear.

"Not at all, Evelyn," Lara said. "And you didn't really need to explain anything." *Unless you terrorized Deanna and killed Donald Waitt.*

Evelyn heaved a massive sigh. "I suppose you're right. My private feelings are my own, aren't they? W-when I found out Deanna was buying the old stone mansion, I couldn't believe it. I thought, well, here's my chance to finally meet her." She paused, her eyes filling again.

"I thought you did a fine job planning that welcome event," Lara said. "Deanna seemed very appreciative."

Evelyn hung her head and shrugged. "But in the end, even that got ruined."

"Not your fault, Evelyn." *Or was it?*

Could Evelyn have planted those worms in Deanna's purse?

Evelyn couldn't have scrawled the message on Deanna's car window. From the time Deanna had arrived, Evelyn never left the room where all the guests were milling about with their tea and snacks.

Uh oh. Yes, she did, Lara thought, remembering that Evelyn had escorted Donald Waitt out to the parking lot. Had she been gone long enough to dig out a tube of her own lipstick and write that cryptic message on Deanna's car window?

Evelyn stood abruptly. "I should go. I've bent your ear long enough. But I want to say one last thing." She lowered her voice to a murmur. "Other than my husband, you're the only person who knows that story about the Hollywood trip. I-I would appreciate it if you didn't share it with anyone. It's embarrassing enough."

Lara hated to promise. What if Evelyn was the killer? What if she'd decided to kill Waitt and frame Deanna for his murder, as revenge for that long-ago fiasco in Hollywood?

It didn't seem possible. Evelyn didn't strike Lara as the kind of person who'd carry a grudge to that extreme. *Although*, she reminded herself, she'd been surprised before by a killer, hadn't she? Maybe she shouldn't be so trusting.

"You have my word, Evelyn."

After seeing Evelyn to the door, Lara closed it with relief. She turned the deadbolt, something she rarely did. Evelyn's revelations had her head whirling.

Lara had read about rabid fans who stalked celebrities. Some had been dangerous. A rare few had killed in pursuit of their obsession. The word *fan* itself came from the word *fanatic*.

She took a long sip from her glass of lemonade. Munster was still licking his ice cube, but he'd been joined by Twinkles, who wanted him to share. Lara smiled and popped another fishy cube out of the ice cube tray. She set it on a separate dish for Twinkles, who immediately claimed it for his own.

Although they weren't siblings, Twinkles and Munster looked somewhat alike. Twinkles was shyer, not so quick to cozy up to visitors. His best bud was Dolce, but lately Dolce had been hanging out with Frankie and Aunt Fran. Did Twinkles feel like the odd man out?

It was one of the challenges of having a multi-cat household. Every cat in the house didn't necessarily love every other resident feline. That's why the adoptions were so crucial. The goal was to match each new cat they took in with the ideal person or family. Every cat was different, so their personalities had to be considered.

Lara and her aunt had vowed from the beginning that they'd never place a cat in a home if they had the slightest doubt. That's why Aunt Fran had surprised Lara when she'd been so insistent about matching Frankie with Hesty.

As it turned out, Aunt Fran had been right. No one could have known Hesty's days were numbered. No one except a certain blue-eyed Ragdoll cat.

It was chilling the way Joy Renfield had picked up on Lara's secret. The more Lara thought about it, though, the more she saw that Joy had only been guessing. No doubt it was part of the tealeaf reader's standard shtick. After all, didn't everyone have a secret or two? It was easy to throw that out and pretend it was etched in the leaves. How many others had Joy said that to?

A sinking feeling gripped Lara's heart. It all reminded her of Gideon. They'd had such a fantastic evening. She hadn't anticipated the intimate talk they'd engaged in well into the night. Considering how long they'd been dancing around the "L" word, it was a conversation that'd been long overdue.

Maybe it had been too soon. Maybe Gid thought she'd pushed things, pressured him into saying what she wanted to hear and not what he actually felt.

Gideon's text had been abrupt—not at all what she'd expected. She'd wanted to tell him all about her visit today with Uncle Amico, how she and his uncle had enjoyed sharing the blueberry buckle. How they'd enjoyed each other's company. How they'd chatted about the old days.

A harsh light suddenly glared in Lara's head.

That was it.

Gideon found out that Lara had questioned his uncle about Donald Waitt. Why that would bother him so much, Lara wasn't sure. She *was* sure, though, that she'd nailed the reason for Gideon's abrupt change in attitude.

She needed to explain. Even if she never saw Gideon again—in a romantic sense, anyway—she had to make him see that she'd gone there with only with the best of intentions.

Had she, though?

In the back of her mind, she probably *had* intended to question Uncle Amico about Waitt's past, and about the Wild Carrot Society. Even though Gideon's uncle had brought up the subject first, Lara had pressed him for more information.

Did Gideon think she'd used his uncle? That she'd baked him that dessert only so she could take advantage of his memory?

Never again, she vowed. The next time she visited Uncle Amico, with or without Gideon, the past would stay in the past. She'd talk only about the present.

Her cell rang on the kitchen table. Tired of talking to people, Lara went over to answer it. The number wasn't familiar.

"You Lara?" a woman's crusty voice barked into the phone.

"I am," Lara said.

"My brother-in-law gave me a message. Said you're writing an article and wanted to talk to me about something."

Lara gripped her phone harder. The amiable Anthony must be her brother-in-law. "Are you Claudia?" Lara asked.

"That's me," the woman said peevishly. "What's up?"

The absence of common courtesy is obviously a family trait, Lara thought.

Now that she had Claudia on the phone, she wasn't sure how to begin. She'd hoped to chat with her face-to-face. This wasn't the ideal way to handle it.

"Claudia, I'm not sure where to start, but I understand you're Jimmy Rousseau's daughter."

"Was," she corrected. "Was his daughter. My dad died a few years ago. Couldn't give up the cigarettes. I warned him over and over, but he kept smoking anyway."

"I'm so sorry to hear that," Lara said. "My dad died a number of years ago. It's very hard, isn't it?"

"Yeah," Claudia said. "Anyway, why do you care about my father?" she asked warily. "Did you know him?" A smile touched her voice. "Were you one of his old flames?"

"Um, no. No, I wasn't an old flame. I didn't know your dad at all. I'm calling because of Donald Waitt. You might have heard his name in the news lately."

Claudia went silent. Then, "Yeah, Donald Waitt. I recognize that name. I heard on TV he got offed in a cemetery. Creepy, right? Like the freaking Twilight Zone."

"It was terrible," Lara said. Should she reveal more?

It suddenly struck her that she was doing exactly what Chief Whitley had cautioned her against.

Loose lips. The accusation rattled in her head.

Should she hang up? Claim she had the wrong person?

"Why're you asking about Waitt?" Claudia said, sounding guarded now. "You hear something about him and Dad?"

In for a penny, in for a pound, Lara remembered her dad saying. Right now, the scale was tipping way over a pound.

"I heard they had an altercation back in high school," Lara explained. "I know it sounds like a long time ago, but —"

Claudia gave out a harsh laugh. "Yeah, like almost sixty years. Why the heck would that matter now?"

"I'm sure it doesn't," Lara said.

"Wait a minute. Are you some kind of cop?"

"Heavens, no," Lara said firmly. That much, at least, was the total truth.

Oddly, the idea that she might be a cop seemed to amuse Claudia. "I think I like you, Lara. You're nosy and just a tad pushy. I bet you don't let people tell you what to do. Am I right?"

Lara smiled to herself. "Kind of," she said, "although I'm not sure I agree with the pushy part."

"Hey, you had supper yet?"

The question took Lara by surprise. "No, but my aunt and I will probably make something at home. She's a bit under the weather."

"Oh."

"Why do you ask?" Lara said.

"I was wondering if you wanted to meet someplace for a quick bite. Maybe you could feed your aunt later."

Claudia made Aunt Fran sound like a house pet.

This was starting to get dicey. Was Claudia trying to lure her someplace where she could get her alone? Now that Lara had the chance to meet her in person, she felt uneasy about it.

Lara admitted it now—she hadn't really thought this through. Instead of asking questions, she should have turned over whatever she'd learned directly to the chief. Let the police deal with it. Hadn't she said many times that catching a killer wasn't her job?

"Lara, listen. I don't know where you live or anything, but do you know where the clam shack is in Tamworth?"

Lara's stomach sank. It was *their* special place, hers and Gideon's. She absolutely didn't want to go there.

"I know where it is," Lara said, "but I don't really eat clams." Fib quotient climbing ever higher.

"Me neither. I hate those slimy things. No, what I meant was, there's a hot dog joint about a half mile down the road from there. They make this sauerkraut topping that's to die for."

Dying. Exactly what Lara was afraid of.

A furry face and a pair of turquoise eyes appeared suddenly across from Lara. Blue sat on the chair directly opposite, her chin resting on the table. The Ragdoll cat held Lara's gaze. Her chocolate-colored ears, facing forward, were dipped slightly to the side.

It was a sign. Lara had seen it before. Blue felt totally at ease, not threatened in any way.

Should I meet Claudia? The thought flew, unbidden, through her head.

Blue blinked slowly, then closed her eyes. Lara had the strange sense the cat was smiling at her.

In the next instant, Blue was gone.

"You still there, Lara?"

"Uh...yes. I'm sure I can find it," she said. "Or my phone can. I don't live that far from the Tamworth line."

"Great!" Claudia gave her directions. "See you in, say, thirty minutes?"

After they disconnected, Lara batted her head with her palm. She never should have agreed to this. She never should have started this inquiry. She never should have given anyone in the Rousseau family her name.

The chief was going to kill her.

If someone else didn't get to her first.

Chapter 22

Blue's blessing notwithstanding, Lara wanted to leave a trail—both a paper trail and an electronic one. She looked up the hot dog place on her cell phone and plunked the address into her GPS. If something happened and the police found her phone, at least they'd know where she'd been.

Lara tore a sheet of paper off the pad that hung next to the house phone. She wrote down Claudia's name—she'd failed to get her surname—and phone number, and the name of the nursery. Everything the police would need if she turned up missing.

She grabbed another sheet of paper and scribbled out a note to her aunt. The hot dog place wasn't that far from here. She certainly had no intention of dawdling over a meal with Claudia. She planned to find out what she wanted to know, eat fast, and bail.

Lara muttered a silent prayer.

She glanced at her phone before she slipped it into her tote. It was only ten to five, early for supper, but she hadn't eaten since morning. She'd had only the scrumptious blueberry buckle she'd shared with Gideon's uncle. Right now it felt like a leaden lump weighing down her stomach.

After quickly freshening the cats' water bowls and plumping up their kibble supply, she headed out to the car.

The sky was an almost cloudless blue. Breezes whispered through the leaves of her aunt's maple, cooling Lara's skin. Tomorrow was supposed to be cooler, even chilly for July. Lara welcomed a touch of colder weather. At this time of year, she knew it would be short-lived.

She jumped into the Saturn, started the engine, then headed in the direction of the clam shack. From there she'd take the side road that led to the hot dog place. It should only be a half mile or so up the road.

The closer she got to the clam shack, the more Lara felt overwhelmed with sadness. She hadn't even spoken to Gideon today, and already she felt as if their budding romance was over. Was she overthinking it? Misinterpreting his curt text?

She hated that she even cared.

Spying the clam shack up ahead, she made a quick left turn onto Crackneck Road. *What a name*, she thought gloomily. She hoped it wasn't a prophecy.

The hot dog place was only a short distance up on the left. When she spotted the sign, she made a quick left turn. She was shocked at the number of cars clogging the small parking lot.

Lots of people. Lara liked that. She took a deep breath and headed inside the beige, flat-roofed building. The AC blasted her in the face.

The scent of hot dogs, mustard, and onions wafted around her. She pulled in a deep breath. She felt suddenly hungry. Something about the smell of mustard always made her ravenous.

Lara looked around at the jumble of booths and tables. Three college-age kids dressed in identical blue T-shirts took orders at the front counter, which had lines at least four-deep. An older man worked the grill, juggling hot dogs, fries, and onion rings with the precision of a surgeon.

Claudia had told Lara she'd be wearing a straw hat with a hot pink bow. Lara glanced all around. In a corner booth, a little boy of about three shrieked with delight as a slightly older girl squirted ketchup at him. Their mom tried to intervene, which only made the little boy squeal louder.

A finger poked Lara in the lower spine.

"Yipes!" She whirled around.

A woman so petite she barely reached Lara's shoulder beamed up at her. "Sorry. Didn't think you'd be so jumpy. I bet you're Lara."

"You'd win that bet," Lara said, unable to suppress a grin. "You must be Claudia."

At well under five feet tall, Claudia peered at her from underneath a wide-brimmed straw hat. Tied around the hat was a bright pink bow almost the size of the woman's head. Her face was tanned to a toasted brown, and her blue eyes sparkled with more than a hint of mischief. Lara held out her hand, but Claudia grabbed her elbow instead and steered her to the booth she'd saved near the rear of the dining area. On the table were two bottles of water and a brown paper bag stained with grease. A stainless-steel napkin holder and a set of condiments sat on the far edge of the table.

Claudia slipped into the booth and pointed at the seat opposite hers. "Sit. I got food for both of us." She plopped her hat on the seat, then removed a foil-covered plate from the bag and set it down in front of Lara.

Despite her misgivings, Lara was intrigued by the woman. She sat on her side of the booth and peeled the foil off her plate. A foot-long hot dog piled with sauerkraut sat next to a mound of shoestring fries. *Junk food to the third power,* her dad would've scolded.

"Looks delish," Lara said.

Claudia ripped the foil off her own plate. "That's their signature topping," she said, nodding at Lara's dog. "Eat first, then we'll talk."

Lara sampled her hot dog. It was messy, but so yummy she didn't care. Her taste buds danced in pleasure at the tangy blend of flavors. The fries were crisp and surprisingly hot. She squeezed a puddle of ketchup onto her plate for dipping.

Claudia tore off a bite of her hot dog, chewed it with gusto, and swallowed. They ate in silence for a few minutes, then Claudia said, "How is it you never heard of this place? You live close by, right?"

An alarm sounded in Lara's brain. *Don't tell her too much.*

Lara swallowed a fry. "I only moved here last year," she said. "I'm still getting my bearings."

"So," Claudia prodded, "you said you live with an aunt?" She shoveled her last four fries into her tiny, bow-shaped mouth.

"Yes, she's a wonderful person. We get along really well."

Claudia nodded and swallowed at the same time. "You're lucky. I live with my husband, and we *don't* get along really well." She laughed, then curled her lip. "You met my brother-in-law, right? Mr. Personality?"

"If you mean Anthony, yes," Lara said, squelching a smile.

"Well, multiply his charming traits by a hundred and you got my husband, Hal. Hard to believe, right? Even more bizarre is that those two jokers make a living selling flowers." Claudia grabbed a fistful of napkins from the holder and swabbed her lips. She crumpled them into a ball and dropped them on her empty plate.

"How long have you been married?" Lara asked. She really wanted to ask her why she stayed with horrible Hal.

Claudia rolled her eyes. "Seventeen glorious years. My dad hated Hal. Knew he was a jerk from the get-go." She shrugged. "I didn't listen to him, though. Just like he ignored my cigarette warnings."

Lara set aside her plate, which was empty save for a few overcooked fries. She didn't want to stray from the reason she'd come here. "Your dad," she said. "Did he ever talk about Donald Waitt?"

Claudia studied her for a moment. "He did, but not the way you'd think. Me and my brother and my mom, God rest her soul, we'd all heard the story at least a dozen times about Waitt throwing the football at Dad's eye. You know that story, right? I'm guessing that's why you're here."

Lara nodded.

"In a weird way, Dad wore that injury like a medal of honor. Sometimes I think he was proud of it. Used to tell his buds it was an old football injury."

"Did his eye have permanent damage?"

"It did—it skewed his vision a little—but it never bothered Dad. He said it gave him more perspective. He was a fantastic carpenter, you know. When he died, he still had orders up the yin-yang for hand-crafted furniture. He never got to finish his projects before the cancer took him."

"I'm awfully sorry," Lara said. "He sounds like a character, and a nice man."

Claudia shrugged, then her face grew serious. "He had his moments. Ma put up with a lot, but she loved him. No one's perfect, right?"

"Right," Lara said, looking away.

Claudia folded her arms over the table and leaned closer. "I remember this one time, Dad was talking to my brother and me about the day Waitt threw that ball in his eye. For once he didn't joke about it. He said Waitt showed absolutely no remorse for what he did, just kept insisting it wasn't his fault." She took a long swig from her water bottle.

Lara's pulse quickened. Maybe Claudia knew more than she realized.

"That was the day Dad told us that other story," Claudia went on, "about the man who was killed in the car crash. 'Course I have no way of knowing if any of this is true, but Dad wasn't one to tell tales, if you know what I mean." She frowned. "Anyway, he told us that about two years after the accident with the football, Waitt was driving his girlfriend to some babysitting gig. It was November, and the road was slick with freezing rain. They were running late, so Waitt was speeding. They were approaching a bridge, I guess, and a car was coming from the other direction. The other driver swerved to avoid hitting Waitt. The other guy lost control and his car went straight through the guardrail and into the river. He drowned before the rescuers could get to him."

Lara felt her stomach turn over. "What a terrible story. Waitt obviously survived," she said.

"According to Dad, Waitt's car made it over the bridge seconds before that poor man went into the river."

"How did he know all that?" Lara asked. "Were there any witnesses?"

"There were two witnesses—a couple driving home from some event at their church that night. They told the cops they saw Waitt's car weaving like crazy before it got to the bridge. The other driver had to swerve to avoid him."

An icy shiver wriggled down Lara's spine. She could only imagine that poor man's last moments—knowing he was crashing through the guardrail with no way to stop.

"Waitt told the cops it wasn't his fault. That his girlfriend begged him to drive fast because she was late for her babysitting job." She shook her head in disgust. "What a creep, blaming it on someone else. Like he wasn't the one at the wheel."

"A terrible, needless death," Lara said quietly, but something poked at her brain. She looked over at Claudia. If it hadn't been for Gideon's uncle, Lara wouldn't have known anything about Jimmy Rousseau, or his family. Claudia had given her some interesting tidbits about Waitt.

Lara didn't picture Claudia as a killer. Why would she take the risk? She'd admitted that her dad's eye injury hadn't adversely affected his life, or his career.

But the car accident. That was a different story.

"Did Waitt ever get charged with anything?" Lara asked.

"Nope. He hadn't been drinking. That probably saved him. Plus, the chick he was with told the cops that even though Waitt had been speeding, his car never swerved. She said the witnesses got that wrong."

One person's word against that of two others.

Claudia's voice grew soft. "Less than a week later, everyone forgot about the accident. No one cared anymore, because the unthinkable happened."

"What was the unthinkable?"

Claudia looked at Lara. "President Kennedy was assassinated."

Lara sagged, absorbing everything Claudia had told her. She glanced up at the wall clock. She'd been gone over an hour.

"Claudia, I really appreciate you taking the time to chat with me," Lara said, digging her wallet out of her tote.

"You kidding? I enjoyed this. Hal's managed to scare away most of my old gal pals, so I'm on my own most of the time." Her expression changed, and Lara saw the loneliness in her eyes.

"Still, I'd like to treat," Lara said. "What do I owe you?"

"I'll agree to that. So long as it's my treat next time. The whole thing with the waters was eighteen bucks, give or take."

Fortunately, Lara had that much in cash. She usually depended on her debit card for purchases. She slid the money over to Claudia.

Claudia scooped up the cash. "Hey, I'm sorry if I came off like a flaming witch when I called you earlier. It's my defense mechanism—bite first, ask questions later."

"You were fine."

"And you better go," Claudia said. "You got that aunt, remember?" She grabbed her straw hat and swung her legs out of the booth. "You're not really writing an article, are you?"

Lara felt her face redden. "No, I'm not."

"What do you do, then?"

"I'm a watercolor artist," Lara said. She didn't want to tell her about the shelter. Not until she was one hundred percent sure of Claudia's innocence. She hoped Anthony would forget she'd ever mentioned the shelter.

"Cool! Better than working with the sunshine brothers at the nursery, like I do." She made a face.

Lara grinned. She liked Claudia. "By the way, working with all those plants and flowers, did you ever hear of Queen Anne's Lace?"

"Yeah, sure, I'm very familiar with it," Claudia said. "We carry it on occasion, mostly during the wedding season. It adds a nice touch to bouquets. I don't think we have any in the shop right now. Why're you asking about that?"

"No special reason," Lara said. Her fib quotient was off the charts now. "I'm working on a watercolor of a wildflower garden and I'm trying to decide if I want to include some Queen Anne's Lace in the painting."

"Go for it," Claudia said. "The white will make the other colors pop."

They cleaned up their table and dumped their trash in a barrel near the door. Claudia stuck her straw hat on her head, and together they walked out to the parking lot.

"Can we do this again sometime?" Claudia said. "Now that I have your number, you don't mind if I call you, right?"

Lara hesitated. "Um, no, that would be great."

She was sure now—well, ninety-nine percent sure—that Claudia hadn't killed Donald Waitt. The mention of Queen Anne's Lace hadn't triggered any reaction in the woman. Not even a blink.

Claudia could, of course, be a sociopath. She might've told Lara exactly what she wanted to hear. The tale about the car crash might've been a total fiction.

Except for something that nagged at Lara's subconscious and wouldn't let go.

Lara stopped walking when they came up beside the Saturn. She jiggled her key chain. "Thanks again for meeting with me, Claudia. Is your car close by?"

Claudia glanced out over the lot. "Yeah, the piece of crap is over there someplace. Only King Hal gets to drive the new car." She turned sharply toward Lara. "Hey, you know what I forgot to tell you? About the car crash?"

Lara's ears perked like a cat's. "No, what is it?"

"That guy who drove off the bridge? Dad said he wasn't alone that night."

"He wasn't?"

"Nope. There was a kid with him. A little boy."

Lara felt her heart shift into overdrive. "Do you know what happened to him?"

Claudia slowly shook her head. "Nope. Like Dad told us, after the president was assassinated, the country went into mourning. No one gave a flying flapjack about the accident anymore."

Chapter 23

On the ride back to her aunt's, Lara forced herself to focus on the road. Over and over, visions of a car sailing over a guardrail into a frigid river invaded her mind.

A man.

A little boy.

The man drowned, but what happened to the boy?

Bits and pieces of the distant past were beginning to form a picture. The problem was, there were gaps. Huge gaps.

She remembered her history. President Kennedy was assassinated on November 22, 1963. Miss Cleary in eleventh grade American History had drilled that into her students' heads.

Lara needed to find out more about the accident. In this case, Googling might not help. By modern standards the accident would be ancient history.

It also might have nothing to do with Waitt's murder.

When Lara had first learned to paint watercolors, she'd often used too much water. The result was a runny landscape, colors melding into one another in messy blobs. The more she tried to cover them with extra paint, the worse it looked. Once she learned to control her brush, to blot it when needed, her skills improved. These days the techniques were second nature, but as a newbie artist she'd made loads of mistakes.

That's how she felt now. In a way, she was a newbie investigator. Not by choice, but by necessity. As professional as the police were, she felt sure they were aiming their efforts in the wrong direction. They worked with evidence, with witness statements, and whatever the forensics people turned up. All the right things.

What they didn't have was a blue-eyed Ragdoll cat with a penchant for pointing out abstract clues.

Whoever murdered Donald Waitt had not only taken a life and devastated a family. The killer had also compromised Deanna's freedom. Undoubtedly, the actress had her faults. Didn't everyone? But she'd taken in two kittens and given them a loving home. In Lara's book, that put her at the top of the "good" list.

Lara was anxious, now, to get back to Deanna's stone mansion. She needed to press the actress on details from the past. Claudia had said that Waitt's girlfriend was in the car with him the night of the accident.

Lara would bet anything that girlfriend had been Deanna.

Deanna had invited her and Aunt Fran to lunch. Maybe they could make a date for Monday. Aunt Fran should be feeling better by then. If not, Lara would go alone.

Her head throbbing, she pulled into her aunt's driveway. A familiar sedan was parked off to the side.

Gideon's.

Lara felt her stomach tighten into a knot. He'd come over so he could ditch her in person. That was Gideon—a gentleman all the way. He'd probably say that it was him, not her. That he needed his space...blah, blah, blah. Either that or he was going to blast her for asking his uncle all those questions.

Heart battering her ribcage, she shut off her engine. She felt heat rise upward from her chest, infusing her face with a hot flush.

Then she saw him. He sat on one of the Adirondack chairs, staring off across Aunt Fran's vacant field. Apparently deep in thought, he didn't notice she'd arrived until she slammed her car door.

Her legs felt rubbery as she walked across the yard. His face grim, he took deep strides toward her. He looked like a model from a men's casual wear catalog. Black hair slightly mussed, cream-colored polo shirt over tan chinos.

Don't say a word. Let him speak first.

He stopped in front of her, close enough that she could see the spot of coffee he'd spilled on his shirt a week ago and couldn't get out to save his life. A giggle escaped her, mingled with tears. He was so hopeless at doing laundry.

"I have only one thing to say." He moved closer, until his face was only inches from hers. "I am an ass."

Lara burst out into laughter. It was the last thing she'd expected to hear.

"Not that I'm disagreeing or anything, but why do you say that?"

"Because I had the nerve to get ticked off when Uncle Amico told me you asked him all kinds of questions today. It was totally, *totally* unacceptable behavior on my part. Who am I to say you can't talk to my uncle? Who, by the way, thinks you're the greatest thing since raisin bagels were invented."

A massive wave of relief washed over Lara. "So that *is* why you were mad. It wasn't because of, you know, last night? The stuff we talked about?"

Gideon's eyes widened. "Last night? Are you kidding? Lara, last night was everything I'd been hoping for. For so long, I've wanted to say so many things to you. It was such a relief to finally tell you how I feel. How I *really* feel." His cheeks flushed pink. "When you said you feel the same way, I think I bumped my head on a cloud up there somewhere."

"You should have known it already," she said softly, her voice snagging in her throat.

Gideon took her shoulders in his hands, then pulled her to his chest. His arms around her, she clasped her hands behind his back. She inhaled his delicious scent—that clean green soap with the stripes he used. She pulled back just far enough to look into his eyes. "Nothing to do with us, but I told quite a few fibs today. But only because I was trying to get information from people."

Gideon laughed, but then shook his head and grew serious. "But see, that's the part that scares me, Lara. You want to help everyone, and I adore that about you, but sometimes you put yourself at risk. If anything bad ever happened to you—"

"It won't, Gid. I've been as careful as I can possibly be. I talked to a woman this afternoon who gave me a lot of good intel. She gave me a lot to think about."

He groaned. "Will you at least fill me in? Maybe if we brainstorm about it, I can offer some ideas."

"That's an excellent suggestion. To say the least, I've had an interesting day."

"It's kind of late for that bike ride. I don't suppose you want to have clams again."

Lara laughed. She told him about her hot dog date with Claudia.

"Hmm. I can't wait to hear all about it. Well, since the coffee shop's closed, why don't we just sit out here?"

She leaned up and kissed him on the nose. "Yeah, but you must be hungry. What if I get us something to drink and make you a sandwich? We have ham, sliced turkey, peanut bu—"

"Ham," he said. "With lots of mayo."

"You got it. First, I want to see if Aunt Fran needs anything. She's been in bed today with a cold."

"Oh, sorry to hear that. Can I come in and help with anything?"

"Only if you want to. Otherwise, sit out here and relax and I'll bring everything out."

He opted to go into the house with Lara. Aunt Fran was in the large parlor with the television on, watching a cable news show with her eyes only half-open. Dolce was parked in her lap. Catalina and her kitten were tucked into the cat tree, gazing out the picture window. Lara didn't see Frankie anywhere. He was probably upstairs on her bed. And she suspected Ballou was under her bed.

"You're back," Aunt Fran said with a sniffle.

"I'm back. Gideon and I are going to sit outside for a while. Do you need anything? You must be getting hungry."

"No, I've been drinking too much tea." Her aunt smiled. "I'm ready to float away. I had a few cookies earlier. Food doesn't really appeal right now."

Gideon popped his head in. "Hey, Fran. How're you doing?"

"I'm okay, but don't come close," she said.

"Yes, ma'am. Can I do anything for you?"

"No, thanks. You two kids go do your own thing." She waved them away. "Don't worry, I'm not going to perish."

Lara pushed Gideon into the kitchen. "Come on. Let's make that sandwich, then I can tell you about my strange day."

Minutes later, they were stretched out on the Adirondack chairs. Lara had poured iced tea for herself and found a beer at the back of the fridge for Gideon. Her aunt must have bought beer for the chief, since she didn't drink it herself. As for Lara, she'd never been a beer drinker. One bad experience when she was in art school had made her swear it off for good.

"Good ham," Gideon mumbled around a mouthful of his sandwich. "Now, tell me what happened today."

Lara went over everything, beginning with her visit to Uncle Amico and ending with her meeting with Jimmy Rousseau's daughter. She remembered afterward to tell him about her strange conversation with Evelyn Conley.

"I told you my uncle has a sharp memory," Gideon said. He swallowed his last bite of sandwich. "But even I can't believe he remembered the story about that Rousseau kid. Isn't it odd how that stuck in his head?"

"Some things do, I guess," Lara said. She sipped her iced tea. "When I asked if he'd ever heard of the Wild Carrot Society, he remembered that, too."

Gideon studied her for a moment. "Uh, Lara, what the heck is the Wild Carrot Society?"

Uh oh. She'd slipped. She wasn't supposed to talk about the flowers scattered at the crime scene. Now she understood what the chief meant about loose lips. It was the unintentional blabbing about stuff that was supposed to be a secret!

But this was Gideon, a man Chief Whitley trusted without reservation.

"I'm not supposed to talk about this," Lara said. "If the chief found out I'm telling you, he'd have me drawn and quartered at the traffic intersection in downtown Whisker Jog."

Gideon reached over and covered her hand with his. "I'm pretty sure that form of punishment's been outlawed," he said. "And whatever you tell me will not go any further. You have my word."

"You never have to give me your word, Gid. With you it's automatic."

She told him about the Queen Anne's Lace, how she'd researched it and stumbled upon the Wild Carrot Society. Finding that tie tack at the library's sale had been a total fluke—almost as if the gods dropped the clue in her lap.

That wasn't the total truth. Blue had led her to that vendor. Lara had been on her way home when the cat had somehow tipped over that box of tie tacks. Lara's tote might have brushed the box, but not with enough force to upend it.

And in that moment, it struck her. How could she ever be totally honest with Gideon if she didn't tell him about Blue? And how could she tell him about Blue without sounding insane?

The tealeaf reader's words popped into her head.

Unburden yourself, Lara. You'll find others more receptive than you think.

She would. Someday. The time just had to be right.

"Did you Google the Wild Carrot Society?" Gideon asked.

"I did, but nothing helpful came up—only a botany site describing the plant. I don't think the group, which was kind of secretive to start with, lasted very long."

Gideon took a swig of his beer, then set the bottle down and pulled out his cell phone. He tapped at it. "I'll make some quiet inquiries tomorrow. Who knows? One of the old-timers I represent might remember it. I'll check out some of the names you gave me, as well. Tardiff, for starters."

"Thanks, Gid. So, what do you think about Evelyn Conley? Why would she come over and spill her guts to me that way? The more I think about it, the more it gives me the willies."

Gideon looked pensive. "I suspect she was overly embarrassed about her granddaughter dropping that bombshell about her scrapbook. She must have wanted to explain so you wouldn't think she was some kind of whacko."

"Celebrity stalkers are often whackos," Lara said wryly.

"Yeah, they can be. From what you described, I'm not sure Evelyn rose to the level of a stalker. She's probably okay, just a tiny bit obsessive."

"In a way, I felt sorry for her. Nonetheless, I don't want to befriend her. I love her granddaughter, though." Lara smiled. "That little girl was determined to read to a cat, even if she had to sneak in."

"Sounds like something you'd have done as a kid," Gideon teased.

Lara laughed. "You're right."

"Lara," he said, his face now solemn. "I think you have a guardian angel watching over you."

Yes, and she has fur and big blue eyes.

"Unfortunately, it doesn't make me worry any less." He took her hand and gently squeezed her fingers. "Honey, I wasn't so much mad at you as I was scared. I don't want to see a repeat of last year's nightmare."

Lara didn't want that either. Even thinking about it still gave her the chills.

"You have to stop stressing. Nothing's going to happen to me. As far as angels, I have several looking out for me."

"I hope I'm on that list."

"At the very top," Lara said, then frowned and sat back in her chair. "Gid, I feel like I'm playing connect the dots here. Except…at least one of the dots is missing, and I don't know how to find it. If I could snag it and connect it to the others, I might have a complete picture. Meanwhile, Deanna feels like a prisoner in her own home. Noodle and Doodle are there with a housekeeper who clearly doesn't relish the idea of cats in the house."

"Honey," Gideon said gently. "I know you're concerned for the kittens. But you've seen for yourself that they're doing fine. Besides, Deanna has something you don't have—resources."

"You mean money."

"Exactly. If she wanted to, she could fire that housekeeper and get a new one in a heartbeat. I'm sure there are lots of people who'd leap at the chance to work for Deanna Daltry and take care of her home."

Lara smiled at that. "That's definitely true, but she seems very defensive of Nancy. I think she genuinely likes the woman."

Which reminded her of something else. Kayla had said Nancy used a different name back in her bank-robbing days. Had Kayla had a chance to go back to the library to research it any further? Lara made a mental note to ask her, although she was fairly sure Kayla had been too busy with family and other obligations.

Gideon fidgeted. "You don't see any way Deanna could have killed Donald Waitt?"

"I considered it briefly, but it doesn't fit, Gid. Why would she kill him on her own property?"

He held out his hands, palms up. "Who knows? Why did he show up at the welcome party? Maybe he tried to blackmail her over something."

Blackmail. Lara hadn't considered that. It brought her back to the theory that someone in Deanna's past had it in for her.

Lara thought back to when Waitt first arrived at the welcome event. He'd looked strained, almost tearful. Not the way she imagined a blackmailer would look.

"I hear you, Gid, but my gut tells me Deanna is not the killer. I think I'll take her up on her lunch invitation, if I can wrangle another one. Maybe I can also get to know Nancy Sherman a bit better."

"You mean, maybe you can do a little snooping about Nancy Sherman."

Lara laughed. "Okay, you got me there. But now that I think about it, couldn't she have had some connection to Donald Waitt? Maybe they were working together. Maybe she agreed to apply for that job so he could get back at Deanna in some way."

"Get back at Deanna for what?"

"That's just it. I don't know. Deanna admitted they dated in high school. That sounds like a thousand years ago, but some people have long memories, especially if they felt hurt or rejected by someone they cared about."

"Anything's possible," Gideon conceded. "But I'm sure the police have already questioned Ms. Sherman, especially if it turned out she's the same person who helped her husband rob banks. Even so, she's an unknown quantity. And I'm still not sure I trust Deanna Daltry. From everything you've told me, I'm not convinced she's revealed everything she knows."

"I tend to agree with that, but maybe for a different reason. I think she might know something she doesn't know she knows. Does that make sense?"

Gideon smiled. "In a way." He reached over and entwined his fingers with Lara's. "Please be careful, Lara. At the risk of sounding like a broken record, why don't you let the police connect the dots? It's their job, it's what they do. And they're very good at it."

"I know, and I'd love nothing more," Lara said quietly. "But I think they're missing something, too."

Chapter 24

It was nearly dark by the time Gideon left. They'd lingered in the yard for a while, enjoying the soothing sounds of the crickets chirping in the field, watching the sky grow ever darker. She'd hated it when he had to leave, even if she loved it when he recited that line from *Romeo and Juliet*: *Parting is such sweet sorrow*.

Lara had felt guilty about leaving her aunt in the house, but she'd checked on her twice and found her resting quietly. With Gideon's help Lara had also fed the cats, but now it was time to perform litter duty. Tired as she was, she whizzed through it. She was putting away the cleaning supplies when her cell rang with an unfamiliar number.

It was Gillian Gardner, the other reference for the Willoughbys Lara had been waiting to hear from. Explaining that she'd been out of town over the weekend, Gillian apologized for her delay in contacting Lara. She'd known the Willoughbys for nearly twelve years, and gave them a sparkling reference.

After Lara hung up, she emailed Bruce Willoughby. "Your application has been approved," she told him, confident that her aunt would agree. "Your references were sterling."

Her phone rang almost instantly. "Thank you, Lara!" Bruce Willoughby said. "You've made our day. Petey's been waiting with bated breath, as they say. Can we pick her up in the morning? I took this week off from work hoping we'd have a cat by now. We already bought a carrier and lots of food and toys. Safe toys," he emphasized.

Lara grinned at his enthusiasm. Monday wasn't an adoption day, but she was fine with the Willoughbys coming by to get Bootsie in the morning.

Then she remembered—Deanna had offered to pay all adoption fees for the entire month. How was that going to work? They'd never talked about the logistics.

"Bruce, the shelter has a sponsor who's offered to pay adoption fees this month. We haven't worked out the details, but I'm going to waive your fee. I'm sure the sponsor will cover it."

"Wow, what a generous offer. But if it falls through, don't worry—just give me a ring and I'll run a check right over to you. Meanwhile, Petey and I will spend the windfall on Bootsie." Bruce laughed. "He loves her name, by the way."

Tears filled Lara's eyes. Another furbaby was going to a great home. It was what she and Aunt Fran wanted when they founded the shelter, yet it was so hard to say goodbye.

Lara grabbed a tissue from the box on the counter and blotted her eyes. Bootsie padded into the kitchen, her green eyes fixed on Lara's face. The cat wound around Lara's ankles and rubbed against her leg.

She knows, Lara thought, lifting Bootsie into her arms. *She knows she's found her forever home.*

"You know, don't you, baby?" Bootsie purred into her neck and Lara kissed her.

Frankie had known, too—the day Hesty was here. He'd ignored his beloved Aunt Fran and homed right in on the elderly man. Almost as if he'd had a sixth sense that his dad had come to get him.

It sounded crazy, but Lara felt it deep in her bones. There was a dynamic at work here. Did it have something to do with Blue?

She put it out of her mind, focusing instead on breaking the news to her aunt. It was good news, for sure, but Bootsie had been with them for nearly a year. They'd both gotten very attached to her.

Lara set Bootsie on the floor, and the cat scooted off into the large parlor. When she looked up, her aunt was staring at her from the kitchen doorway. She looked ghostly pale except for her nose, which was bright red.

"You don't look well at all, Aunt Fran. Do you want me to take you to urgent care?"

Aunt Fran put up a firm hand. "No, and don't get close. There's no point in both of us being sick. I thought it was a mild cold, but it's turned into a worse one. But that's all it is, and they can't prescribe anything for that. Besides, I don't have the strength to sit in that waiting room."

Lara sighed with exasperation. She'd learned over the past several months that her aunt was stubborn about doctors. The only one she was inclined to obey was her orthopedic surgeon, who happened to be tops in her field.

"Sit, then. I'll heat you some soup. We have chicken and stars, chicken noodle, creamy tomato—"

"I'll take the first one," her aunt said, dropping heavily into a chair. Dolce immediately appeared at her feet and climbed into her lap. "I thought I heard you talking to someone about Bootsie."

Lara pulled a can of chicken and stars out of the cupboard. "I was talking to Bruce Willoughby. Aunt Fran, Bootsie is finally going to her forever home. Isn't that wonderful?"

"It is," her aunt said in a gravelly voice. "But oh, how I'll miss her."

"I will, too." Her throat tight, Lara plopped the contents of the can into a bowl. She popped it into the microwave and opened a box of crackers.

"Would you grab me a tissue, Lara?"

Lara plucked a handful from the box on the counter and gave them to her aunt. "It means we're doing something good, here, Aunt Fran. Each cat we place with the right person or family means we can take in another one. Or three." Lara grinned.

Aunt Fran was quiet. She ate a spoonful of her soup, then said, "I know we have a unique kind of shelter here, and limited space. But we haven't taken in a cat since Frankie. Maybe enough people don't know about us yet."

"You're right, and we said we'd talk about it. But you have to get better first. Let's give it a few more days, then we'll come up with a game plan. We might be able to ease the overload for one of the area shelters."

Her aunt gave her a wry smile. "Remember how things were a year ago? I was a mess, wasn't I?"

"Health wise, you were, a bit," Lara admitted. "You were dealing with much worse than a summer cold, that's for sure. But look where we are now, how much we've accomplished."

Aunt Fran sneezed into a tissue. "I need to head back to bed."

Lara helped her upstairs and got her tucked in. Dolce and Frankie joined her, framing her on either side like a pair of fuzzy bookends.

Downstairs, Lara made herself a cup of peppermint tea and went into her studio. She'd ignored working on her watercolors for way too long. It felt as if she hadn't painted in a week.

She set the painting of the wildflowers in Deanna's yard back onto her easel. She gathered her supplies and went to work. After a few haphazard strokes, she pushed all of it aside.

I can't concentrate, she thought glumly. *This just isn't coming together.*

The Willoughbys would be by in the morning to pick up Bootsie. Lara removed her colored pencils from the drawer in her worktable. Her mind skittering in different directions, she sketched a five-by-seven likeness of

Bootsie's furry face, emphasizing the cat's big green eyes. It worked up quickly. This type of sketch always did. When she was through, she slid it into a cardboard mat and then into a plastic bag. If the Willoughbys opted to have it framed, an inexpensive standard size would fit.

Lara went over to the shelf where she'd tucked the Wild Carrot Society leaflet. She'd never had a chance to finish reading it. She turned each yellowed page with care. It was apparent that it had been written solely for men. A key paragraph jumped out at her:

Your flower, when worn, is a symbol of safe harbor. Wear it proudly and often, as you may be approached one day by a woman seeking asylum. Yes, asylum. Make no mistake—no man has the right to strike or abuse his wife. The police will dismiss it as a domestic dispute, but you may not. If approached by a woman in fear of her husband, assure her of safe harbor. We will assess her needs and quietly arrange for her relocation, and that of her children if need be.

Safe harbor, Lara mused. This was serious stuff, especially for the 1960s. When did places like women's shelters first become available? She wasn't old enough to remember that far back.

The pamphlet also encouraged members to recruit others, but with a careful eye toward true sympathizers. For sure it had been a secretive group, even if their purpose had been a noble one.

Wilbur Tardiff had been a visionary, Lara decided. Ahead of his time. Back then, some might have called his views extreme. But how did he recruit members? How did he know that a new member might not be an abuser himself?

Maybe that was why the group disbanded. Without the internet and other social media, communication among the members would have been dicey—limited to written notes, or telephone calls, or secret meetings.

Wait, though. What did Uncle Amico tell her?

The man who started it died, and no one wanted to pick up the ball. His death seemed like a bad omen.

A bad omen. What the heck did that mean? Why had the others been afraid to carry the so-called ball?

Lara sighed, frustrated. She closed the leaflet and tossed it on her table.

She reached for her mug. Her tea had already cooled. She started to loop her fingers around the handle when it tipped over onto the floor. A puddle formed, minty and fragrant.

"Ach," Lara said, adding a few curses to the mix. "Now how in the heck did I do that?"

She reached for the roll of paper towels she always kept in her studio and sopped up the tea. No harm done, just another mess to clean. The wood floor needed refinishing anyway. *A project for another year*, she thought.

Lara felt something breeze past her ankles. She looked down, but saw nothing.

"I'm definitely going nuts," she muttered to herself. "Or maybe I've already arrived."

Chapter 25

Sherry looked like a different person when Lara went into the coffee shop at seven the next morning. "You made it!" Sherry squealed. "I thought for sure I wouldn't see you again till all the drama with Deanna Daltry was over." She set a steaming mug of coffee in front of Lara, along with a bowl of half-and-half packets.

Lara stared at her. Her friend's black hair fell around her face in a shiny, stylish bob. Her makeup was more subtle than usual, applied in earth tones that emphasized her cheekbones. It was the first time in a while Lara had seen Sherry care about her looks. She'd always been a take-me-or-leave-me kind of person.

"Sher, your hair came out great today. Very pretty."

Sherry shrugged. "Kellie told me it was time to ditch the railroad spikes. I decided to give it a try. Truth be told, this 'do is a lot easier to take care of." A flush crept up Sherry's neck and into her cheeks.

"Well, it's very becoming." Lara didn't want to make a big deal of it. Sherry was sensitive about receiving compliments. She'd always suffered from lack of self-esteem. Plus, Lara suspected Sherry's new friend had something to do with her makeover.

"As for the drama," Lara said, plopping half-and-half into her mug, "I'm hoping that part is over. The kittens seem to be doing well. Deanna invited Aunt Fran and me to lunch yesterday, but I had a lot of other things going on, so I asked for a rain check."

"But the cops haven't caught the killer yet!"

"I know, but I can't do anything about that, right?" Lara crossed her fingers under the counter. The fibs just kept on coming. "I'm going to have to eat and run, so can I have a blueberry muffin? I've got a family—a dad

and a little boy—picking up Bootsie this morning, so I need to get back."
She felt tears push at her eyelids.

Sherry's face fell. "Aw, sweet little Bootsie's leaving?"

"Don't say it that way. She's going home with some lovely, kind people.
She's on her way to a happier life."

"How's Fran taking it?"

"Right now she's fighting a cold, but she took the news pretty well. She
knows it's our goal to place cats in loving, forever homes."

"But she still doesn't feel well?"

Lara took a sip of her coffee. "Her cold spiked yesterday, but I noticed
this morning she was breathing better. I think she's on the mend."

Sherry scooted off to give her mom Lara's muffin order, then came right
back. The coffee shop door opened, dispensing three telephone workers.
Sherry waved to them, and they tipped their hardhats at her. "It's getting
busy," she said, "but you and I still need to chat. You haven't caught me
up on how the G-man is doing."

"The G-man?"

"Yeah, I decided that's a good name for Gideon."

Lara laughed. "I'm sure he'd love that moniker," she said, hoping to
deflect the question.

Sherry shot a glance at the door. "Maybe we can talk later, after work.
What's your day looking like?"

"Adoption this morning, then Kayla, our new gal, will be working today.
I want to sit with her and go over some ideas I have for the shelter. Since
she's studying for her vet tech degree, she's the ideal person to bounce
things off of. And she loves cats more than any other animal."

"I can't wait to meet her." Sherry lifted her gaze toward the door,
slumping when a pair of white-haired seniors strolled in.

"Does *he* come in on Mondays?" Lara asked in a low voice.

Sherry looked at her for a long moment, then sagged. "He has for the
past three weeks. Thing is, he doesn't really have a set schedule. He's in
sales and has different routes every week."

Lara didn't want to pressure her friend with more questions. Sherry's
luck with men had been about the same as Lara's, at least until Lara started
seeing Gideon. "Well, I hope he comes in today."

Sherry's face brightened with a shy smile. "Yeah, me too."

Daisy Bowker rushed out of the kitchen and plunked Lara's muffin
down on the counter. "Hi, Lara! Give my love to Fran! Gotta run."

"That's another thing," Sherry said, leaning over the counter. "Mom and
I have been arguing over hiring some help. We're doing this all ourselves,

every day, and it's killing us. Even if I wanted a life, when would I have time for it?"

"Your mom disagrees?"

"Yeah, she doesn't want to spend the money on an employee. We do okay here—we keep the bills paid—but we're not exactly rolling in money. I get what she's saying, but at some point I want to have a life. The thing is, she works her patoot off every day. I guess she expects me to do the same."

Lara's heart went out to her. Sherry worked hard every day, too. She needed and deserved time for herself.

"I wish I could help," Lara said.

"Ah, don't worry about it, cat lady," Sherry said lightly. "I shouldn't even have whined about it."

They agreed to talk later and plan a date for an evening out.

Lara gulped the rest of her coffee, shoved in the last crumbs of her muffin, and headed back to her aunt's.

* * * *

"Well, good morning," Aunt Fran said. She sat at the kitchen table, a cup of tea and a slice of dry toast in front of her. Dolce, the perpetual lap cat, rested in the folds of her summer nightgown.

"Hey, you're up already?" Lara said. "I was going to bring some breakfast upstairs for you."

"I wanted to get out of bed," Aunt Fran said. "I can't stand being so idle."

"When you're sick you need to rest," Lara scolded.

"I'm better today. I can feel the cold slinking away. I only wish it would run away instead of taking its time."

Munster strolled into the kitchen and gazed up at Lara. She lifted him, covered his face with kisses, and set him down again.

"Today's the day, isn't it?" Aunt Fran said, her face creased in sadness.

Lara sat down at the table adjacent to her aunt. "I know, but it's a good day," she said gently. "Thanks to your taking her in as a rescue, Bootsie has known love and a safe household. Now she can be the only cat for a family who wants desperately to lavish her with even more love."

Aunt Fran sniffled. She dabbed her eyes with her napkin. "I know. Logically, I get all that. It's just so hard—"

Cold germs notwithstanding, Lara rose and hugged her aunt. "Get dressed and meet the Willoughbys this morning. You'll feel better about the adoption when you see them with Bootsie. By the way, where is the lady of the hour? She disappeared right after she ate this morning."

"When I came downstairs she was in the large parlor. She was sitting on the arm of the sofa, staring at the door to the back porch. Isn't that strange?"

She knows it's her special day. She knows this is the day Bruce and Petey are coming for her.

"Cats do have a sixth sense," Lara said.

Aunt Fran smiled. "I'll get dressed. I can't meet Bootsie's new people in my bathrobe, can I? A quick shower might refresh me, too."

Her aunt finished her tea and went upstairs to shower and change. Lara went into her studio. On her tablet, she logged onto the administrative folder she'd created for the shelter. Thanks to the new app on her tablet, she was able to print out the particulars of Bootsie's history, along with her medical records.

With Kayla now on board, Lara thought it might be time to invest in a laptop dedicated solely for shelter use. Her aunt didn't find the tablet easy to navigate. Besides, they needed something that new employees—trusted ones like Kayla—could also use.

The Willoughbys arrived at the shelter promptly at nine-thirty. Petey's face glowed with anticipation. He held up a bag of cat treats. "I'll give her one in the car, and more when we get home," he said. "Right, Dad?"

Cat carrier in hand, Bruce Willoughby grinned and ruffled his son's hair. "Right, buddy."

Lara felt her eyes tearing up. She handed Bruce the folder containing Bootsie's records and the colored-pencil sketch.

"You did this?" he said, staring at the sketch.

"I did. I'm an artist by profession," Lara explained.

"This place gets more awesome by the minute. Cat lady, for sure," he said with a chuckle.

"Let me grab my aunt—and Bootsie. Aunt Fran is the original cat lady, and she's anxious to meet you. And…Bootsie's been waiting as well."

Bruce quirked a look at her.

The moment Lara opened the door, Bootsie shot into the room like a feline projectile. Petey dropped to the floor, and Bootsie leaped onto his lap, rubbing her furry face against his rosy cheeks. Lara had to swallow back the boulder in her throat.

Aunt Fran came down the stairs just as Lara started to go up. Dressed in lightweight summer pants and a loose-fitting blouse, she looked classic and charming, even if her face was a bit too pale and her nose a bit too red. "They're here," Lara told her in a hoarse voice.

They both went out to the back porch. Lara made the introductions, but her aunt refused to shake hands. "Summer cold," she told Bruce Willoughby. "I'm probably not contagious any longer, but I don't want to risk it."

"Totally understand," Bruce said, holding up a hand. "My son is so happy," he told the women quietly. "I can't even explain how much this has meant to him. To both of us. I mean, I know there are lots of cats that need good homes, but Petey and Bootsie—look at them. They're like soulmates."

"They are, aren't they?" Aunt Fran said, her eyes shiny. She reached out and scratched under Bootsie's chin one last time.

After the Willoughbys had tucked Bootsie into her new carrier, Bruce handed Lara a check. "You said you had a sponsor covering the adoption fee, so this is a donation."

Lara glanced at the check, her heart skipping. The check was for double the normal adoption fee.

"Thank you, Bruce. This is very generous. Once Bootsie is settled in, send us a pic of her in her new home and we'll post it on our board."

"You got it." He gave them a thumbs-up and waved his son toward the door. Lara paused in the doorway and watched Petey skip out to his dad's car. His little feet barely touched the ground.

"If only there were more homes like that for cats," Aunt Fran said, her fingers pressed to her eyes.

"They're out there, Aunt Fran," Lara said and slid her arm around her aunt's shoulder. "It's our job to match 'em up, like we did today. So far, I'd say we've done a pretty good job of it."

Aunt Fran sniffled. "You're right. Don't mind me. I'm going to wallow a bit today while I get used to Bootsie being gone. In fact, I never even read yesterday's paper. I think I'll peruse it while I have another cup of tea."

"Great. I'm going to work on some projects for a while. Kayla should be here by eleven."

They parted ways, and Lara went into her studio. She grabbed a pad of lined paper—something she rarely used—and dug a pen out of her supply drawer. There were three shelter matters she wanted to work on.

The first was the feeding of the cats. She'd been reading more about multi-cat households, and wondered if she should create a feeding station. Right now, none of their cats had health issues, and none were overweight. But if a cat with special needs came into the mix, it was something they'd have to consider. Plus, the kittens ate food designed specifically for them. It wasn't unheard of for one of their adult cats, usually Munster, to sneak a sample from their dishes.

Lara wrote it down as one of the matters she wanted to discuss with Kayla.

The second item was that of household and outdoor toxins. Doing the research on Queen Anne's Lace had made Lara more aware of plants and other everyday items that could be deadly to cats. Even the most devoted feline lovers weren't always in tune with every poison that was out there. With Kayla's help, Lara wanted to draw an easy-to-read cheat sheet, complete with colored sketches of the offending items.

Last of all—*and most fun*, Lara thought—was creating a program where kids could read to cats. Trista's visit had sparked the idea, and Lara was anxious to run with it.

She was adding the task to the list when her cell phone chirped and flashed a familiar number—Deanna's.

"Hey there," Lara greeted the actress.

"Hi, Lara. How was your day yesterday?"

"Yesterday?" *Strange question*, Lara thought. "It was fine, really busy. This morning one of our adult cats was adopted, so Aunt Fran and I are still getting used to it. Bootsie had been with us for nearly a year."

"Bootsie. Yes, I remember her—a sweet little girl. I hope she went to a good home."

"An excellent one," Lara said, grateful for the prompt. "Speaking of good homes, how are the kittens doing?"

"As adorable as ever, and happy, too," she added quickly. "They have the run of the upstairs now, but don't worry—I watch them carefully. As I mentioned, I hope to introduce them to the downstairs this week. As you might have guessed, this is a big place. And you've barely seen any of it! Which brings me to the reason I called. Do you and Fran have a busy agenda today? I told Nancy to hold off making that quiche until you and Fran were free to have lunch with me. I was hoping you could both make it today."

Darn. This was exactly the opportunity Lara had been looking for to get back to Deanna's, but now Aunt Fran was sick.

Lara had questions, so many questions she wanted to pose to the actress. Truth be told, she also wanted to see for herself that Noodle and Doodle were thriving. And though she was anxious to do some planning with Kayla, a day's delay wouldn't hurt.

"Deanna, I could definitely make the time today, but Aunt Fran's been fighting a cold. I think she'd prefer to wait until she's back to her old self."

"Oh, that's a shame."

The note of desperation in Deanna's voice sent an alarm through Lara. Was she that lonely in that big old place? Or was it something else? Maybe she'd grown fearful of Nancy Sherman and needed to confide in someone she trusted.

After a long pause the actress said, "Lara would you come alone then? I, well, I have kind of a surprise. I called that tealeaf reader, and she's coming as well. Nancy will supply the food, and Joyce—Joy—whatever her name is, will supply the tea. You and I can schedule another lunch next week when Fran's feeling better."

Lara smiled to herself. No doubt Joy had gone all aflutter when Deanna called her. Lara was happy for her. The woman had seemed incredibly lonely.

"Can I eavesdrop when you have your tealeaves read?" Lara teased.

"Sure, why not," Deanna said with a laugh. "It'll be fun."

Visions of the kittens swam in Lara's head, clinching her decision.

"Deanna, I accept your invitation. With pleasure."

"Excellent! I told the tealeaf lady one o'clock. That'll give Nancy time to work her magic in the kitchen. She's a marvelous cook. Wait till you taste some of her concoctions."

Chlorine-free, I hope, Lara thought.

"One's fine. Can I bring anything?"

"Only yourself, and tell Fran I wish her a speedy recovery."

After Lara disconnected, she dashed into the kitchen. She told her aunt about her date at the mansion with Deanna.

"Lara, I don't mind at all being left out of the luncheon. The thing I'm concerned about is your going there alone."

Lara smiled, but her heartbeat quickened. "Come on, Aunt Fran. Now you sound like Gideon. You're a pair of worrywarts."

"We worry for a reason. Something about Nancy Sherman still bothers me. We haven't quite figured her out yet, have we? I've been meaning to ask Jerry about her, but I haven't seen him since I got sick."

"Aunt Fran, look at it this way. If it's true that she helped her husband rob banks, that's all the more reason I should check on the kittens. This gives me the perfect excuse, right? Besides, what can she do with Deanna and Joy right there?"

Her aunt blew out a long sigh. "At least I'll know where you are. But text me when you're leaving, okay? And if you get a chance, take a few pics of Noodle and Doodle."

"Yes, ma'am," Lara said with a mock salute. "And now I need to gussy up for tea and luncheon at the manor."

"What about Kayla?"

Lara glanced at her watch. "She'll be here in about twenty minutes. I'll explain where I'm going. She's totally capable of working independently. I have every faith in her."

Her aunt smiled. "I do, too."

Chapter 26

Taking advantage of the slightly cooler day, Lara had donned a patterned, scoop-neck peasant blouse—another eBay bargain—and a pair of gauzy, butter-colored pants that were straight out of the 1980s. Her wardrobe couldn't compare with Deanna's, but then, it didn't have to.

Kayla had been more than agreeable to taking over the shelter duties on her own for a few hours. Lara had spoken briefly to her about the topics she wanted to discuss, each one eliciting a smile from the young woman. Kayla promised to come up with some preliminary ideas and make notes. If she was disappointed at not being invited to Deanna's, she didn't let on. She graciously wished Lara an enjoyable lunch. Lara also remembered to ask her if she'd gone back to the library to research Nancy Sherman. As she'd suspected, Kayla hadn't had a chance to go back there, but promised that it was high on her "to do" list.

On the way to Deanna's, Lara's phone pinged with a text. She made a mental note to check it before she got out of the car.

When she reached the mansion, she navigated the Saturn along the circular driveway and parked directly in front. Another car was parked up ahead, at the point where the driveway curved. One of those old VW bugs.

Lara took a moment to gaze at the mansion through her car window. She loved the way the ivy wrapped around the offset stone column, embracing it with a blanket of lush green leaves.

Such a peaceful scene.

Almost too peaceful, Lara thought. As if time had stopped and frozen everything in its path. Something was out of place. What was it?

Lara glanced at her watch—it was ten to one. She remembered she wanted to check the text message on her phone, and pulled it out of her tote. The name attached to the text made her smile. Gideon.

She tapped it, and read his message.

> *First of all, miss you! Hey, will you call me? I*
> *have some info on that society we talked about.*
> *Kisses.*

Excited, Lara punched his number. "Gid?"

"Hi, sweetie. You got my text."

"I sure did. My heart's pounding a mile a minute."

"Listen, I lucked out. I have an elderly client, a crusty old-timer who changes his will at the drop of a hat. He was in here this morning. I asked if he'd ever heard of that society we talked about. Not only did he know of it, but the founder was his next-door neighbor."

"Gideon, that's unbelievable. What did he tell you about it?"

"We already knew the founder was Wilbur Tardiff. My guy knew him and his family quite well. In fact, he took a family photo for them on Christmas Eve, not long before Tardiff died. He thinks he might have a copy at home. If he finds it, he's going to come back with it."

"Gideon, this is good information. Can I call you back later? I'm about to join Deanna Daltry for a tea party-slash-luncheon at her mansion. She invited the tealeaf reader, Joy, to join us."

After a pause Gideon said, "Have fun, Lara, but be careful, okay? I'm still not convinced of that woman's innocence. Text me if you need anything."

"I will, and don't worry. Deanna's a well-known and beloved figure. She certainly isn't going to harm me. She'd have to answer to her fans, right? Besides, I need to see those kittens. For my own peace of mind."

After promising to give him a full report later, Lara disconnected.

Lara was right on time for her date with Deanna, but now her head was spinning like a toy top. She hoisted her tote onto her shoulder, and was opening the car door when a face appeared in the driver's side window.

Lara shrieked and tried to pull the door shut, but the man gripping it was stronger. She recognized his grizzled beard and shaggy hair. He was the man she'd caught peeking inside the Saturn the day of the welcome event for Deanna.

He reached in and grabbed her arm. "You have to come with me. You have to help!"

"Let go of me," Lara demanded, even as terror rushed through her veins. "I don't have to go anywhere."

The man let out a sob. "Yes, you do. You have to make it stop."

He dragged her by the arm, ignoring the pummeling she was inflicting on it. When they reached the top step, he yanked her toward the front door.

It was open about three inches.

That's what was out of place. The door should have been closed.

He rushed inside and pulled her behind him. She stumbled into the vast entryway, blinking at the abrupt absence of sunlight. A smell like burned eggs assaulted her senses.

Noodle and Doodle. Where were they? She had to get them out of there.

The man still had her arm in a vise-like grip. His face looked wild, his eyes red-rimmed and puffy. To their left was another doorway, its carved mahogany door hanging open about a foot.

He pushed through it, tugging Lara with him.

The room was stunningly furnished with antiques. A fainting sofa upholstered in plush velvet sat beneath one of the Roman-style windows. Thick carpets, ornately patterned, covered the dark wood floor.

A low piecrust table with carved legs sat in the center of a cluster of three tapestry chairs. On the table was a tea set Lara recognized immediately. The butterfly finials danced atop the teapots as if trying to escape their captivity. A roll of duct tape rested on the table, along with a pair of scissors.

Deanna was slumped in the head chair, her ankles and wrists bound with duct tape. A longer length of duct tape was wrapped around her chest, pinning her to the chair. Her face the color of flour, she wept quietly.

Lara gave a start, and her feet wobbled.

To Deanna's left, Joy Renfield sat in one of the tapestry chairs. Her eyes looked glazed. Her lipstick was the same shade as the message scribbled on Deanna's car. A gun sat in the voluminous folds of her tie-dyed muumuu.

"I'm sorry, Lara," Joy said earnestly. "I didn't want you to be a part of this. I wish Deeny hadn't invited you. I specifically told her I wanted time alone with her." She shook her head and looked at her watch, her lips curving into a sad smile. "At least you're on time. Deeny said you'd be here at one, and you're right on the button. I don't like it when people are late. It's very, very bad when people are late. Isn't it, Deeny?"

Deanna cried harder and nodded.

Lara tried to swallow, but her mouth was desert dry. Her arm was still trapped in her captor's iron grip. "Joy, whoever this is, tell him to let me go."

The man sucked in a noisy sob. "Make her stop," he rasped in Lara's ear. "Please make her stop."

"Where are Nancy and the kittens?" Lara demanded.

"Nancy?" Joy's brow furrowed. "Oh, you mean the housekeeper. Don't worry about her, Lara. She won't be troubling us."

"Are the kittens with her? Where are they?" Tears blurred her vision.

"Stop yammering about them. They're fine. Since you've already ruined things, sit down and keep your trap shut. I already set up a chair for you." She nodded at the vacant chair. "I'm going to pour us some tea and tell us all a story. It's a story that comes with a lesson, doesn't it, Deeny?" Her voice rose on a note of hysteria, sending a cold chill through Lara.

Deanna's head dipped in the slightest of nods.

"I'll warn you, though. It doesn't have a happy ending. Except for the princess over here." She reached over and slapped Deanna's arm. "You've been enjoying quite the charmed life, haven't you, princess?"

"Joy, I wanna leave," the man whined, his opaque brown eyes overflowing with tears. "Can't we go now?"

"Not yet, Will," Joy said gently. "We have some unfinished business. Then we can go. Okay?"

Lara forced herself to smile at the man. "Will, is that your name? Will, I think Joy wants to hurt…Deeny. Can you find a phone and dial nine-one-one?"

Will shook his head, sobs racking his chest.

"Shut up and sit down, Lara. Will isn't going to help you. You're only upsetting him." Joy's face softened. "Bring her over to the chair, honey. She needs to learn some manners."

"I wanna go home, Joy. You said we could have ice cream."

"We can, sweetie. As soon as we're through here, okay?"

Will pushed Lara over to the vacant chair. She sat down hard, every limb feeling like molten lava.

Joy poured tea into three cups, one for each of them. "Sugar, Deeny? Oh wait, never mind. You won't be able to drink with your hands like that, will you? Lara, sugar?"

"I don't want tea," Lara said quietly.

Joy pursed her lips and glared at her. "How rude. And after I set out a cup for you." She plopped two sugar cubes into her own tea, her other hand resting on the handle of the gun.

Lara considered her options. She could run like the devil and try to get help. Or she could try to overpower Joy and get the gun away from her.

Neither option was promising. She'd already found out how strong Will was.

Her cell phone was in her tote. Where *was* her tote? Had she dropped it outside when Will roughhoused her into the mansion?"

"Joy," Lara suggested, as if they were at a real tea party, "why don't you give Will the gun and have him put it in your car for you. That way it will be safe and we can enjoy our tea. I think I will have that sugar cube after all."

Joy tossed her head back and laughed. "Safe? Oh my, that's priceless, but don't try to manipulate me, Lara. As for the sugar cube, you had your chance. Now you can just drink it bitter."

She's speaking like an angry child.

Joy sipped from her cup. "Mmm, excellent. Chamomile's always been my favorite. Now Deeny, tell Lara what we learned today about being late."

Deanna lifted her head. Terror shone in her gray eyes. "That it's im-impolite," she said in a ragged whisper.

"Good. What else?"

"Th-that it...hurts people," she said dully.

"And how does it hurt them, Deeny?"

"I-it makes other people late, and th-then they have to rush to get to the Thanksgiving play." Deanna broke off into tears.

"Stop bawling. And what happens when they rush to the Thanksgiving play?"

"Joy, please, listen to me," Deanna said, crying harder now. "I'll give you whatever you want. I'll buy you a pretty little house and you can—"

"A pretty little house?" Joy slapped Deanna's arm again. "Do you think that makes up for the misery we suffered?"

"Joy," Lara interjected. She waved a dismissive hand at Deanna. "Never mind about De...Deeny. Tell me the story. I haven't heard it yet. I-I'd like to hear your side of it."

Joy appeared to consider it. She looked at her watch. "I don't suppose we're in any rush. You may as well hear the ugly truth."

Lara let out the breath she was holding. "Thank you."

"When I was a kid, Deeny used to babysit me. She was a fun babysitter, too, weren't you, Deeny? My favorite part was when she let me read her Hollywood magazines. She always brought a few with her so we could drool over all the stars."

Joy's gaze shifted to the side. Lara made a quick scan of the room, hoping to land on something she could use as a weapon.

"But Deeny had one problem," Joy went on. "She could never be on time. Of course, if Mom and Dad were only going out for dinner, it didn't really matter. What's fifteen minutes, give or take, right?"

Deanna's eyes fluttered, and she slumped. Lara was afraid she'd passed out.

"Then one day my sister Pauline found out she was going to be Priscilla Alden in her school's Thanksgiving play. Dad was so excited. He couldn't wait to take our whole family to see her perform, even my Aunt Agnes. My uncle had beat up my aunt so many times she had to come and live with us."

Lara closed her eyes and tapped into her memory. The photo—the one in Joy's shop. In the picture, a row of stockings hung on the mantel behind the family, so it could have been taken on Christmas Eve.

Christmas Eve. The flowers. The Wild Carrot Society.

The few final dots connecting…

"Joy," Lara said softly, "are you Wilbur Tardiff's daughter?"

Joy snapped her head at Lara. "You…knew that?"

"Not until a minute ago." She forced a smile. "I know what your dad did, though. He tried to help abused women. He was a courageous man, wasn't he?"

"He was, in every way." For the briefest of moments, Joy's eyes softened. Almost immediately they morphed into a pair of dark brown marbles.

Lara looked over at Will. He'd dropped to the floor and now sat crossed-legged, his head cradled in his arms. If only she could persuade him to call for help.

"Go ahead, Joy," Lara urged. "You were talking about the play."

Joy licked her lips. "Two days before the play, I came down with the flu. Dad said I'd have to stay home with a babysitter while they went to the play. He felt bad for me, but I honestly didn't mind. I loved it when Deeny babysat us. This way I'd have her all to myself. We could read her magazines and watch TV and put makeup on. But Deeny never made it that night, did you Deeny?"

Deanna was silent. Lara prayed she was all right.

"Deeny and her boyfriend Donald were too busy necking in his car to be on time. My mom had already taken my sisters to the school. One of the other parents had driven them. Dad had to wait for Deeny before he could leave, so Will stayed with him. Gosh, he was such a cute little boy. Smart as all get-out, too. He could do simple arithmetic when he was four years old. We all spoiled him."

"Couldn't your dad find someone else to sit for you?"

Joy fingered the gun. "When the play was about to start, Dad finally brought me over to a neighbor's house. After that, he and Will headed to the school. I never saw him again." Tears streamed down her cheeks.

"I'm so sorry," Lara said.

"We were almost there," Deanna cried, her shoulders heaving with sobs. "If he'd only waited. We were almost there!"

"Dad never drove fast," Joy said, her voice a scary monotone. "He was always so careful. But that night he had to drive fast. He didn't want to miss Pauline's debut."

With the tidbits she'd gotten from Claudia, Lara guessed the rest. The road was slick with freezing rain. Wilbur skidded on the bridge, crashing through the guardrail. He drowned before anyone could rescue him. And Will?

"Joy, I know about the accident," Lara said.

Joy shook with rage. "Dad drowned in the car. Do you know what a horrible death that is?" She rocked forward, and the gun shifted slightly. "They thought they'd lost Will, too, but at the hospital they revived him. He'd been under water too long…"

And suffered brain damage, Lara surmised.

"They sent Will home from the hospital on the morning of November twenty-second. Hours later, President Kennedy was shot. No one cared about us anymore, not even about Will."

"I'm sure they cared, Joy."

"You're wrong, Lara." She said it in such a quiet voice that Lara's heart wrenched. The sad little girl was now a vengeful woman, determined to make someone pay for her father's tragic death.

"Mom couldn't deal with Dad's death. She was a young widow with four kids to raise. And Will—" She shook her head. "Seven months later, she met a man at church—Kenneth Renfield. He was kind to her and attentive to us. That is, until the ink dried on the marriage certificate.

"He ran our home like a drill sergeant. Mom cringed every time he spoke. We had chores galore. Our favorite TV shows were banned. He insisted on adopting us so our last names would be the same as his—he said it gave him more control. He used the college money Dad saved for us to start up his own business. You know what he said? Girls didn't need college. They're supposed to be homemakers. His business failed, of course. He went through all of Dad's savings, what was left of it."

"What about the Wild Carrot Society? Couldn't your mom ask them for help?"

Joy gripped the gun. "You know about that?"

"I stumbled on it by accident," Lara said.

"It was a joke. None of them would help us. They didn't really believe she was being abused. Dad would've been ashamed of all of them."

"Why did you kill Donald Waitt?" Lara asked, eyeing the gun.

Joy's lips flatlined. "He was driving that night. He could've made sure Deanna was on time, but he didn't because he wanted to make out with her. He didn't care about any of us. No one did. Besides, I wanted it to look like Deanna killed him."

"Is that why you sent him those threatening texts that supposedly came from Deanna?"

Joy looked at her. "How do you know all this?"

"I-I think it was in the paper."

"When I was seventeen I left home. By then, I didn't care anymore, either—not even about Will. For a while I lived on a commune. You know, Lara, I really wish you hadn't come here. You're a nice lady, but now you've created a big problem for me." She shrugged. "One thing you don't need to worry about—I'm not going to shoot Deanna. There won't be any blood spatter on the walls."

Lara nearly fainted with relief.

"I'm going to duct tape her nose and mouth shut. That way she'll know how my dad felt when he drowned in that icy river."

"*Nooooo.*" The sound came from Will, guttural and heartrending.

Deanna jerked in her chair. "For the love of God, Joy, I was sixteen years old. I never meant to hurt anybody. I was a silly, stupid girl. Can't you see that?"

Still clutching the gun, Joy reached for the roll of duct tape.

In the next moment, a flash of cream-colored fur skidded across the piecrust table and knocked the tape to the floor.

"What the—" Joy stared at her hand as if it had grown talons. "How did I—?"

Lara's heart pounded so hard she thought it might bubble up through her lips. Blue batted at the roll of tape as if toying with a mouse. The tape changed direction and skittered away until it rested underneath a sideboard.

Stunned, Lara froze in shock, her limbs refusing to move. She knew Joy couldn't see Blue.

A noise at the front door penetrated her brain, but her eyes were fixed on Joy. She needed to free Deanna so they could get out of there.

"Lara!"

Lara looked up to see Gideon rushing into the room. He stopped short, nearly tripping over the carpet, his sharp gaze taking in the scene. He whipped his phone out of his pocket.

Her eyes now closed, Joy gripped the handle of the gun and pressed the barrel to her temple. "I'll be with you soon, Dad."

Lara and Gideon lunged at her simultaneously, but before they could reach her Will was already there. He flung himself at his sister, sending her chair toppling backward as the gun discharged in a deafening blast.

Will lifted his sister's shoulders and crushed her to him, his sorrowful wail echoing off the papered walls.

"Gid, we need help," Lara said, her own face streaming with tears.

"Already done," he said.

By then Blue had vanished. Gideon went over to Will and pulled him gently away from his sister. "It's okay, son. Let her go so we can get her some help, okay?"

His body still racked with sobs, Will nodded and lowered her gently to the floor. Joy lay on her back, unmoving, except for a tiny flicker of her eyelids. Blood seeped from a wound on her temple.

"I think she's only grazed," Gideon said, "but she needs to get to the hospital."

Lara looked around frantically, then spied a crocheted throw folded over the back of the fainting sofa. She went over and grabbed it, then bent over Joy, tucking it around her neck and shoulders.

Gideon's face was white. "Lara, are you okay?"

"I'm fine, but Deanna needs help, too, and I have to find Nancy and the kittens." She turned to Will. "Will, do you know where they are?"

His face blotchy, Will nodded miserably. He pointed at the ceiling.

Lara jumped up and raced out of the room, passing Chief Whitley jogging through the front door. "Help's on the way," he said.

"In there," Lara gasped out, pointing at the room. The burned egg smell was stronger now, more like scorched metal. "Ne-need ambulance," she added and dashed up the stairs. "And shut off the stove before the whole house goes up in flames!"

Lara took the stairs two at a time and flew down the hallway. When she reached Deanna's bedroom, she found the door closed. She turned the knob and almost fell into the room.

Nancy lay on her side in Deanna's bed, her hands tied tightly with rope and secured to the bedpost. A strip of duct tape covered her mouth. Her wig had slipped backward, exposing a scalp graced with only thin wisps of hair. Noodle and Doodle were nestled in the curve of her chest, purring as if they didn't have a care in the world.

Nancy looked at Lara with a mixture of pain and relief.

"Let me get this off," Lara said. She peeled back the duct tape as gently as she could.

Nancy winced, then gasped out a shaky breath. "Thank God," she said and took several deep breaths. "Is Deanna okay?"

"She's fine, but she needs to go to the hospital and get checked out. You do, too. An ambulance should be here any second."

Lara struggled with the rope, which had been tied in multiple knots. After she managed to untangle the last one, Nancy sat up and rubbed her wrists. "I'm sorry, but I have to c-cry now. I didn't dare do it before—I was afraid I'd suffocate."

Lara leaned over and hugged her. "You cry all you want. I think I'll cry, too."

That's how the paramedics found them—both women hugging each other with tears streaming down their cheeks. Nancy blotted her face with the back of one hand, her other hand curled lovingly around both kittens.

"Aw, those little guys kept you company, didn't they?" one of the paramedics said.

"They kept me from going insane," Nancy blurted. "Th-they seemed to sense that I was in trouble." She stroked Noodle's head, and then Doodle's, before the paramedics transferred her to the stretcher. One of them adjusted her wig so that it sat straighter on her head. "Thank you," Nancy said. "Do I really need to go to the hospital?"

"We recommend it, ma'am. Besides, your boss wants to be sure you're okay."

Nancy looked once more at the kittens. "Will they be okay here?"

"I'll take them home and bring them back here as soon as you and Deanna are ready," Lara promised. She waved at the stretcher as it rolled down the hallway.

Gideon's face appeared in the doorway. He'd gotten some of his color back, but he still looked stricken. He moved toward her, and in one swift move wrapped her in a giant bear hug.

Lara laughed and cried at the same time. "I still don't get why you came over here. Did you have a flash of ESP or something?"

"I'm honestly not sure myself," he said. "I was gobbling down a quick lunch at my desk and I opened a bottle of iced tea. Then my client, the one I told you about, came back with that photo. I knew right away where I'd seen it before."

"The one in Joy's shop," Lara supplied.

"Yeah," he said. "It bothered me, big time. But…there was something else. I was trying to connect the dots, as you put it, when my iced tea bottle flew off my desk. I swear, I wasn't anywhere near it. It was like…it jumped off my desk on its own."

Lara smothered a smile, her mind picturing a certain Ragdoll cat lighting a mental fire under Gideon.

"Long story short," Gideon said, "something about the tea stuck in my head—the photo, the tealeaf lady, your tea party-slash-luncheon at Deanna's. It was like someone was whispering—no, more like bellowing in my ear."

"Must've been my guardian angel."

Chapter 27

"Now that my taste buds are back," Aunt Fran said with a grimace, "I'm not sure I'll ever want tea again. At least not for a couple of weeks." She pushed aside her cup and drank a mouthful of orange juice. She smiled down at Dolce, who sat in her lap, and stroked the cat's neck.

"I second that," Lara said. "I swear, I can still smell the chamomile in that tea Joy poured for herself. I hope I never smell it again."

Two days had passed since Joy Renfield tried to kill Deanna. The network cable trucks were back, clogging the roadway in front of the mansion. Late yesterday, Deanna had come out and given a statement to the reporters. Gracious and penitent, she gave a truthful account of everything she remembered about that cold November night. She expressed deep sorrow for Joy and her family, as well as for Donald Waitt's loved ones.

"Poor Deanna. Hollywood's late date for sure," Lara said. "I can't help wondering, if she'd been on time that night, would Wilbur Tardiff still have had that accident? Would it really have made a difference?"

"We'll never know," her aunt said. "It's one of the mysteries of life. Many people believe that everything in life unfolds exactly as it's supposed to."

"Maybe," Lara said soberly, gripping her coffee mug, "but I like to think that the choices we make contribute at least a little to our fates." She grinned when she saw a familiar face peeking through the screen door—a face that made her heart waltz around her chest.

Gideon stepped inside and leaned down to hug Lara, then went over and hugged Aunt Fran. He plunked a white bakery bag on the table, then helped himself to a chair.

They hadn't seen each other since Monday, although they'd shared a zillion texts and calls. After Joy, Deanna, and Nancy had been loaded into separate ambulances, a state police detective had sat with Lara and gotten her entire account of what happened from the time she'd arrived at Deanna's until the moment the police had invaded the house. Hours later, she'd driven home, limp with exhaustion, Noodle and Doodle tucked safely inside her carrier.

Lara peeked inside the bag. "Bagels? Where did you get them?"

"A new place opened up on Elm Street. Thought we'd try them."

"Uh oh. Competition for the coffee shop?"

"Nah, I don't think so. Totally different type of place. There's cream cheese in the bag, too."

Lara helped herself to a cinnamon bagel, which had already been sliced in half. "Yum. So, how did your meeting go this morning?" She pulled out a silver packet of cream cheese and spread it over one of the halves.

Gideon had been asked to confer with Chief Whitley and two detectives from the state police. They wanted his statement as to what he'd witnessed on Monday.

"First, I'll tell you what I learned. Joy is recovering. They expect to release her from the hospital either tomorrow or Friday. After that she'll be transferred to a different hospital for evaluation. And after that…well, her fate will be in the hands of the criminal justice system."

"I can't imagine she'll avoid prison," Lara said. "I have to say, though, my heart still aches for her. When her dad died, her childhood died with him. I don't think she ever had a moment of joy after that."

Gideon nodded. "Strange, because she was named Joy. I sat with her at the hospital yesterday when she gave her statement to one of the homicide detectives. She still believes Deanna was responsible for her father's death. She spilled her entire life story to us. I have to say, it was one of the saddest I ever heard. Mind if I grab a cup of coffee?"

"Sure, sorry," Lara said. "My brain is on idle today. There's a fresh pot on the stove. The mugs are on the counter."

Gideon helped himself to coffee. When he came back to sit down, Munster had stolen his chair.

Gideon laughed. "Hey, did you reserve that seat?" he teased. He lifted Munster with his free hand, sat down, and set the cat in his lap. "There, now we can both sit." He ruffled the fur on Munster's neck.

"You were telling us Joy's story," Lara reminded him.

"Right. From the time Joy's dad died, neither she, nor her siblings, nor her mom ever enjoyed a day of peace. Her stepfather was a taskmaster. He treated them all like servants. After she graduated from high school, she took up with a guy who made his living dealing marijuana. They ended up traveling to California, living on a commune. After that they drifted, and eventually split up."

"What about Will?" Lara asked. "Where did he end up?"

"That's a sad story, too," Gideon said and took a sip from his mug. "The mom died sometime in the late seventies—from a broken heart, Joy firmly believes. Both of Joy's sisters had long since moved out of the house. Eventually the two girls got an apartment together and took Will to live with them. He enjoyed doing odd jobs, helping people with yard work, things like that."

"Where was Joy all this time?" Aunt Fran asked. "Did she stay in California?"

"She did until the early nineteen-nineties. Never married. No kids. After her younger sister died, she came back to New Hampshire and settled in Moultonborough. By then Will was living with their sister Pauline, but they were struggling, surviving mostly on help from the state. Pauline succumbed to alcoholism a few years ago. That's when Joy took Will to live with her."

Lara remembered the fear etched on Will's face when he'd dragged her into the house that day. Her heart broke for him, too.

She tore off a piece of her bagel and held it aloft. "Gid, when Joy was telling me about the night of the accident, something occurred to me. How could she have remembered it in such detail? She was only seven or eight, right?"

"You're right," Gideon said. "She was seven when her dad died. I don't think she did remember it. Over the years, her mother told the kids the story so many times that it became ingrained in her head. The mom blamed Deanna and Donald for the accident, and for all their subsequent troubles. Joy never let go of that."

"Then Deanna moved back to town," Lara said, surmising the rest. "Joy saw her chance to get revenge for all the years of pain her family suffered." She popped the piece of bagel into her mouth and chewed thoughtfully.

"Exactly. When that article went in the paper about Deanna moving into the old stone mansion, all those feelings of rage came back. Joy began to plot."

Lara filled in the missing pieces. "When she found out the Ladies' Association was having a welcome event for Deanna, she must have begged Evelyn Conley to let her supply the tea."

"Yeah, no doubt."

Aunt Fran raised an eyebrow. "Not to tell tales out of school, but I know for a fact Evelyn is a world-class penny-pincher. I'm sure she jumped at the chance to save the association a bit of cash."

"So, Joy's the one who wrote on Deanna's car window?" Lara asked.

"Not quite. She had her brother do it while she was inside serving tea. She wrote out on a piece of paper exactly what he should write. Poor guy. He was only doing what his sister told him to do. He thought he was helping her. That paper and the lipstick were found under the front seat of her car."

"And he must have put those worms in Deanna's purse, too."

Gideon chuckled. "Guess again. Your buddy Evelyn came into the police station yesterday. She wanted to 'come clean' as she put it. Turns out she paid one of the two server boys to dig up those worms and stick them in Deanna's purse. I guess she was still mad at Deanna for that imagined snub all those years ago."

Aunt Fran looked quizzically at Lara. "Hmm, you never told me that story."

"Sorry, I was sworn to secrecy. Loose lips, remember?" She sat back in her chair. "I can't help thinking, is revenge truly that sweet? Is it worth it to hold on to all that anger for decades of your life?"

"I guess it is for some people," Aunt Fran said. "But it's not a healthy way to live. Not in my book, anyway."

Gideon looked solemn. "Some people, like Joy, can never forget. It devoured her life. I contacted a friend of mine this morning, old law school buddy. He's going to represent Joy."

"Is he good?" Lara asked.

"Dynamite," Gideon said. "Nevertheless, Joy committed one premeditated murder, and attempted to commit a second. That'll weigh heavily against her."

Lara's thoughts drifted. She hadn't been able to get Joy out of her head for two days. Not only because of the nightmare that took place at the mansion. Joy's words that evening in the tea shop had been haunting her.

Unburden yourself...you'll find others more receptive than you think.

Joy looked at her aunt, and then at Gideon—the two people in the world she cared for most. Something clutched at her heart, and she felt her eyes getting misty.

"You okay, honey?" Gideon said quietly.

Lara nodded. She reached over and covered his hand with her own. In only a week's time, they'd grown so much closer. It thrilled her and frightened her at the same time.

"I'm very okay, and very lucky. Look at everything I have, everything I've been taking for granted. I'll never take it for granted again."

Gideon grinned at her. "Okay, now you're getting philosophical," he teased.

"I'm only getting real," Lara corrected with a smile.

But I'm not ready to tell either of you my secret, not yet.

For now, I'm the only one who can know about Blue.

"I can't stop thinking about Wilbur," Lara said. "In his own way, he pioneered a kind of shelter for battered women. It just didn't work out the way he'd hoped."

"His own sister-in-law was a victim," Gideon said. "I'm sure that's why he was so passionate about the cause."

Lara took a sip of her coffee. "In a way, it reminds me of what we do here, taking in cats who've been discarded or mistreated. We give them care and a safe haven, just as Wilbur wanted to do for abused women. In his case he was a bit ahead of his time, but he had the right idea, didn't he?"

"I agree, with all of that," Gideon said. "Joy told the police she scattered those flowers around Waitt's body to remind the world of what they'd lost."

A thought struck Lara. "What's going to happen to Will?" she asked. "Other than Joy, he has no family left."

"I'm not sure. That's up in the air," Gideon said. "I'm not even sure where he is right now."

Lara sat back in her chair again. The cinnamon bagel called to her, but her appetite had fizzled. She couldn't help wondering what she'd have done in Joy's place. Would she have made similar choices?

Gideon finished his coffee, set Munster gently on the floor, and rose. "Hey, I gotta run. My schedule's jam-packed today." He went over and kissed Lara. "Bye, sweetie. Call you later, okay? Bye, Fran."

After his footfalls disappeared down the porch steps, Lara looked at her aunt. She felt a distinct blush creeping into her cheeks. Aunt Fran looked away discreetly, but a knowing smile perched on her lips.

"Hey, I gotta run, too," Lara said with a smile. "I'll clean up the dishes, and then—I have a very special delivery to make."

Chapter 28

"Special delivery!" Lara grinned and held up the cat carrier.

Nancy and Deanna stood in the doorway, Nancy sporting a raven-black wig that accentuated her pallor. Both women's eyes beamed when they saw the kittens. "We couldn't wait till you got here," Deanna said. "Oh, look at them, Nancy. Their little noses are pressed to the screen. I think they know they're home. Don't you, darlings?" she cooed to the kittens.

Lara set down the carrier and hugged both women. She'd learned from Deanna that the housekeeper suffered from a hereditary hair loss condition, which explained why she owned several wigs.

Nancy shifted her gaze to the cat carrier. "I can't wait to see our babies again. It seems like they've been gone forever, doesn't it?"

Lara marveled at the change in Nancy. *The miracle of the kittens*, she couldn't help thinking. She unzipped the screen on the carrier and released the kittens. Nancy immediately scooped up Doodle, and Deanna did the same with Noodle.

Deanna kissed her kitten's head. "Um, Lara," she said, shooting a look at Nancy, "we hope you don't mind, but we're changing their names. We're going to call them Bogie and Bacall."

"Those are great names!" Lara said. "I heartily approve—not that you need my approval."

Nancy laughed. "See, I told you she'd like them."

Nancy Sherman, Lara had learned, had formerly been known as Adele Nancy Harrison. After serving a light sentence for her part in several bank robberies—something she'd done under dire threats from her husband—she'd changed her name to a combination of her middle and maiden names. It gave her a sense of privacy she couldn't otherwise have found.

They brought the kittens upstairs and settled them in Deanna's room. "We're going to keep them here for a few more days, since this is the room they're most familiar with," Deanna explained. "After that we'll gradually introduce them to the rest of the house."

Tears filled Nancy's eyes. She set Doodle—now Bogie—down on Deanna's bed. "When I was tied to that bedpost, I was so terrified. I thought for sure it was the end of me. But these two darlings, they knew better. They wouldn't stop purring, and I knew, somehow, it was going to be okay."

Deanna pressed a finger to her eye. "All right, Nancy, enough is enough," she said sternly. "You're going to make me cry again, and I just put on my makeup."

Lara giggled. These two were perfect for the kittens. How had she ever doubted it?

The scent of fresh paint tickled Lara's senses. Faint sounds drifted from one of the other rooms. Before she could ask, Deanna set Noodle—or rather, Bacall—on the bed next to her brother and slid an arm through Lara's. "Come with me."

Deanna led her down the hallway to a room at the end. The door was open. Each piece of furniture in the room had been covered with a sheet. One wall had been painted a cerulean blue; the others were a muted lilac. A man stooped over a paint can, his brush poised in mid-air. Deanna knocked lightly on the doorjamb. "May we come in?"

The man rose to his full height and looked at them. "Yes, you can. Come in," he said shyly.

Lara stared at him in shock. "Will?"

He nodded and set his brush down. Recognition flashed in his eyes, but then he offered a tentative smile. "I'm painting my room blue. Do you like it?"

"I love it," Lara said. "That's a dazzling shade of blue."

"Will is going to live here and help us around the house," Deanna explained. "He's a pro at tending the flowers and the lawn. He also builds the loveliest birdhouses. Wait till you see them."

"I'll make you one, if you want," he said softly.

"Hmm," Lara said. "I think I'd like that. Can you build a green one? I live with my aunt, and I think she'd love green. We can hang it in our maple tree."

"A green one," Will repeated. "I can do that."

"We'll leave you to your painting, Will," Deanna said kindly. "Nancy will call you when lunch is ready."

"Bye, Will," Lara said.

When they were out of earshot, Lara said, "Deanna, I am so impressed with your generosity. He already looks at home."

Deanna's eyes took on a haunted glaze. "That man suffered needlessly, Lara—and I'm to blame, at least partly. He deserves a comfortable home with people who care about him."

"I don't agree that you're to blame," Lara said. "But I feel sure he'll be happy here, as much as he can be with his memories."

"He already has his own bathroom," Deanna said, "but eventually he'll have his own entrance, too. My architect is coming by this afternoon to go over the design. I've also arranged for Will to speak to a counselor. I think it'll help him deal with everything he went through with his sister." She looked down at her clasped hands. "Truth be told, I'm going to see one myself. I'm hoping it will give me some perspective."

"So, no more movies?"

"No more movies. Though if the right role came along"—she shrugged—"who knows? Coming back here has helped bring my life into focus. My family's gone, but I've made some fabulous friends." She winked at Lara. "I want to start feeling things and doings things like a real person. I don't want to be that caricature of a so-called seasoned actress anymore. Those days are gone, and good riddance to them."

"I totally get that." Lara gave Deanna a quick hug. If she didn't leave soon, she was going to burst into tears. "I'd better go. Lots happening at the shelter these days. Kayla—you remember our assistant—is helping us design a program for kids to read to cats. We're hoping to get it started before the kids go back to school."

"What a marvelous idea," Deanna said. "And before I forget, since I agreed to pay all adoption fees this month, I'm going to have Nancy send you a check. It will be large enough that you'll have some left over. You can use it all for the shelter."

"Thank you," Lara said. She heard her phone ping with a text.

After bidding both women goodbye, Lara hurried out to her car. She dug out her phone. The text was from Sherry.

> *Hey, cat lady, you better get in here today. I got a*
> *date Saturday night and I need some serious girl*
> *talk. By the way, he loves cats.*

Lara giggled to herself. She texted back.

> *Tentative approval given. Please follow up with*
> *deetz.*

* * * *

Lara drove home with a range of emotions churning through her head. Mostly they were positive ones, but occasionally one of the bad ones managed to sneak through.

When she made the turn onto High Cliff Road, she flicked a glance at the rearview mirror. A car she didn't recognize was following her.

The car tailed Lara until she swung the Saturn into her aunt's driveway. The driver of the car, whoever it was, moved past the house and pulled into the shelter's small parking lot on the other side.

Had someone gotten the adoption days confused?

Lara hopped out of the Saturn and slammed the door. After the events of the past few days, her nerves were still on edge. Instead of going inside the house, she jogged across the backyard to the other side, over to the shelter's entrance. The driver of the car, a woman, was easing herself out of her front seat.

Lara waited, and then her jaw dropped in surprise. "Mildred?" It was Hesty's neighbor, the kindly woman Lara hadn't seen since the day they'd discovered Hesty's body together. She dashed over to her and gave her a firm hug.

"I'm so glad I caught you home," Mildred said, her long gray hair swirled atop her head in an old-style bun. "I wasn't sure what day you did adoptions, and I'm not too good on the internet, so I took a shot."

"Come inside," Lara said, escorting her onto the back porch. "Can I get you some lemonade? Have a seat, Mildred."

"Oh no, I don't need anything." Her eyes shiny, she lowered herself onto one of the padded chairs. "I still miss Hesty," she said. "You didn't really know him, but I did. He was a rarity, Lara—kind and funny and cranky and irreverent all in one bald-headed, wrinkled body."

Lara's eyes welled at her description. "He was a good friend, wasn't he?"

"He was the best. Anyway, I know I'm taking up your valuable time, so I might as well just come out and ask you. Is it okay if I adopt Frankie?"

It was the last thing Lara expected to hear. "You're interested in Frankie? Mildred, I-I think that's wonderful. But you haven't even met him!"

"Well, I guess that's why I'm here. To meet my new best friend. I've had cats before, and they all lived to a good old age. It's awful hard when they pass on, but I miss having a cat. My home is small, but it's neat and comfy. I won't let Frankie go out. He'll stay inside where it's nice and safe."

Lara reached over and touched Mildred's hand. She uttered a silent prayer that Mildred was the right match for Frankie. "Stay right here," she said. "I'll go get him."

She found Frankie sprawled on her aunt's neatly made bed. "Come on, sweetness," she said and gathered him into her arms. "A very special friend wants to meet you."

She carried him downstairs and through the large parlor. When they reached the back porch, he squirmed in her arms, his nose on full alert. The cat sprang from her grip and into the meet-and-greet room, leaping directly onto Mildred's lap.

"Oh my, that was fast!" Mildred chuckled, tears in her eyes. She pulled the cat closer and hugged him. "No wonder Hesty was in love with you. You're just a little ball of heaven, aren't you?"

Choking back tears, Lara decided right then—she would put Mildred's application on a super fast track. With luck, Mildred could take Frankie home by the end of the day.

Lara wasn't worried. A furry Ragdoll face peeked over the edge of the table from the chair to Mildred's left. Blue fixed her eyes on the pair and gave her slow, trademark blink.

Outside, a car door slammed. Lara went to the doorway and peeked through the glass pane. Kayla had parked her gram's car next to Mildred's, and was pulling something out of the back seat. Lara racked her brain. Kayla wasn't scheduled to work today, was she?

Kayla pushed the car door closed with her foot and trotted toward Lara. In her arms was a deep cardboard box, open at the top. She wore a look of alarm, as if her life hung in the balance.

"Lara, we have to help them. Pleeease," she begged.

"Help who—?" Lara started to ask, then saw the contents of the box. Five furry kittens, nestled on a towel, mewed pitifully as they tried to scale the box.

"Oh, look at them," Lara said, her heart melting. She lifted out a furry gray kitten and cuddled it to her chest. "Where did they come from?"

"My gram's neighbor's niece brought them over. The niece found them in the Dumpster at her office building. The *Dumpster*, Lara! The neighbor told her I was a vet tech student and would know what to do with them."

"Bring them in," Lara said. "We'll get them settled in our isolation room. I'm sure they're hungry. How old do you think they are?"

"Six, maybe seven weeks," Kayla said and carried the box inside. Lara closed the door behind her. "They're old enough to eat wet kitten food— God knows what they've been surviving on—but we'll need to watch them carefully. Also, I checked their ears, and I think they have mites. They need to see the vet, ASAP."

"I'll call Amy and ask if she can see them today. Where's mama kitty?" Lara asked, feeling the kitten's tiny claws sink into her jersey top.

"No one knows, but I'm going to try to find out. I'm going over to that office building after I leave here."

For the first time, Kayla noticed Mildred sitting at the table with Frankie curled in her lap. "Oh—hi. Are you—?"

"I'm Mildred, and I hope I'm Frankie's new mom."

A logjam of emotions clogged Lara's throat. She couldn't imagine her life without this shelter, without being there for the felines who found their way into the care of her and Aunt Fran. Her aunt's words came back to her.

Many people believe that everything in life unfolds exactly as it's supposed to.

Still clutching her tiny charge, Lara placed a hand on Mildred's shoulder. "Mildred, I *know* you're Frankie's new mom," she said. "An angel out there in the wild blue yonder just whispered it in my ear."

Lara's Blueberry Buckle

Ingredients for cake:
¾ cup white sugar
½ cup (8 tablespoons) butter, softened
1 egg
½ cup milk
2 cups all-purpose flour (preferably sifted)
2 teaspoons baking powder
½ teaspoon salt
½ teaspoon grated lemon zest
1 teaspoon vanilla extract
2 cups fresh blueberries

Ingredients for streusel topping:
¼ cup white sugar
¼ cup brown sugar
⅓ cup all-purpose flour
½ teaspoon ground cinnamon (or to taste)
¼ cup (4 tablespoons) butter

Directions for cake:
Preheat oven to 375 degrees F
Grease an 8-inch or 9-inch square pan
In a bowl, blend the flour, baking powder, and salt
In a separate bowl, beat together the butter, the ¾ cup sugar, egg, vanilla, and lemon zest
Alternately add the milk and the flour mixture to the sugar/butter mixture
Add blueberries, stirring only enough to blend
Pour batter into pan

Directions for streusel topping:
In a small bowl, blend the white and brown sugars, flour, and cinnamon
With a fork or pastry blender, cut in butter until mixture is crumbly
Sprinkle evenly over the cake batter

Bake at 375 degrees F for 40 to 45 minutes until a toothpick inserted in the center comes out clean. Cool on wire rack, then serve right from the pan.

If you enjoyed *Claws of Death*, be sure not to miss the first book in Linda Reilly's Cat Lady Mystery series

Here, killer, killer, killer…

For the first time in sixteen years, Lara Caphart has returned to her hometown of Whisker Jog, New Hampshire. She wants to reconnect with her estranged Aunt Fran, who's having some difficulty looking after herself—and her eleven cats. Taking care of a clowder of kitties is easy, but keeping Fran from being harassed by local bully Theo Barnes is hard. The wealthy builder has his sights set on Fran's property, and is determined to make her an offer she doesn't dare refuse.

Then Lara spots a blue-eyed ragdoll cat that she swears is the reincarnation of her beloved Blue, her childhood pet. Pursuing the feline to the edge of Fran's yard, she stumbles upon the body of Theo Barnes, clearly a victim of foul play. To get her and Fran off the suspect list, Lara finds herself following the cat's clues in search of a killer. Is Blue's ghost really trying to help her solve a murder, or has Lara inhaled too much catnip?

Read on for a special excerpt!

A Lyrical Underground e-book on sale now.

Chapter 1

Lara Caphart paused at the foot of the wide porch steps and stared up at the old Folk Victorian. She was startled, and oddly relieved, at how little the place had changed. The white wicker settee still sat on the wraparound porch, its colorful cushions now sun-faded. A hanging planter, devoid of any foliage, dangled from a metal hook in front of the green-shuttered window.

She glanced over the yard she hadn't laid eyes on since she was eleven. The lawn was a bit unkempt, and the shrubs along the base of the porch needed tending. Lara easily recalled the days when Aunt Fran had kept everything trimmed and tidy—postcard pretty, in fact.

Heart thwacking against her chest, Lara slowly climbed the steps. Could it really be sixteen years since she'd seen her aunt? She tapped her knuckles on the wooden doorframe, lightly at first, then with a tad more vigor. After a wait of at least two minutes, the door creaked open. She took an involuntary step backward. "Aunt...Aunt Fran?" she asked with a slight gasp.

The woman clutching the doorframe in one hand and a gray-spotted kitten in the other tottered sideways. "Well, if it isn't the prodigal niece, returning to her roots. To what do I owe the pleasure? Did someone tell you I was dying?"

All at once, Lara felt tongue-tied. She didn't need a psychic to tell her that her aunt was in trouble. It was etched, like cut glass, in the hollows beneath her aunt's green eyes—eyes that at one time had looked at Lara as if she were the niftiest thing since peanut butter on toast.

"No. I, um..."

"I suppose Sherry called you about my knee problems," Fran Clarkson said, a bit more softly. "I can't imagine why else you'd have driven all the way up here from Boston." With a sigh and a slump of her thin shoulders, she opened the screen door. "You may as well come in."

"Thank you." Lara stepped inside the once-familiar kitchen, a room where luscious aromas like cinnamon, apple, and cloves once lingered in every corner. But today a sour smell permeated Lara's senses—an odor she'd never before associated with her aunt. According to Sherry Bowker, Lara's bestie when she was a kid, some of the folks in town had begun calling Aunt Fran the crazy cat lady.

At that moment, Lara noticed her aunt was grasping a cane in the hand that clung to the doorframe. Without a second thought, she cupped her hand firmly under her aunt's upper arm and guided her to a padded chrome chair at the head of the Formica table. "Why don't I take this little furball for a while?" Lara asked, gently removing the kitten from her aunt's hand.

"Thank you," her aunt said quietly. "That's Cheetah you're holding, if you're interested."

Lara felt herself bristling at the comment, but quelled her annoyance. "Of course I'm interested. Haven't I always loved your cats?" *All cats?* She tucked Cheetah under her chin, reveling in the softness of the darling kitten.

Aunt Fran's eyes misted with a faraway look. "That you have," she said. "You'd best set him down now. If he starts to get antsy, which he will, you'll get a sample of his razor-sharp claws."

Very gently, Lara set Cheetah on the floor. The kitten scooted away toward the jumble of food bowls lined up near the sink.

"I wasn't expecting you," her aunt said, her tone slightly accusatory. "I suppose I could make some tea—"

Lara held up a hand. "Why don't I take care of it, Aunt Fran? You sit for a while, okay?"

Aunt Fran nodded her assent. Lara stripped off her faux-suede jacket and draped it over the back of a chair.

It felt strange, rummaging through her aunt's glass-front cabinets, the way she had as a child. She found the tea bags exactly where they'd always been—in a battered tin container advertising Hershey's Cocoa.

Within minutes, two cups of steaming tea sat on the table in front of them. To Lara's delight, a thin gray cat leaped up from under the table and onto her lap. "Oh my, and who are you?" Grinning, she stroked the cat's head and was rewarded with the revving of a purr engine.

"That's Bootsie." Aunt Fran smiled wanly. "She's Cheetah's mom. Bootsie and her three-week-old babies were found by a state DPW worker on the side of Route Sixteen, tied inside a trash bag." Her face darkened at the memory.

"That's terrible!" Lara said. "How did you manage to rescue them?"

"The worker was one of my students, back in the day. He knew exactly where to bring those poor abandoned cats."

He sure did, Lara thought.

"One of the kittens didn't survive. But Cheetah and Lilybee were tough little darlings."

Another cat strolled in to check out the commotion—a long-haired black kitty who made a beeline for her aunt's lap. "And this is Dolce," Aunt Fran said, stroking the cat.

"Which is the Italian word for sweet," Lara piped in. "I live in the North End, above an Italian bakery. In fact, I work at the bakery part time…in exchange for rent I can actually afford," she added dryly. "My landlady owns the studio apartment upstairs."

Lara knew she was babbling, but she wasn't even close to achieving a comfort level with her aunt. There was a time when they'd been as close as mother and daughter.

"I see." Aunt Fran stirred her tea thoughtfully. "I assume you're still painting?"

"I am," Lara confirmed. "Mostly watercolors." She took a sip from her teacup.

For a long moment Aunt Fran was silent. Then, "So what are your plans? Are you here for any particular reason? Or is this just a casual visit?"

Her aunt's tone stung. Lara swallowed back a lump. "I don't have any plans, per se, Aunt Fran. I…I mean, Sherry did call me. She and her mom are worried about you. Extremely worried."

Sherry Bowker and Lara had known each since childhood, from the day they entered first grade together at Whisker Jog Elementary. But the summer after Lara had completed sixth grade, her family moved away. She and Sherry were devastated—they missed each other horribly. Lara had been especially lonely, moving to an unfamiliar school in another state. The girls kept in touch by letter, and later by e-mail, until they both graduated high school. It was during Lara's hectic art school years that they lost the thread of communication. Then one day, about five years ago, Lara plunked her old friend's name into a search engine and discovered that Sherry and her mom had opened a coffee shop in downtown Whisker Jog. She contacted her, and was thrilled to get an instant response. Every summer now, Sherry and her mom took a day off to drive to Boston for a lunch/shopping expedition with Lara.

Lara realized her mind was wandering. Her aunt obviously knew that she and Sherry had been in touch.

Aunt Fran's gaze skimmed Lara's face. Her eyes brimmed with tears. "It's been so long since I've seen you. I don't know what to think."

Lara sucked in a hard breath. She didn't want to cry. "I know, but I'm here now and I want to help with the cats. How many do you have?"

"Eleven. Two of the kittens—Callie and Luna—are afraid of people, and one adult male is feral. The kittens are young enough to socialize eventually, but Ballou won't go near a human."

Lara inhaled, then winced inwardly. She didn't know how many litter boxes her aunt had, but from the scent coating her nostrils she felt sure all of them needed to be cleaned and changed. "Aunt Fran, will you rest while I check out the litter boxes and clean things up a bit?"

With a sag of her shoulders, her aunt nodded. "That... would actually be a big help. The supplies are in the utility closet, next to the bathroom."

Lara grinned. "I know exactly where that is."

It took Lara the better part of two hours to scrub and replenish the twelve litter boxes scattered throughout the house. Fortunately, she'd found a pair of rubber gloves under the bathroom sink, along with earth-friendly cleaning supplies, trash bags, and scads of paper towel rolls.

Her heart melted at the sight of the furry faces watching her as she worked. She would have to learn all their names, if she was here long enough.

By the time she was through, the rooms smelled minimally better. In the kitchen, she collected the myriad food and water bowls, washed them, and replenished them with kibble and kitten food. She'd been relieved to find her aunt's cabinets well stocked with cat food. Lara wondered how her aunt shopped for supplies with her knees in such bad shape.

It was already two thirty, and she was starving. She headed upstairs and knocked softly at her aunt's bedroom door, which was slightly ajar. "Aunt Fran?" she called.

"Come in, Lara."

Her aunt was sitting in her padded rocking chair reading a paperback thriller. Dolce rested in her lap, looking every bit like a furry black shawl.

Lara had to swallow to keep her composure. The room was almost exactly as she remembered it, with its braided scatter rugs and white, iron bedstead, a handmade quilt folded at the foot of the bed. The white-painted dresser, its oval mirror silvered in places, sat in the same corner. From where she stood, Lara could see her own reflection.

"Come on, I'm famished," Lara said. "I'm treating you to lunch at Sherry's. She doesn't know I drove up here today, so we're going to surprise her."

Her aunt frowned and rubbed her left knee. "I don't think so, Lara. I walk very slowly, you know. It takes me forever to get in and out of a car."

"I'll help you," Lara cajoled. "I'm not going without you."

* * * *

Bowker's Coffee Stop sat in the center of Whisker Jog's downtown block, about a half mile downhill walk from Aunt Fran's home at the end of High Cliff Road. So far Lara had only seen photos of the place, supplied by Sherry via her smartphone or on the coffee shop's Facebook page. The pictures, Lara realized, failed to capture the cozy essence of the inviting cafe.

The walls were painted in swirls of pastel, graced with vintage photos and artifacts from the 1960s. On one side of the shop was a counter lined with bright-red stools. Square oak tables and padded, mismatched chairs made up the rest of the seating. Daily specials were announced on a standalone chalkboard framed in pale-green distressed wood.

The moment Lara and her aunt approached the counter they were rushed and assaulted.

"Oh my God, I can't believe it!" Sherry Bowker, her short black hair poking the air in gelled spikes, raced around the end of the counter and threw her arms around Lara. She squeezed and rocked back and forth until Lara laughingly begged for mercy.

"Sherry, this place looks wonderful," Lara said.

"Thank you." Sherry hugged Lara again and then looped her arm through Aunt Fran's. "And Fran, you haven't been here in like, forever," she said in a mock-stern voice. "I'm so happy to see you."

Aunt Fran smiled and allowed Sherry a quick hug. "I'm glad to see you, too, and my pal Daisy over there." She waggled a hand at her old friend Daisy Bowker, who was busy serving a table of four. Daisy's face morphed into one of sheer joy when she spotted Lara and Aunt Fran.

After more hugs were doled out, Lara and her aunt settled onto stools at the counter, which, Aunt Fran explained, was easier on her knees. Sherry instantly produced two steaming mugs of coffee, along with two of the oversized sugar cookies Daisy was known for. With Halloween only a few weeks away, today's cookies were shaped and frosted like mummies. Lara couldn't help giggling as she bit off a chunk of the mummy's frosted arm.

"Eating dessert before you've even ordered lunch?" Aunt Fran asked wryly. "I guess some things never change."

Lara smiled, feeling her nerves loosen. For the first time since she'd arrived in Whisker Jog, she thought her aunt looked almost happy.

They both ordered tuna salad sandwiches and sipped at their coffee. Between serving customers, Sherry and Daisy took turns plying them with bits of local gossip.

Aunt Fran waved at a table of four opposite the counter. Its occupants— two women, an older man, and a teenage girl—returned the greeting. The girl, who looked about thirteen and sported aqua-tinted hair, smiled curiously at Lara. Lara smiled back and took a napkin from the dispenser on the counter. The girl's face intrigued her—oversized brown eyes, roundish cheeks, slightly large ears lined with silver studs. And that hair.... She removed a pencil from the depths of her flowered purse and began to sketch.

Sherry sidled up to the counter and leaned over to sneak a peek at Lara's handiwork. "Hey, that's Brooke you're drawing, isn't it?"

"Brooke?" Lara said.

Sherry laughed. "Sorry. You haven't been introduced yet. Brooke Weston is the girl sitting at that table over there." She tilted her chin at the table of four. "They all belong to a book club that reads the classics. Brooke comes here directly after school every Wednesday so she won't miss any of the discussion. The coffee shop closes at four, but sometimes I stay a bit longer so they can finish up without feeling rushed."

"That's nice of you," Lara said. "But why don't they just have the club at the library?"

Sherry smiled. "They like it better here. Can you blame them?"

Daisy came up beside her daughter. "So, Fran," she said, "I've been thinking about you, sweetie. Have you been able to plant your tulip bulbs yet?"

"I don't think I'm going to get to it this year, Daisy. The bulbs were shipped to me last week, but they're still sitting in burlap bags out by the shed."

Tulips! That's right—Lara remembered now. Back when she was a kid, Aunt Fran was known for the gorgeous tulip varieties that skirted her house from front to back along the brick walkway. Apparently she'd kept up the tradition.

In fact, Lara remembered one year when she "helped" her aunt plant a row of the bulbs, only to learn that she'd stuck them all in the ground upside down. Instead of getting annoyed, Aunt Fran had only laughed, ruffled Lara's curls, and said "Oh well, next year you'll get it right."

But there never had been a next year. Lara's folks had moved out of state, and she'd never seen Aunt Fran again.

Until now.

Lara didn't want to embarrass her aunt by bringing up her current physical limitations. Instead, she made a mental note to try to plant the tulip bulbs before she returned to Boston.

Daisy went off to clear one of the tables. Lara was putting the finishing touches on her napkin sketch when the door to the coffee shop swung open. A broad-shouldered man wearing a red-and-black-checkered jacket strode in. His bushy eyebrows matched his thick white hair, and he wore the look of someone quite enamored with himself. "I'll take a black coffee to go," he said to Sherry in a rather rude tone.

A muscle in Sherry's face twitched, but she gave him a sharp nod. With a quick tilt of her head in his direction, she shot Lara a meaningful look.

Who's that? Lara mouthed to her aunt, after he strode off.

Aunt Fran leaned closer to Lara. "Theo Barnes," she whispered. "I'll tell you later."

The man's hard-looking blue eyes scanned the room, and then he sauntered over to the book club table. "So how are all my buds today?" he said in a voice like a sonic boom. He touched the younger woman's cheek, eliciting a smile from her. The older woman beamed up at him, and with a theatrical motion he took her left hand and kissed it. Then he clamped a meaty hand onto the shoulder of the club's sole male member, a sixty-something with a pasty complexion who cringed visibly at Barnes's touch. Barnes leaned over and growled something in the man's ear. The man nodded, slunk out of his chair and stalked out of the cafe.

Barnes came up to the counter to collect his takeout coffee, stopping between the stools where Lara and Aunt Fran were seated. Lara stifled a shudder. Barnes was standing far too close for her liking. She looked at her aunt, whose face had gone pale. Lara was about to tell Barnes to take a hike when he announced, "I need to talk to you, Fran."

"I don't think so," Aunt Fran hissed at him. "You've talked quite enough."

Barnes's piercing eyes shifted and rested on Lara. "My proposal stands, my lovely, but I think I can make it even sweeter for you. We *will* chat later. I promise you that."

Aunt Fran squeezed her eyes shut and said nothing.

With a smug look, Barnes reached across the counter and took the lidded paper coffee cup Sherry was holding out. Then, without so much as a thank you, he left.

"What an oaf," Lara said after the door closed. "I mean, could he have been any louder?"

"Theo Barnes is the town bully," her aunt murmured. "I'll tell you about him when we get back to the house."

"But he didn't even pay for his coffee!"

Sherry slid two plates in front of Lara and her aunt. "Don't worry about it, Lara. He never does. He thinks he owns the place."

"He does own the place." Daisy came up behind her daughter. She reached under the counter for a bottle of spray cleaner. "Unfortunately, he's our landlord. For now, anyway. But that's not for you to worry about. You two go ahead and enjoy your lunch."

Lara looked down at her tuna salad on wheat. A pile of rippled chips and two pickle rounds sat beside it—exactly the way she liked it. She set aside her pencil sketch and dived into her lunch. The tuna salad was perfect—lightly seasoned, and with just the right amount of celery and onion to give it crunch. Aunt Fran nibbled at hers, but with far less gusto.

Lara was attacking the last bite of her sandwich when her aunt, who'd barely eaten half her lunch, suddenly pushed aside her plate. "Why are you here, Lara?" she asked quietly. "I mean, why are you *really* here?"

Lara felt a hard lump form inside her stomach. The cats weren't the only reason she'd driven to New Hampshire. Sherry had confided that a local businessman had been harassing her aunt, making her life a living nightmare. She hadn't given details, but Lara now suspected she knew who it was.

Theo Barnes.

In a voice that came out shakier than she intended, Lara said, "I came because I want to help you. Because I care about you."

"You care about me," Aunt Fran said flatly. "Isn't it strange, then, that I haven't seen or heard from you in sixteen years."

Her aunt's sudden vitriol surprised Lara. Feeling tears push at her eyelids, Lara snatched up her crumpled napkin and blotted her eyes. "I don't know what else I can say, Aunt Fran. I care and I want to help. Can we talk about this back at the house?"

Aunt Fran looked suddenly flustered. "Of course we can. I shouldn't have brought it up here." She reached into her purse for her wallet, but Lara quickly covered her hand.

"No, Aunt Fran. It's my treat, remember?"

"Actually, it's our treat," Sherry said, coming up to the counter. "When you walked in together, I was just...so glad to see you both."

"Thank you, Sherry," Lara said.

Since Aunt Fran hadn't eaten her mummy cookie, Sherry slipped it into a paper bag and handed it to her. "You'll both come back tomorrow, right?"

"You bet," Lara said.

Aunt Fran only smiled. "I'll try."

Lara helped her aunt off the stool. Just then, Brooke, the teenager, excused herself from the book club and dashed over to them.

"Hey, are you Lara?" she asked, beaming as if she'd spotted a rock star.

"I am, and I understand you're Brooke."

"Yup. Guilty as charged. Your hair is like, so gorgeous. Is that the natural color?"

Lara laughed and fingered a coppery strand. "It is," she said, charmed by the girl's bluntness. "I'm glad you like it, but I wouldn't mind doing with fewer curls. By the way, I have something for you." Lara handed her the napkin sketch.

Brooke pushed a strand of aqua hair behind one ear. "You drew this?" she asked, gawking at the napkin. "It looks just like me!"

"Lara is an artist," Aunt Fran put in. Lara detected a hint of pride in her aunt's voice.

"Can... I mean, *may* I keep it?"

"You sure can," Lara smiled at her. "It was a pleasure meeting you, Brooke."

"This is so cool!" She gave it back to Lara. "Would you bring it back to the house for me? If I put it in my backpack it'll get wrinkled."

"Um, yeah, sure," Lara said, perplexed.

"Thanks!" And then to Aunt Fran, "See you in a few, Ms. C."

Meet the Author

Photo by Harper Point Photography

Raised in a sleepy town in the Berkshires, **Linda Reilly** has spent the bulk of her career in the field of real estate closings and title examination. It wasn't until 1995 that her first short mystery, "Out of Luck," was accepted for publication by *Woman's World Magazine*. Since then she's had more than forty short stories published, including a sprinkling of romances. She is also the author of *Some Enchanted Murder*, and the Deep Fried Mystery series, featuring fry cook Talia Marby. Linda lives in New Hampshire with her husband, who affectionately calls her "Noseinabook." Visit her on the web at lindasreilly.com.

Printed in the United States
by Baker & Taylor Publisher Services